THE RAIN BARREL

THE RAIN BARREL AND OTHER STORIES

GEORGE BOWERING

TALONBOOKS   VANCOUVER   1994

Copyright © 1994 George Bowering

Published with the assistance of the Canada Council

Talonbooks
201 - 1019 East Cordova
Vancouver, British Columbia
Canada V6A 1M8

Typeset in Garamond at Pièce de Résistance Ltée. and printed and bound in Canada by Hignell Printing Ltd.

First Printing: March 1994

Some of the stories in this book have been published previously:

"The Creature" in *The Capilano Review*; "Rhode Island Red" in *Rampike* and in *Parallel Voices* (Quarry Press, 1993); "The Rain Barrel" in *The Great Canadian Anecdote Contest* (ed. George Woodcock, Harbour Publishing, 1991); "The Stump" in *Beyond Tish* (ed. Douglas Barbour, NeWest Press/line 1991); "Staircase Descended" in *West Coast Review* and *90: Best Canadian Stories* (ed. David Helwig and Maggie Helwig, Oberon Press, 1990); "Being Audited" in *The Bumper Book* (ed. John Metcalf, ECW Press, 1986); "Desire and the Unnamed Narrator" and "Familiar Admonitions" in *Descant*; "Feller at the Sunsplash" in *Brushes With Greatness* (ed. Russell Banks, Michael Ondaatje and David Young, Coach House Press, 1989); "October 1, 1961" in *Taking the Field* (ed. G. Bowering, RDC Press, 1990); "The Described" in *Matrix*; "Spread Eagle" in *Rampike*; "Little Me" in *West Coast Line* and *Canadian Short Stories* (China); "Nadab" in *Border Crossings* and *Das Magazin* (Germany); "Diggers" in *Das Magazin* (Germany). Drawing on p. 261 by Thea Bowering.

Canadian Cataloguing in Publication Data

Bowering, George, 1936-
    The rain barrel and other stories

ISBN 0-88922-345-9

I. Title.
PS8503.O875R34 1994   C813'.54   C94-910117-6
PR9199.3.B68T34 1994

Contents

These stories are dedicated to Southern Okanagan High School, which expelled me in grade twelve, so I could get something done outside.

THE RAIN BARREL

When I was eleven years old my parents and I spent a lot of the summer fruit season on a big orchard in Naramata. It was so big that it was called a fruit ranch. My uncle managed this place and lived in one of the houses on it. At the northeast corner of this house there was a rain barrel. It didnt rain very often in the Valley, but you could depend on a deluge to damage the cherry crop, and maybe another terrific downpour in peach season. In between there might be an early morning shower from time to time.

But everyone who lived on an orchard ten miles from the nearest real town had a rain barrel. They knew where to put them to get nearly all the rain that hit the roof. Women liked to wash their hair in rain water because the regular water in the Valley was full of minerals. You couldnt make the softest soap lather up.

An eleven-year-old boy does two things with a rain barrel. On cloudy days he sticks his head in and yells for the marvelous echoes. On bright sunny Valley days with puffy white clouds he looks at the reflections of the puffy white clouds. We should stay in the past tense. These were the two things he did in the days before boys watched television, which was slow to get to the Valley, but which now controls the imagination there, with moving images of the mean streets of Detroit. *And that person is a long way past eleven years old.*

One day that boy was watching the puffy clouds slide over the surface of the water, when all of a sudden the reflected sky was filled with the huge shaggy head of God.

He turned and looked behind him. He looked above him. He decided to look in every direction. He could see tractor smoke rising from between the trees fifteen rows to the west, but no human beings.

He looked back into the rain barrel. There was God's face again, maybe closer than the clouds, maybe just bigger than the clouds.

Then he was in the water, face first. Grabbed by the ankle and tipped in. A prince struggling to get back out. In his kicking and underwater yelling he made it harder than it need be, but he got out, all wet in the good morning sun.

He looked around again, and saw his uncle with his normal friendly creased face and grin, carrying something that needed fixing. He was just coming out the kitchen door of his house.

The eleven-year-old boy looked carefully at his uncle's face. It did not at all resemble the reflected face of God. He looked at the water again. It was still rippling, so any reflection was just a *little plane of chaos*.

He decided to wait until the water became a simple mirror again. But a squall brought in dark low clouds from the east, and soon it was raining into the rain barrel. Next thing he knew his mother was telling him to get in out of the rain. What could he do? When he was eleven years old his mother's word was law.

BLITHE TREES

"Havent I told you a thousand times that it's better to be mysterious as far as your lineage goes?" she asked him.

She was trying on rings, silver, gold, old dull stones in settings from the olden days. She always told him that she could not tolerate metals on her skin. But a woman was expected to have rings, and to wear some of them.

"In these days, anyway," she said. "You want to be interesting. It is as if you have no name, isnt it? Odysseus said he had no name, and his son was given a beautiful beach at Antium. You have a name borrowed from me when necessary."

"That's what you always tell me," he said.

He was twelve years old. His voice and his limbs were changing, but he had no idea what they would change into, no model. His nose was a lot like PB's, but what did his eyes resemble, or whose?

"Nameless, you claim a great heritage. That is certainly to be preferred over being the son of a small town mayor, or a shoe merchant, or a school choirmaster, wouldnt you say?"

She had never promised him anything, never told him that she would reveal his history when he was of age, never told him that he would one day stand face to face with a stranger in a mirror.

She was trying on her rings, at the open window of her sitting room. Outside the window the apricot tree was heavy with green fruit, and a breeze turned the leaves, silver and green, not silver, but a green notion of silver. He stared into the jewelry case, willing her to pick up the emerald.

"Who am I?" she asked, asked someone out the window. "I am your dam. I am a shameful presence in their midst, an unmarried artist. I am the daughter of a great man. I am a seed pod carried by a careful stream. You see, I am many women, and all of them your mother. You have many mothers. What does it matter whether you have one father or a tradition?"

When she said artist he knew she meant poet. He knew nothing about such things. She offered now to rub the top of his crewcut head. He moved his head till her hand went back to the jewelry. She picked up the emerald.

"Well, that's nice," he grumbled. "You have a choice of things to be. I dont even get to tell my best friend what my real name is."

"Neither does he, dear. You will know what I mean in the years to come."

At least that was almost a promise.

She put the emerald back and closed the box. The scent of cedar departed through the window. He turned and went to his room, to his books.

In the middle of the Depression she broke her engagement with a famous young poet and left Philadelphia almost forever, but unlike her friends, she turned her back to the ocean and went westward. She left her father at the station in Philadelphia and sat beside a window for five days, watching all the countryside in her father's picture books drift by. She fetched up in an orchard that had been planted fifteen years before. She was twenty years old. Her friend was nineteen. Her friend's mother was forty-five.

They were an odd entourage in the valley full of fruit trees and undeveloped lake beaches. PB had no illusions about the neighbours and the people in town. She knew that these hard-working folk, as they probably liked to be called, would be talking about the three females newly in their midst. A beautiful girl, a tall gangly girl with bobbed hair, and a striking woman of a certain age. Three females with enough money despite the Depression, to rent a cottage in a widower's orchard. And to operate a motor car.

A motor car is what Sandy's mother called it.

Sandy's mother was a very careful and very unreliable driver. She never got the Ford from their gravel driveway onto Highway 97 in less than five minutes, sometimes even getting out of the car and looking down the road both ways. Sandy, on the other hand, would have been terrific in a Flivver at Atlantic City. That's what PB always thought. She had been to Atlantic City more than once in her life, or so she was told, and didnt remember anything except one memory she was always told about, a young man dipping something into a jar and taking it out to make rainbow bubbles float in a stream away from him.

PB never even wanted to try to drive the motor car. It was one of the very few new vehicles in the valley, and a mystery to her. Sandy might as well have been Phaeton and she one of his sisters, locomotion was that much a puzzle to her, a puzzle and a bit of a terror.

But neither was she devoted to their little cottage. In fact it was pretty, the sort of blossom-surrounded quaintness imagined by people in the cities back east. It was settled right in the middle of the young orchard, apricot trees on one side, taller cherry trees to the edge of the lawn in front, apple trees stretching up the slope behind the chicken pen in back, and dark prune trees on the fourth side. The tree blossoms followed one another in an orderly schedule, white cherries first, then the apricots and the prunes—finally the pink apples. When a light breeze swept through from the north, the air, even inside the house, was a river of perfume. The three women would bring chairs out onto the lawn, and sit, knitting and tatting, smoking white cigarettes that Sandy's mother made, five at a time, on a clever little machine. They hardly ever talked about the past, seldom about the famous young poet, never about the source of their money. They told stories about ancient Greece, or prose glosses of the recently-translated *eddas*, or inventions set behind the almost bare brown hills behind their orchard.

And PB walked there, because she could still walk strongly in those days, dressed in what the local people would have to call a costume, jodhpurs and scarves, wide-brimmed hats and wrappings around her ankles. Walked, this visitant, nearly six feet tall, among the ground cactus and the sage brush, around ancient crumbling rocks left by glaciers, around greasewood showered with narrow dark leaves in the summer and standing as dark twisted branches in the winter, perfect, if she only knew, for sudden hot campfires such as any ambient gods would notice and appreciate. For she was, she thought, walking in search of gods or at least their messengers, looking for a poem that would owe nothing to Europe, nothing to the smoking cities of the east.

Once in that first year she saw a coyote, and later gave herself the gift of considering him a god or at least a messenger. She knew nothing about the stories the valley's Indians told about coyotes. This animal stood across an open area of burnt couch grass, his tail toward her but his head turned to look. She took a few quick steps toward him (she assumed that the animal was male, as one did in those days, about animals, about poets), and he loped away a little, his rump rising with each easy jounce. She stopped and sat on a rock, taking off her hat and settling as

14

best she could on the aged basalt. The coyote faced her and sat, his tongue hanging out, a kind of grin on his face. She wondered for a long time what his grin reminded her of, and one morning she remembered the smile that was always, when he spoke to her, on the face of Andrew Gray the Scottish composer. And so poet and wild creature regarded each other. She spoke to him in her language.

"I thought you a dog, but you are too much the colour and shape of this place," she said. "I wondered were you a wolf, but you are not serious enough, are you?"

The coyote smiled. He ducked his head and leaped up and away.

"Yes, you remind me of someone," she said, not rising.

He reminded her too of herself, of course, and that may have been what she meant.

She had to walk in these low hills, climbing sometimes to the second bare brown bench, and other times struggling her way along the willow-sided river, had to make these excursions for almost a year before the first poems came.

And when they came they were not Greek, they were not European, they were not from the smoky cities of the east. But they were not regional descriptions of this dry sagebrush valley, either. Still, they were not eruptions of the human heart, and they were not expressions of the self-engaged soul. Those are some of the things they were not, but what were they? They were things no one had seen or heard in the past few centuries, so PB sometimes showed them to Sandy and her mother, but asked them not to talk about them, especially not to talk about the things they were not.

In the summer in this valley the air was hot and clean. When the sun went down the air cooled and the rocky cliffs that had baked all day gave off their heat, to the hand, to the nearby face. In the winter the air was cool and crisp and dry, so that puddles in the road would be a surface of thin ice with nothing underneath, a pleasure to crack with one's steps. In the winter Sandy would deliberately run the high narrow tires of the motor car through the crisp puddles.

In winter and in summer the air of the valley was clean and dry, and objects seen through the air were clear and sharp. PB's short poems were like that. She was an outcast from the east, taken to walking in dry air. People here spoke of the blue of the valley, the sky bluest blue, the hills, the lakes, the air, blue. They said it was a Mediterranean blue.

> The speckled rock
> broken, thin salt
> drifts over a new surface.

> Sage, whipped round my ankles!
> Ah, wind!
> Ah, who are you,
> to meet me in this place?

She did not carry pen and paper to the hills or the river or the orchard. She found the poems there, perhaps, and brought them home with her to the stucco cottage and wrote them swiftly or slowly at the window table. If she saw a finch at the birdfeeder she might let the bird into her poem. Through the year of 1937 she wrote many poems at the window table, and carried others home that she never put to paper. She burned many poems in the spring of that year, and in the late autumn she consigned whole booklets of verses to the kitchen stove. Still, she saved numerous poems that people later would call hard and crisp, but they were never hard and only sometimes crisp. People did not know quite what they were. They were only vaguely aware of the absence of the things that they were not.

In the valley, or at least in the nearest village, there was nobody to show the poems to. So she showed some of them to her friend and her friend's mother, and that was it.

Until she sent four of them to the famous young poet back east. She never considered sending them to her Moravian father, although she wrote letters to him once a month.

On the last Saturday morning of every month she wrote four pages to her father, making sure to tell him about the rocks and the clouds when there were some, about the birds and the foliage and the latest condition of the fruit trees. Then Sandy would back the "flivver" out of the faded wood garage and turn it around, and they would drive to the post office in the village. They had a box at the post office, though they could have had their letters and catalogues and newspapers left in the mailbox at the bottom end of their gravel driveway.

The valley was made of a little soft dirt on top of ancient crumbling rocks. Some of the rocks in the hills had old writing on them, runes rather, usually hidden with the thinnest possible cover of light grey lichen. Tall gangly PB found this writing, images of human beings, arrows, wild animals, other items lost to time; and she memorized them, so that when she returned to her peach-coloured cottage she could draw them on paper and send them to her brother. Never to her father. This she withheld from him. Her brother Ira had tried to live in the scant woods of Pennsylvania. He read books from Canada, about men who put on furs and cooked in pails filled with water made from melted snow.

She looked among the bulges of rock for a picture of her coyote or writing done by his friends, but never found them. This she understood to mean that it was left for her to make his portrait, with words. She never did. She hoped that this abstinence would bring him again to the faded brown bench where they had met. She did not see him for over a year, though she found his spoor, she thought. She never wrote a poem about her coyote, but she wrote poems for him. These she sent to the famous young poet back east, and wondered whether he would ever know the identity of her muse.

One day at the post office in the village she was handed an envelope with British stamps on it. The famous young poet was in London, listening part of the time to Mr Auden and Mr Spender, subjectively screening out their social politics, and instructing the unknown younger poets who had never read any of the lesser-known poets of Italy and "Provawnce."

She was happy to be here in the ancient west. They had made the right decision. Here she would be instructed only as she required, or only as she was startled anew by the earth.

One day she bent her costumed lanky body and with her long fingers picked up a field mouse. She put it into the pocket of her peculiar long skirt and almost forgot it. From time to time on the way home she slid the ends of her fingers into the pocket and touched the rough fur of this creature. It did not offer to bite her. She felt as though the gods or at least their messengers had seen her passing a test that was not even offered to most of the hard-labouring people of this new place.

When she got home she did not go inside the cottage, but straight to the gray chopping block beside the wood pile. There she kneeled and took the mouse out of her pocket. It lay on the smooth wood, dead, its eye mercifully closed. A fat white worm protruded from its abdomen.

The next time they went to the post office in the village there were two letters from London. One said that the famous young poet had received her four poems and thought that they were better than anything he had seen her do before she had left. The second letter said that they were great poetry, that they were better than anything he had seen from their generation, and that he wanted to see more.

She wanted to be placid, but she held the two envelopes to her chest on the way home, and she took out the letters and read them often over the following week.

For a reason she did not understand or question, she did not give the letters to Sandy and her mother to read. She told them that the famous young poet was principally concerned about whether they, the frontierswoman, and he the Old Country aesthete, were still engaged. She said that his language was a little intemperate and that she was embarrassed to show his words to them.

So their life in the dry valley continued. Her father sent her the regular cheques that family affairs had regulated. Sandy's mother had probably the largest bank account in the village, and several accounts back east. Sandy took up watercolours, and was often to be seen somewhere among the trees or in the yard, capturing the low hills and the higher hills with long gentle brushstrokes. Sandy's mother wrote letters, took the sun that shone brightly every day, and spent hours at the stove, cooking badly.

PB continued her hikes, visiting places that had become important to her, and exploring new ground at least once a week. But she also grew interested in the work of the orchard. They rented their cottage from the orchardist who had lived in it until he had built a large house farther back off the highway.

The orchardist and his sons grew accustomed to working under her gaze. She generally sat a row away from them, on an upturned apple box, or she strolled about, appearing and reappearing while the men attended to the growing trees. In the late winter they came out with long pruners and lopped off small branches, while the youngest son, striped electrician's gloves on his hands, yanked the new suckers off the trunks.

"Time to prune the prunes," this boy said, more than once.

She watched them thin apples. When a man was finished with a tree of Jonathans there would be a carpet of the smallest green apples on the tromped grass under the tree, some in the furrows of the disked earth. She stayed out of the orchard when they were spraying. From her apricot window she watched them with their hoses, sending green poison up into the high branches, emerging from a day's work covered with the green stuff themselves, coughing as they trudged home for an early dinner. PB hated the odour of the spray, which stayed in the air for days, and which she could detect a month later when she held a green Macintosh apple to her nose. Some of the orchardists were experimenting with sprinkler systems, but the crew on this "fruit ranch," as these places were often called, still went to the place where the irrigation ditch was met by their syphons, and opened some little gates. PB liked to watch the first of the water find its way down the furrows between the trees, much of it sinking quickly into the dry earth. In late June the first crops were picked, the fat cherries from the tallest trees in the orchard, dark Bings and Lamberts and the yellow Royal Annes. The three women were told that they were welcome to all the fruit they could eat, and they loved cherry season. Every June, just before the cherries were to be picked, there would be a terrific electrical storm, and a downpour of warm rain that would collect on the cherries, swelling them and splitting them, dashing annual expectations of a bumper crop. The orchardist called this phenomenon the proof of the existence of God. PB liked him for having the patience to say such things.

But her favourite month was August, season of peaches and pears. She wrote a poem about the heat of August, the weight of pears and grapes, the rough god she knew was loose in the orchard. This poem would do much to make her famous for a while, before her poems and herself were forgotten except by her friends and the people she would meet when she worked in the village during the war. This poem, too, she sent to the famous young poet.

In cherry season of 1938 she received a letter from him, saying that he had sent her first four poems to the most important new poetry magazine in America, and that they would publish them. This letter too she did not show to Sandy and her mother. But in pear season the magazine itself arrived at the village post office, probably the first issue of that magazine ever to appear in the southern part of the valley, at least. There they were, a poem for her coyote, and the others. On the first page of the magazine were the words "Four Poems by P.B."

"Imagine this," said Sandy's mother, her happiness undisguisable. "And we may see you every day. We made the right decision in coming to this country."

But she would be gone in less than a year.

One September morning she was not the only poet in the valley. She met him during one of her hikes. This sunny day the scent of ripening apples rose from the orchards that stretched as far as she could see, and the breeze that blew across the bench carried alternating perfumes of apples and sage. She was wearing her high boots because this was traditionally the season for rattlesnakes. They would doze in the sun, and wake in momentary confusion if you stepped near them. She kept her head down more than usual, so that by the time she saw him she was nearly in his arms.

Waking from her own preoccupation, she must have looked a little vexed. She was not used to encountering other people up here. Tall in her boots, she looked at him from above. He was sitting on a flat boulder, with a stone in one hand and some kind of tool in the other.

"My gosh, you're a tall one," were his first memorable words to her.

"What are you doing in my garden," she asked. She was bashful as always, but one way of handling bashfulness is to engage in vocal artifice.

He held up the stone and showed her the design on its flat side. It was a small sea shell, or an insect such as one had never seen.

"This little fellow was nicely settled here quite some time before it became your garden," he said.

She did not like him, and she was attracted to him. He was very handsome, and this fact did not make her antipathy and his attraction any easier to reconcile. He spoke with a the kind of British accent that one associates with tweed coats at inefficient country houses. In fact he was wearing a smooth old tweed coat at this first meeting, along with high laced boots and corduroy breeches. He wore no hat, a mad Englishman, she thought, and his hair was thick and curly. It looked as if he had brushed it at dawn, and it had been struggling to break free all morning.

When he got round to enquiring of her her name she said that it was Artemis.

"I must be dreaming," he said.

He was an archaeologist who was tired of Europe. Like her, he had come out here to be contrary. Holding to an original theory, as all famous archaeologists will, he was looking for something a Spaniard horseman might have dropped on the dry ground here while Robert Jenkins was exhibiting his severed ear at Parliament. So far the Spanish had to be considered meticulous about their equipment, but in the meantime, he was finding some interesting evidence of very old Indian habitation in the region.

"Very old is a phrase that we archaeologists are hospitable to," he said. When he smiled his military mustache spread across his face.

I am still pretty young, she thought.

But she fell for him anyway.

His name was Richard Morrison, of the Bristol Morrisons. He was once a teacher of antiquities at an important university, and an amateur poet. When he left pedagogy to become a freelance digger, he coincidentally became a more serious and successful poet. When PB met him he had published in all the best of the new magazines in Britain, and would soon see publication of his first book of verses. Not from one of the big houses, of course. He was a modern.

He took her as a student first, showing her what to look for under the lichen on rocks, how to see arrow heads in the tumble of stones at the river's edge. She began to comb her hair over her small ears because he remarked on their peculiar shape. She took him as a teacher, then as a friend. Then she took him as a lover. She showed him that she could not cook. He admired the poems she would show him, and he showed her his own. She did not mention that his poems were not quite as good as hers. After a while they mentioned the famous young poet, who was now living in Paris.

In April of 1939 she married him in the little Anglican church in the village. In August Sandy and her mother returned to New York, and the couple took the stucco cottage in the orchard filled with peaches and pears. In September Andrew Morrison went to England to join the Royal Fusiliers as a Lieutenant. Now PB had to walk four miles into the village, or depend on the orchardist or his younger sons for a ride in their smelly old truck. After she got her first letter with English stamps, she wrote a poem for her husband.

What are these trees to me
if you are taken away,
what are these dark stones
if you lie on wet earth?

In my garden
the rain beats on ripe apples,
small animals crouch underground,
what is the sun round edge of clouds
if Endymion be gone from the air?

Still she did not read the newspapers, and she did not tune the radio to the war news. When people in town or the family in the orchard raised the progress of the fighting she would not reply. Soon people began to treat her carefully. It was agreed among them that she had been offered too great a shock with what they called a "whirlwind" romance and a sudden loneliness. She read his letters and the poems in them, and she knew that any one of them might have been sealed and despatched by a man now dead.

The boy played with the food she had prepared so inexpertly. He had never known any other cooking, save the meat and potatoes and carrots served at the local cafes. This was 1958, long before interesting restaurants were to come to the south end of the valley.

"Could Morrison have been my father?" he asked.

She was using her fork to pick up one little tooth of corn at a time. She smiled and pointed her fork at her son.

"Could have?" she said, teasing him. "Are we talking just about could have? Well, let us say maybe he could have and maybe not."

"Did he ever see me, Morrison?"

"Or did *you* see *him*? I do not know whether he ever saw you. I do not know whether he bothered to look. But you have seen him, yes. When you were three years old, when we lived in Philadelphia."

The boy had stopped eating entirely, though there was food of some sort on his plate, and even on his fork.

"Morrison was a reporter in New York then."

"Not reporter," she said, as if instructing a pupil. "He was a correspondent. For the *Times*."

"The times, the times, the times," the boy mumbled, his chin on his chest. He used to mumble this way when he was younger, when his legs hung from the chair and his feet did not touch the floor.

In April of 1940 PB was lying in the hospital of a small city slightly to the north. Morrison's daughter was born dead. She resembled a perfect new human being except for the curious lack of breath and heartbeat. The labour had gone on for more than twenty-four hours. PB was a strong tall woman who had played basketball for her highschool in Philadelphia. But the little girl, whose kicks PB had felt in her enormous body, was never to take a breath of valley air.

PB stayed in the hospital for two weeks, and there was no one she knew who could visit her. If the orchardist had had a wife perhaps she would have asked to be driven up for a visit. The men were not the kind of people to visit in the hospital. Especially in such embarrassing circumstances, a young woman with full breasts and no child.

She had not made or bought many baby's things, and had been given only a few gifts. That was good, somehow.

Her husband was somewhere in Africa. Her daughter was nowhere at all, unless there was a Limbo. She lay alone, on her side, looking out the hospital window at a cherry tree in full blossom.

For three years people in the village or south of it were surprised when they saw her, walking along the river, or trying to learn to drive the "flivver" that Sandy's mother had left behind. She would disappear from sight for months at a time, and rumours moved with the breeze up and down the treefruit highway. She had gone to Vancouver to become a character on the street. She was back where she came from, taking up the high society life in New York and Boston. She had locked herself inside her house and was living on apricots and the wild asparagus that grew between the trees.

They did not see that she caught the train from time to time, when it stopped at the packing house behind the orchard where her cottage nestled. This was a fruit train that stopped at all the packing houses, but it always had one passenger car. It would meet the tracks that ran east and west through the city to the north, and there PB would take up her reserved roomette and settle in for the ride to the coast. There she met the train that travelled south to the bare hills of California. There she spent her days in labour over the rush of poems that came to her in those years, and some of her nights with a very famous British novelist, short story writer, and poet. He was, many people thought, a great novelist, and she never showed her fiction-writing to him, but she was the better poet.

He was B.P. Oliver, a name that struck terror into the souls of puritans all over the English-speaking world. He wrote shamelessly of the passions that made people's lives blossom suddenly and then wither. Where PB was reticent, and concentrated a life's yearning into eight short lines, Oliver exfoliated, repeated himself, blustered, explained. His photograph, with bushy beard and poorly-tied neck-ware was active currency all over the world. PB laboured in secrecy. He trumpeted his humble beginnings, and made fun of her gentle background. She fell for him completely. Almost completely. She thought that he was a fool or at least an ass. But she also thought she knew that he was a great man.

He had left Britain years earlier, and never expected to go back. He had wandered and domiciled on all the continents save Antarctica. He had been living in the U.S. for four years before he came north for his one trip to her stony home.

There he strode the hills in his woollen suit trousers, waving a stick in front of him, prepared for rattlesnakes.

"In Sicily I had golden snakes for companions. In India I stared down the king cobra. In Australia I found killer reptiles in the latrine," he said. "I am not likely to be cowed by these little fellows."

PB was happy that he never once saw her coyote. She did not know for a fact that she saw the same animal each time, but she liked to think so.

For he never did what the other did. She was very fond of that coyote for many reasons, she thought, but chief among them was his grin. The very famous British novelist did not smile, and he certainly never laughed. In San Francisco the Scottish Andrew Gray was writing music criticism, and dining whenever possible with them. Andrew Gray smiled whenever he spoke to her. He often laughed as Scotsmen are not supposed to laugh, and he often laughed at himself. But the very famous British novelist did not laugh, and certainly never at himself. That was perhaps the reason why so many others laughed at him, even while they were impressed by his onrushing paragraphs. Sometimes he moaned, sometimes even growled. Often he was given to long silences, though she knew that the paragraphs were expanding in his head. She took him to her bed in the little cottage with the blossoms at the windows, and there they were serious and not altogether successful.

For it was true that she did not smile either. It was a strange and ominous relationship, and she never spoke of what they did or what they said, except years later when she cast him in one of her late unread novels. She spoke of the "fire-blue eyes in his burnt out face," and gave him the name she had always wanted for herself, Nico. Nico Flame, she called him, so that anyone who read the novel would know who he was, but not what he was. Hardly anyone read the novel.

"That novelist, Oliver, was in this house?" asked the twelve-year-old. He was making scrambled eggs and toast for their late Saturday breakfast. She was in the front room, reading a month-old newspaper from England, in which she had turned first to the book pages. The brace for her leg was half-hidden behind her chair. Mother and son had to shout a little to be heard.

"He was here for one visit. He said the dry climate agreed with him. He had tuberculosis, you know."

He knew. He knew as much as he could. It was because she and her son lived without anyone else that he could ask things about his mother that most boys would not.

"And you saw him in California?"

"When I went to California we would see each other, certainly."

The eggs were ready. He made them with a little milk in them, and when they were done he shook pepper on them. He took the two plates into the front room. Scrambled eggs and slices of beefsteak tomatoes.

He handed her the ironed and slightly starched napkin that she liked to insist on. They did this every Saturday morning, before he walked into the village for the movie. He tried to slow down his eating so that he would not finish before she had made any headway.

"B.P. Oliver might have been my father?"

She finally took a forkful of egg, to provide her with a short silence. When she spoke it was with the mock-lecturing tone she favoured on such occasions.

"As you know, his writing is filled with energetic advice about living and making love and grasping what you can of passion, etcetera. But it is common knowledge that he never had any children. They may not have been able to put up with babies in the house."

The boy took their plates to the kitchen. When he returned he stood behind his mother's chair. Her hair was done up the way Greek goddesses have theirs done in the books they both pored over.

"But," he said, "in terms of time, in terms of time—"

"Time," she whispered, She was looking out the window. Her hands were on the arms of her chair. Bright sunlight faded the carpet, at least temporarily. "Time, time, time, time."

"It's possible," said the boy.

"Tell yourself," she said, "you are the child of time."

She could not remember quite what it was like to be pregnant, waiting for the baby, waiting for it to become visible, waiting for her to be completely composed and separate and regardable. It was as if the stillborn child was not and then had not been. Now she spent longer time in the making of a book. She watched for the shaggy god she knew was in the apple trees. She thought she saw an angel in the mist of a bright morning's sun-shower. The poems came steadily but they were not all poems for the book. The book grew and the famous young poet, now back from Occupied France, back in London, was writing to her and urging a manuscript. So she spoke to the blue eyes in San Francisco, and she wrote a letter to Morrison, a soldier labouring in some theatre of war, a letter which was never to be answered, and she argued with the famous young poet in London, till there was nowhere else to turn, nothing else that she could do. She completed the book, she typed the manuscript, starting with the first four poems. In Europe and Asia and Africa people were dying in explosions as war machines roared through their villages and cities. How could a woman in an orchard in the only quiet part of the planet complete a book of poems?

> The shadows of these branches
> are twisted
> after many a wind, after
> many a cold winter.
>
> The apples are sweet
> to the powerful teeth, the news
> does not sour them, death
> in your far country
> does not sour them.
>
> Where the great sea foams
> and angry men
> flail it with chains
> these shadows are white.

As her body had once given up flesh that became other and was put away soon, now her hands delivered the manuscript. She mailed it to London, and the people there told her that if the printer in Plymouth could procure the paper, the book would be published in 1943. During her walks in the orchard, along the river, or in the hills, she often murmured the name of the printer in Plymouth.

She was filled with aspiration. She grew sweeter while waiting to see this book. She paid the rent on her cottage, and she entered the community. She overcame her bashfulness, she did her hair in braids piled on top of her head, and volunteered for every war project in and around the village. She drove the "flivver" as well as she could, visiting people who might buy war savings bonds or need to know where to send their scrap metal.

Metal fell on the shelters of warriors elsewhere.

She was consumed by aspiration. Or it was consumed by her. She read all her most dear texts. "And I took the little book out of the angel's hand, and ate it up; and it was in my mouth sweet as honey: and as soon as I had eaten it, my belly was bitter." She woke each day a new person and each was filled with aspiration in her own way. She longed for this book from England that would have to be carried by fearful sailors on the North Atlantic convoy.

One day late in 1943 she drove the "flivver" over wet asphalt into the village, to mail her letters to Sandy and to Andrew Gray, and there was a box for her at the post office. She placed it in the trunk of her car and continued all day to aspire while she performed her duties to the community, to the "war effort." She drove back home in the falling darkness, and carefully, slowly, put away the vehicle, spread food for tomorrow's birds, brought in some firewood from the shed. Then she put away her coat and hat and gloves. She made herself a pot of tea and some toast with damson plum preserves. Then she fetched the sewing scissors and cut the twine on the package. She put the English stamps in the envelope in which she saved stamps for the youngest son of the orchardist. Then she took some tea and a bite of toast. And then she unwrapped the books.

There were twelve copies, plain and beautiful, with the two words of the title and the two letters of the poet's name in clear black type on a dust jacket the colour of August sagebrush.

She held her first actual book in her long fingers. And watched it fade. It faded. This was attainment, but it was *very* not hers. She was not disappointed. It was just that this was not her aspiration—it belonged to someone else, to someone she had been a year ago, and then six months ago, and then perhaps yesterday. She would put the book on *important* the shelf. There would be copies on those tables in London and San Francisco and somewhere in Africa. She would leave one copy for a while on the table beside the apricot window. It was someone else's beautiful book.

She was not disappointed. How could she be disappointed in someone else's book? Now someone else had had one child, nearly, almost certainly, and one book, poems that she herself knew well. She looked on the last page and saw the name of the printer in Plymouth, and then put the book on the table. The other copies she placed on a shelf.

He visited her on her seventy-fifth birthday. There was no family other than the two of them, and Claire, but there were several friends and their husbands. None of these friends had ever really read any poetry. They met each other to play bridge and tell stories, to recall events from a pioneer valley, to smoke forbidden cigarettes on the back step.

He flew all the way from London to be with her on her seventy-fifth birthday. She was wearing a birthday costume, something that spoke of the middle east in the middle ages. She was still very tall, and not bent at all. It was the first time he had been in the cottage for a decade.

"These walls are still standing," he said.

"Clever boy," she said.

He winked at her while she walked with her slight limp, away to talk to "the girls," as she condescended to allow herself to call them. He went outside with Claire for a stroll through the orchard, looking for some trees that might have been there forty years before. Some of the orchard had been removed to make way for ground crops. Most of the acreage had been converted to miniature trees, an economic decision made through much of the valley during the years when the financial panic there was just beginning. Around his mother's cottage there were still the old yard trees, but he was looking for a stand, old twisted branches where a god might rest himself. He found a few old cherry trees still acting as a windbreak along the highway. But he had to settle, he told himself, for a secular fruit ranch.

He stayed with them for two weeks, and allowed the very image of London to sink below the horizon. Before he left he asked her seriously for some new poems. She said she had not been writing anything since "retirement age," but she did put a small book into his coat pocket. He had had no idea that there was a new book. He would read it on the plane. He hoped dearly that the poems would be perfect.

On the day that her second book arrived at the post office, there was also a letter from Ottawa. She knew what it was before she opened it. She saw Morrison's shattered body on a stretcher, carried as fast as they could manage by two soldiers in steel caps, objects exploding in the background. She saw his eyes become dull. She listened to hear whether he spoke anything of her.

But it was her brother. In a place called Anzio. That night she looked it up. It was a fine sandy beach. She remembered being there when they were children, learning to count: *uno, due, tre, quattro.*

Ira. When they were children she called him Chip.

She thought she could write a poem for him. But she did not. She read the encyclopedia. For a while she stopped reading the newspaper. She read about Italy in the encyclopedia. Sandy's mother's encyclopedia.

When they were nine and ten, they went to hear the children's choir in Saint Mark's. The children sang Christmas songs they knew and Italian songs that only sounded familiar. The cardinal arrived and the children beamed as they were taught to do. Officious nuns scurried around backstage, where Chip had found a place to stand, nuns pushing children into place, silencing little girls who had not made a sound between songs. The cardinal smiled, a gift of his high office. Everyone did as they were supposed to do. The children sang *Adeste Fidelis*, and it was perfect, it filled the old brown bulby edifice, and then everyone went outside into the square.

It was snowing! Children broke ranks and raced about in the provisionary snow, making little snowballs and hurling them awkwardly at one another. PB and Chip stayed close to their parents and watched with gratefulness. They thought, despite what their father said, that there might be a God, in Italy at least.

Uno, due, tre.

She put one copy of the new book on the table beside the apricot window, and the rest on the shelf with the six copies that remained of her first book. The cover was elegant, simple, the colour of dry meadow grass. It was difficult to believe that someone might be reading it in a shadowed room in London, in Philadelphia.

Next day in the village post office she received a blue envelope with British stamps on it. Inside was a letter from Morrison's lawyer. Morrison wished to inform her that he was initiating procedures that would make their separation legal and prepare the way for their divorce.

That made two pieces of mail from England on consecutive days.

The letter did not say where her husband was now. Her last letter from him had been written on the south coast of the Mediterranean Sea. She presumed that he had crossed from there to Italy, but were the British in Italy with the Yanks and the Canadians? Sometimes she imagined Morrison dead on the fine sand of Anzio. Other times she imagined him with a swagger stick and little objects on his shoulders, strutting in front of younger soldiers standing in rows, like a little orchard made of scratchy brown wool. Sometimes she pictured him entering a doorway with a thin dark girl, and then she stopped imagining him.

When they were nine and ten she and Chip visited Nero's Villa at Anzio, at Antium. They saw the great statue of Apollo Belvedere, their mother said. They asked her whether it was the real one, the first one, but she did not tell them. Was Circe ever here, PB asked her Mennonite mother.

When PB began to read the newspapers again, she became fascinated with the maps. Every week in the newspapers the map of Europe and the map of Asia changed. In Europe the black part where the Germans still ruled grew smaller, shrinking from all sides. The white and gray areas came closer together, and large curved arrows showed the latest movements of the Americans and Canadians and British, eastward and northward. The arrows from the east had hammers and sickles beside them. In Asia the islands were sources of the curved arrows, or their targets. The black islands grew fewer. In the newspapers the changes were good news. The generals were exuberant. History was moving in the right direction. On the ground in the black areas there were many broken buildings, and under the mountainous weight of the broken buildings there were young girls with bare legs. PB continued to knit and to collect metal. She wrote letters to soldiers she did not know. That was what they called the "war effort." She did not write as if she were a poet. She did not mention the things she was mentioning in her poems. She did not mention, either, her brother or her husband.

And in the last year of the war she received a letter from her mother. Her father, whom she had left on the station platform in Philadelphia was gone, gone in a month of good news. His Moravian funeral had passed while the letter was being carried westward. There was no reason to go to Philadelphia.

A week later she received a letter from Sandy and Sandy's mother. They said that the funeral was quiet. They said that there was a piece in the newspapers in Philadelphia, on the middle pages, after the news about Europe and Asia.

PB climbed to the second bench above the valley floor, and walked and sat and looked at the bright sun on the brown grass. She did not know that she was looking at the grass, but when she brought her mind back to looking from her gray eyes, she saw that she was looking at the coyote. It was looking at her, its tongue hanging far out of one side of its jaws, its grin. Was he, on these occasions, the visitor, or was she? She stared and stared, and when again she returned to looking from her eyes, the coyote was not there.

When the black area was no bigger than a city block and the war was folded into history in Europe, she was in San Francisco. The very famous Mr Oliver was in Mexico for the moment, but the smiling Mr Gray had a cottage in Berkeley.

"I dont suppose that my father could have been Count Zizendorf," the boy shouted from the kitchen, where he was drying the day's dishes.

"Dont be cheeky," she said. "It does not become you. You are, remember, a miracle boy."

He put away the tea towel and walked as any twelve-year-old might walk, into the little sitting room. He was, as he often was, eating a peach. With a look alone she indicated that he should not eat it over any furniture or carpet. He held his head and the peach out the open window.

"Oh? At school I am your normal C-plus," he said, juice on his face.

"To my everlasting sorrow."

"What were you?"

"About a C-plus."

"Some miracle," he said.

He was going to be quite tall when he grew up, she could see. At twelve years he had not yet developed the clumsiness that plagued her all through her school years, as she grew to stand taller than her teachers and yet felt that she held nothing in her head. All through school she read a book she had found in the attic of an abandoned house, *Between Two Worlds* by a man named Philo. She had thought that it would be something like H.G. Wells, but it was something else. She knew, because she had found it so strangely, that none of her classmates and none of her teachers would know about it. Then they would never read the books she would write while they were living in their houses.

"Perhaps miracle is too sentimental a word," she said, and he could see that now she was serious again.

So he waited for a while, reached his arm fully outside and with a backhand motion threw the wet peach pit across the lawn into the grass of the orchard. Her new book, a kind of little novel, perhaps, was lying on the round table. He saw the permission in her eyes and looked at a few pages.

"Maybe you could tell me what nationality I am," he said. "I mean we are always filling out these forms. and they want to know what nationality."

"What do you write?"

"Canadian, like everyone else, just about."

"All right then," she said.

"But what am I really?"

"I dont know," she said. Not because she didnt know where he had been born. Not because she didnt know well enough who his father was.

"Is Claire my father?" he asked.

"Shut up," she said.

The sun shone warmly in Berkeley, but looking west across the bay she could see clouds roll over the city, roll toward her, and stop halfway across the still new bridge. Over there the people wore coats and tried to hurry up and down the steep streets. In Berkeley PB sat in a garden with a fortunate kumquat tree and read Euripides and wrote a few lines of poetry. Every second day she went to the university swimming pool and laid her long body in the water, swimming two more lengths each time.

With Andrew Gray she went to concerts across the bay and at the university. In the pool she would remember the music and strike out at the water in front of her while attending to the rhythm and the melody inside her. She found herself swimming beside a young woman, a girl with hair so short that one could see the perfect shape of her skull. They swam, and afterward, they walked together down Shattuck, sometimes stopping for lemonade, for tea. The girl's name was Claire, and her last name was well known in the financial district across the bay. PB waited a month, and then gave her a book of Euripides.

That was one of the three important things that happened while PB was in California that year, just after the war. B.P. Oliver came back from Mexico and was sometimes around, but that was not as important as it might have been. The second important thing was that PB again began to carry life inside her. At the pool she was amused and a little alarmed to see her belly gradually fill out.

Her brother was dead. Her father was dead. Her daughter was dead. Her husband was gone. Sandy was in Philadelphia, with a husband who belonged to clubs.

PB did not want to go through it all again. Better to tear it out of her now and fill her with drugs. But she went to the pool every second day, and watched herself, if it was herself, grow. Young Claire massaged her back before they swam. It was very helpful. Where did she learn that?

Then there was the third important thing that happened to her there in California. A polio virus entered her body by way of her throat. From her alimentary tract it was absorbed into her blood and lymphatics, whence it was widely disseminated and ultimately reached her central nervous system.

She could not go to the pool any more. She lay in bed and tried to read, but her fever would not allow Euripides. She had a sore throat, a headache, nausea, and then aching legs. So they knew what it was. The university doctor asked her whether she were pregnant, and he said that pregnant women were especially vulnerable. I have always, she tried to say, been vulnerable. But she fell, all day long, into and out of a sleep that brought her restlessness for this moment to a relief. When she opened her eyes she thought she saw the face of Claire, here in the house. It was Claire, she thought, who moved her legs for her.

"My daughter?" she whispered. And the three men did not know what she meant.

"Do you think there is a Limbo?" she asked once, when she could open her eyes and speak a sentence. But no one answered her.

Take me to the valley, she heard herself say. But she did not know for certain whether she had said it aloud. In the hospital she looked out the window and saw a tree. It may have been a cherry tree. It may not. Claire's hair was very short, and it had the colour of someone she remembered. Claire removed her white mask and smiled for her, and it was the only genuine smile among them all.

Now she was in the same hospital room she had been in before, or she was not, and she would lose her daughter again. She did not want to see her this time. She could not feel her own legs now, but Claire moved them for her. Claire massaged her back.

The news came that her father had died and people had performed a respectful Moravian funeral. Can you drive a motor car, she asked Claire one day late in 1946.

Can you find the eggs the hens hide in the tall grass? *Uno, due, tre.*

So somewhere he was born. He would never see his birth certificate. He would grow up in the valley and move away. His mother gave him a name out of Latin, but he would move away and call himself (GB) and write poems. Why not? In fact he would write some of hers when he wrote a story about her life. He would think he was writing some of hers.

sets the stage for the rest of the stories

Rhode Island Red

Trust me, this will take only a fraction of the time it would take to write and read a novel, but there will be order somewhere here, faint order, human traces anyway.

If you were not in the South Okanagan Valley in the fifties you will not be able to picture the scene I am picturing. But you can say this on the other hand, that no matter how well we think we are remembering scenes of thirty years ago, whenever we are given the opportunity to check those memories, we are invariably wrong, sometimes a long way off.

So I will have to do a little description, I guess, at least to get this going. The consolation will be that we will no longer have to listen to the voice delivering the goods in sentences that start with the first person singular pronoun. I like pronouns, but that one is not my favourite. Description, then. But be aware, wont you, that description will not bring you the authentic look or feel of the place.

We are three miles, because they still used miles then, south of the village of Lawrence. Lawrence could have been called a town, but the people who lived there persisted in calling it a village because that was cheaper when it came to taxes. No one could tell you how that worked, but everyone seemed to think that it made good sense.

Three miles south of Lawrence, let us say, in November. The orchards are just beginning to turn skeletal, the season's fruit-picking finished weeks ago. Just across Highway 97 there is a funny-looking apple tree. It owns perhaps only seven dry curled brown leaves, but there are apples hanging all over it. These are over-ripe apples, brown and wrinkled. If the orchardist working on his tractor up by the house were to drive down here and bump the tree's trunk with the front of his machine, he would find himself in a rain of apples that were useless except to the health of the soil covered right now with slick leaves.

He would probably also notice the chicken hurling its head at the pebbly ground beside the blacktop, and carry it under his arm back up the dirt road to the home yard.

There is no fence between this orchard and the highway. Fences are only a nuisance around the kind of farm on which workers are always moving ladders or trailers covered with props or empty boxes. As every orchardist along the road has said at least once, you dont need a fence to keep apple trees in, and any fruit thieves that come in uninvited at night are going to have to get used to rocksalt in the ass. The kids around Lawrence figured that every orchardist had a shotgun loaded with rocksalt or worse standing by the back porch door along with the baseball bats.

Most families had chickens in their yards in those days. Even in town, where people would make little chicken runs out of chicken wire, with a roof of chicken wire to keep large dogs out or to keep the chickens in. It seemed normal to the narrator of this story, for instance, to keep chickens in the yard. When he was a kid in the South Okanagan in the forties he had to feed the family chickens. That was enjoyable, whether throwing grain on the ground for those flailing heads, or dumping the slop and watching them spear the corn cobs.

This chicken was a Rhode Island Red, a general-purpose breed created in the United States of America. It had a rectangular body and brown feathers of the shade called by parents red. By descent it had come from distant forebears in the jungles of Malaya. There were no roads through the jungles of Malaya in those days.

One time the narrator of this story planted some of the wheat that he normally would have fed as grain to his family's own Rhode Island Reds, and it grew. When the wheat plants were about three feet in height his younger sister pulled them out of the ground and threw them into the chicken coop. He still wonders, today, what made his sister think of doing that. The orchard in which their house stood contained lots of long grass, so she must have understood something about "wheat" when she ripped up his experiment to feed it to the chickens. Something about language. If he were to ask her now she would just treat it as an old family joke. Why did the sister pull the wheat?

These families in the south Okanagan kept chickens for eggs and for chicken meat. That is why the Rhode Island Red was so popular. It produced lots of meat, and brown eggs, thought by superstitious rurals to be superior to white eggs in the matter of nutrition. White eggs were for city folks who also betrayed their personal biology with white sugar and white bread.

The sperm lives in the hen's oviduct for two to three weeks. Yolks originate in the ovary and grow to four centimetres in diameter, after which they are released into the oviduct, where the sperm is waiting. Whenever we found a red dot in an egg we said "Aha!" In the oviduct the egg also picks up the thick white and some shell membrane. Then it heads for the uterus where the thin white and the hard shell are added. The making of an egg takes twenty-four hours. Orchard moms are proud of hens that lay an egg every day. They are amused by the biddies that hide them in the yard instead of leaving them in the coop.

Now, what about this one Rhode Island Red pecking away at pebbles and organisms at the edge of Highway 97? We certainly, I would think, cannot call her (or him if it is a capon) a central character in this little fiction. A figure at the middle of things, perhaps, but not a central character. A chicken does not have character. Unless you want to ascribe character to this Red's pecking and wandering away from the rest of the birds around the house, all the way down the dirt road to this shallow ditch beside Highway 97.

It is nowadays simply Highway 97, and not too much different from its condition in the late fifties. But in those days it was both Highway 97 and Highway 3, the alternative Trans-Canada. The two numbers, adding up as they did, really satisfied a teenage boy who lived in and around Lawrence, but he does not appear in this story. There is a human being, you will remember, sitting on a tractor, doing something of value up near the yellow stucco house, where the rest of the Rhode Island Reds and the Bantams are.

If this fowl were a central character, as it might have been were the story a fable, it would have to be set down in a significant setting for the unrolling of the narrative. Fables do not have characters, but only figures. Though Aesop's fables, for instance, are told in an attempt to mould character in their young listeners, one can hardly ascribe character to, say, a grape-eating fox. If one were supposed to think about him in terms of character, a child might ask, "Why does this fox desire to eat grapes, especially grapes that are out of reach?"

In any case, even though we refuse character to the young hen in this instance, we can say a few things about the nature of the setting she had pecked her way into. The most salient because unusual feature, as far as she was concerned, was the highway. It was a normal western asphalt or tar macadam road, what is called in the trade a flexible surface. Gravel of fairly consistent size is covered with hot bituminous material that penetrates the spaces between the little stones and then cools and hardens. If you are a quick driver you can just see a ribbon, as they say, of gray, or if it is the first month of a new highway, a ribbon of black. If your local member of the legislature is in the government's cabinet you will see more black than do people in other places. If you are a kid walking along the highway you can see the stones in the mix, and you have always wondered how many of them were Indian arrow heads. If you are a chicken pecking seeds and gizzard gravel into your interior, you will never get a pebble out of that hardly flexible surface.

There *was* a quick driver a few miles south, just passing Dead Man's Lake, heading north, probably going to the Coop Packing House in Lawrence.

He was driving a truck cab in front of a big empty trailer that was equipped with a refrigeration unit, which could be seen from the outside, a big square item on the top of the front of the trailer. The doors were open on the trailer, so one knew that the refrigeration was turned off right now. If the truck went by you slowly enough and you were on one side of the road you would be able to see the other side of the road for part of a second right thru the trailer. At the Coop there would be some men and lads in cold storage ready to load the trailer of the truck with boxes of Spartan apples. Then the doors would be closed, the refrigeration would be turned on and the truck would head to a large city grocery store chain whose name could be understood by anyone who could read now that the doors on the trailer were slid shut.

This truck was proceeding northward at about fifty miles an hour, which was the speed limit at that time as long as the road was straight, which was not often the case. Its driver was an old army veteran named Stiffy. He lived in the city where the grocery store chain was located, but he spent a majority of his days in the cab of his truck, trying to catch small town radio stations on his radio, stopping at roadside cafes where other rigs were stilled. He had had a conversation at Rhoda's Truck Stop in Castlegar this morning.

"Stiffy. How's it hanging, you old bugger?"

"Cant complain, Buddy. Cant complain."

The other driver's name was not Buddy. Stiffy called him Buddy because he couldnt remember his name, if he had ever known it. He called most men Buddy.

"I think I'm getting too old for this line of work," said the man.

"Know what you mean."

"No future in it either."

"Gettin' to be near time to pack it in and take it easy. Find out what my old lady does all day."

"Wouldnt know what to do with myself."

"Hah, I know what you do with yourself six or eight times a day, you old bugger."

"No, really. Guy owns the old bowling alley in Coleman. Been thinking of moving there, buy him out, live off the fat of the land."

"Oh yeah, bowling is getting more popular every day, they say."

"You know anyone goes bowling?"

"You know anyone wants to buy a Kenworth, one-quarter paid for?"

That was the conversation at Rhoda's, or most of it. During all that talk the driver we are interested in, if that is not an overstatement, was spooning up some chicken soup and biting at a grilled cheese sandwich. He often ate those things at Rhoda's, and something very much like that at the Orchard Cafe in Lawrence.

Now he was about ten miles south of Lawrence, braking behind a farmer in a rusty pickup truck halfway down Graveyard Hill.

In the high insect season trucks like that, and other traffic as well, brought about the demise of countless insects—fruit flies, grasshoppers, the black and yellow caterpillars that travelled the highway in huge groups. It was not high insect season now, but there were still some grasshoppers, those fleecy ones with wings that allowed them to fly in awkward trajectories. Despite the wings there were some dead grasshoppers on the macadam, perhaps a head squashed flat but a thorax still complete. The chicken in question was out on Highway 97, looking for body parts of grasshoppers.

There is a well-known benefit to this kind of diet. If you get your eggs from some large city grocery store chain you are likely to find, on opening them, that the yolks are pale yellow. If you boil them before eating them, you probably notice that the shells crack in the hot water. Those are eggs produced by chickens who are kept all their lives in the company of other chickens in small cages over conveyor belts. If you have your own chickens, and if they are allowed to forage, to eat bits of garbage and insects, their eggs will have tough shells and dark yellow or even orange yolks. They will taste a lot better than the grocery chain eggs. It wont matter whether they are white or brown; they will be higher in nutrition than those city eggs.

Stiffy's truck was no longer stuck behind the farmer's pickup. The farmer had become nervous about the sheer metallic weight behind him, and pulled off the road, without signalling. Now there was a 1949 Pontiac sedan behind Stiffy's trailer-tractor. Inside the Pontiac were four members of the Koenig family: Mr Koenig with his sunburned face and gas-station hat, and three of his teenaged children. The children were not in school because Mr Koenig was taking them into Lawrence to get their shots. At the beginning of the school year in September there had been a nurse at the school giving out shots, but the Koenig teenagers had not been in school. They had been picking apples as fast as they could till it got dark in their father's orchard. Now there was not an apple at the Koenig orchard except for the boxes of Spartans in the Koenig basement. Eighteen boxes of Spartans, and one box of Romes.

The Koenig kids did not care if they missed their shots. But there was a family in the orchard next to the Koenigs which had a son in an iron lung at the Coast. Mr Koenig hated to think about him.

Two of the Koenig kids were in the back seat. One, the oldest and strongest, was in the front seat beside his father. His face was not as red as his father's. He had been born in this valley.

This is the sort of thing the Koenig teenagers were saying:

"Murray told me the needle is yay long."

"Oh sure, did he tell you it's square?"

"What the hell do you know? When the doc says roll up your left sleeve, you always have to get some help from me."

"Listen, if you werent a girl I'd bash your teeth in."

"Just try it, jerk."

"Knock it off," said Mr Koenig.

The road was never straight for longer than a few hundred feet. It looked as if they were going to have to follow the big truck all the way into Lawrence. Maybe they could pass him around the Acre Lots, but by then they were just as good as in town anyway.

Trust me, we are nearly there, and you will admit, I think, that there is some kind of order here. Human traces and some poultry thrown in. That's a bad choice of verb. Let's just say some poultry added.

The poultry in question was now two-thirds of the way across Highway 97, trying unsuccessfully to back up and scratch at the surface, but finding better luck with its plunging head. There had not been any traffic for five minutes. That was unusual for that part of Highway 97 even in the fifties. People near the road could not help noticing, when that happened from time to time, a feeling of peculiarity, as if the location were being *prepared* for something. Now that the tractor was just sitting up there beside the house, you could hear the telephone wires singing above your head.

48

Then Stiffy's truck appeared both to ear and eye. Its tires played a high note that would not descend. Stiffy saw the Rhode Island Red, saw it lift its head and fall momentarily on its tail as it turned to run back to its home side of the macadam, saw it disappear under the front of his machine. He did not see what a witness, had there been one, might have seen. The blur of red-brown feathers emerged behind the truck's long trailer, the living chicken picked up by the wake of hot wind and thrown high in an awkward arc into the air. It did not sail, nor did it soar. It was a roundish bird in the low sky, not flying but certainly falling now, and as it did, along came the Pontiac sedan. Mr Koenig knew that it was a chicken. He even knew it was a Rhode Island Red. He had no idea how it had got where it was, hurtling toward the windshield of his car. He jigged the car slightly to the right, but the course of the hen was eccentric, and it became a smash of feathers and blood and claws and noise in front of his face where the glass became a white star. The car with four Koenigs in it was still moving to the right, and now the front right tire crunched into roadside gravel. Then the car went straight as the road went straight for a little while but in another direction. The Pontiac, having travelled for a moment at fifty miles an hour through long grass, stopped all at once against a leafless apple tree. If it had been the tree just to the left, the car would have been deluged with brown fermented apples.

All this made a noise. Stiffy, a half-mile north in the cab of his Kenworth, didnt hear any of it. But the orchardist and his wife did. It would not be long till they were both out of the house. Today they, like other people in the Lawrence vicinity, would be finding out what had happened. Tomorrow they would be thinking about why. Then they would talk about this event for a long time. Many of them would mention it in letters. As later events intervened they would sometimes ask each other a question or two about this one.

FAMILIAR ADMONITIONS

You want to know about Robbie? There was a child that just plain would not take a bit of advice. You could talk till you were blue in the face, but would he listen? Listen, that boy would wait till you were finished and then run right out and do just the opposite of what you told him. I never knew such a child for defying.

•

Those ones with the slightly knobby skin seem to be a little more spherical than these red and green ones.

These red and green ones are more sensitive to being dropped on the floor.

Those knobby ones with the blatant colour are, as far as I know, never used to convey an image of a maiden's breasts.

I said that they are only slightly knobby; some of them dont seem knobby at all, but rather smooth.

These red and green ones often still have their stems on them, which is never true of the others.

Nobody ever says you are the slightly knobby one of my eye, or comfort me with slightly knobby ones.

While I believe that they have all been kissed by the sun, I think that some of them rely on it a little more than others do.

Do you like that word? Convey?

•

You talk to the people at that place. They'll tell you what fun it was to have him at first—he wouldnt get up in the morning and he wouldnt go to bed at night. It was as if he didnt care about his health, like he was satisfied to be slow upstairs, if you know what I mean. I mean that might not be the school you'd want to send your kid to, but it's still a school.

•

Look at all these eggs.

There must be dozens of them, some hidden in the straw, others in the dark corners, quite a few in plain sight.

Figuring the law of averages, half will be female chicks and half will be males.

We will make all but about four of those into capons and let the rest enjoy life.

I'll bet there are about four dozen eggs here.

That'll be twenty-four hens and twenty-one capons and three cocks strutting around the yard.

Let's say those twenty-four hens lay six eggs each.

That'll give us just about two hundred chickens before we know it.

If we can keep up this rate, sooner or later we will find a female with some nice molars in her jaw.

•

They tell us he still thinks he's at home here, or he pretends like he is. There's times I wish he was, maybe just in the summer. But that boy is getting awfully big. They have people there who know how to handle big people like that. I mean it's not just a question of his dad and I. He could hurt himself too. Fact he does, from time to time.

·

Oh god, I hate this.

I can never have myself a bowl of cereal without getting milk all over the table and my chair and half the kitchen floor.

Other people can do it; little kids in television ads pour milk on their vile pastel cereal while looking in the other direction.

I have a friend who is legally blind, and I have never seen him lose a drop of milk.

Ah god, oh jeeze, why me, why me, why cant I just once in my life get the milk from the fridge to the bowl safely?

It's not as if I am not careful about expenses, I who will walk twelve blocks rather than feed a parking meter.

So here I go again, get the dishcloth and start wiping the table, the chair, half the kitchen floor, my shoes.

Oh jeeze, oh jeeze, oh jeeze, I'm sick of this, why do I even try, ah god . . . .

You're going to say it isnt the kitchen floor I'm worried about. This all stands for something else. Say whatever you want.

·

He had this thing about the car, always wanted to take the car out for a spin. For one thing it was illegal because of his age, and now, well, there's no way he's going to be allowed behind the wheel of a car. But he was always on about that. I think he wanted to drive that car more than he wanted anything else. His dad let him drive the tractor once or twice. But he couldnt even figure out how to run a horse and wagon.

•

I should put a huge sign on this thing, inside and out:
CLOSE THE DAMNED DOOR.

I really hate this.

First I have to come out here and close the door, and then it's up to me to go and find the damned horse.

I suppose people think barns are just decoration for tourists, and horses are shut inside barns by accident.

So leave the doors wide open and let the beautiful animals run free through nature and along the neighbour's creek.

People call up and say did your horse get loose again. I say what does he look like. They say a roan. I say no, he's more tan-like.

I dont know why I even bother to shut this damned door; it's not as if it's easy.

It isnt one of those fancy new electric doors the tourists have waiting for them at the end of their trip.

I bet people dont leave their garage doors open so their station wagons can get away on them.

I suppose I should make a point of going to the barn every fifteen minutes, to make sure the door is closed.

Then who would do all the stuff needs doing around this place?

•

They tell me he likes to do more than his share of the chores at that place. Fact they allowed as to how he's been sitting for less classes all the time and doing chores instead. I wonder if he thinks that doing chores will get him in good with the real grownups and maybe they'll let him come home for real. Well, I cant help thinking maybe he will. But you'll have to ask his dad about that, only I wish you wouldnt.

•

Of course if I was that horse and some idiot left the door open I'd be long gone too.

He is one hell of a smart horse; it didnt take me long to find that out.

I always used to see him pushing things, pushing a gate open with his head and shoulders, pushing other horses away so he could get at the hay.

Someone in the family tried to turn him into a dray horse, tried to get him to calm down and accept wagon traces.

He would never put up with it; he as much as said go get yourself a different-coloured animal.

One day during apple-picking the tractor broke down and there was a trailer full of apple boxes needed hauling.

I figured if he wouldnt pull that wagon maybe he'd give it a push.

So I lined him up and whacked him one.

He just grinned at me.

But he was still standing there, shoulders against the high end of the wagon.

I gave him a little Scotch thistle right in the tender part under his tail.

He pushed all right. He pushed the wagon right over on its side.

When they came with the neighbour's old spare tractor we had to spend most of the afternoon picking up apples and sorting them.

I'll never forget that horse's grin; I've tried for ages to imitate it, but I cant get it right.

•

Well, you've talked to him at that place. Does he sound like a dangerous boy to you? He's got a friend there, a fellow his own age who's mostly blind. Far as I've heard he takes care of that boy, watches out for him. You wouldnt be able to get too close to that blind boy without declaring your peaceful intent.

Apparently that boy's blind from his brother shooting him in the head.

·

I got into more trouble in that damned barn, especially when I was a kid, which wasnt long ago.

The manure pile used to be about five steps away from one end of it, but then we found out the flies made the trip back and forth.

The manure pile was in layers—manure, straw, manure, straw, and so on, up to about one and a half kids high.

I used to check it out for pitchforks and then take my broad jump, jumping and yelling "Muscatel!"

I would run the length of the barn loft where I had a path, and out into the sun and over the gap, kerplunk, right on top of the pile.

Heap, my mother called it; dung heap.

A leap in the heap, I called my event in secret. A jump in the dump.

But then we moved it, because of the flies; I mean flies and milk, eh?

I forgot all about it.

I had given up checking for pitchforks because I had never once seen a pitchfork in the manure pile.

I picked up speed, and yelled "Zamboni!" and in the middle of the air over the gap I saw it wasnt a gap anymore.

I hit the ground on my back and lay there for about an hour because I was the only one home.

Just lying there on the last little scraps of the oldest part of the manure pile, flat on my back.

I could hear the flies but after it got dark I couldnt see them.

·

There's times I think he's a lot smarter than we give him credit for. I never have been able to understand what they're talking about when they talk about that stuff. I mean it seems like there is one thing called intelligence and another thing called something else, maybe like figuring out how to handle the world. Or fit into it. Now a lot of the boys in that school havent got either of those things. But I have a feeling he's as smart as I am at least. I'm just lucky I never had any trouble fitting into the world.

·

I imagine that any young fellow brought up on a farm has a special attachment to the manure pile.

For instance, you could always find some perfect horse buns for throwing, usually because they rolled down to the bottom of the hill.

Not too wet, not too dry, not too heavy, not too light, not too small, not too big, just a little dry on the outside.

Usually I would throw them at the barn door, or the clothesline post, or if there were crows around, at the crows. Never the chickens.

Sometimes I would catch shit if they found too many broken horse buns all over the place.

So you would never throw them anywhere near the house.

One time the dogs were snoozing in the dusty July sun right at the base of the clothesline pole.

I was a pretty good thrower by this time, my first horse bun hit the clothesline pole about head level on a basketball player.

One dog opened one eye for one second; the other one waited for his turn, I guess.

My second shot missed the pole altogether, but my third one smacked into it right next to a dog ear that took a twitch.

Then I got carried away. I wound up like a baseball pitcher and fired one right into the ribs of the eye dog.

What happened next was very fast, less noisy than I would have wanted, and painful at last in the kitchen where the Mercurochrome was kept.

I can tell you that is the last time I want to see my blood on an animal's tooth.

●

I mean you've talked to him. Do you think his dad did the right thing, putting him in there with all those other special students they call them? I remember one time he sat right here at this table telling me about Darkest Peru. He wanted to go to Darkest Peru, he said, and he told me all about what it was like, all those strange animals and those Indian priests walking around those mountains in robes and bare feet. Made me kind of wonder how many different kinds of places there are in the world.

●

It wasnt just the stuff coming out of a horse that got me into trouble. It was the stuff going in the other end, too.

It's not as if I ever tried to get out of my fair share of work around here, nothing like that.

You think I should say there instead of here. Well, that too, if you want.

I have probably worked harder than any of those others at least during my lifetime, however long that is.

I have spent a lot of hours in that hay field over there, the other side of the barn.

Over there.

Just one time, maybe two, I was a little bit what you might call slow.

The machines were all at the garage or rented out to other spreads, so we were cutting by hand, with the old scythes from out of the back room in the garage.

That kind of work is fun at first, but you get hot, and thirsty.

So I went for a little swim up at the hole.

And fell asleep for a little while.

Later I said how about finishing tomorrow but they said the haying was set for today in that field.

So I swung that thing in the dark.

If you dont think that is a scary activity, try it sometime, I mean in the complete dark with no moon.

I was afraid I was going to put the sharp end into some stomach, a person or a creature anyway.

So I sang loud all night long, a song I made up about scything in the dark, all about look out.

You never want to do that for the first time, and I never want to do it again.

•

But what could you do? He shot Lightning, and then he had that accident he said with his foot, and then he was pointing the .30-.30 right at his dad. We were lucky to get out of that all alive, which you would know if you knew the things that have gone on around this part of the country the last ten years or so. Seems as if with a rifle you dont have to worry any more about how people might not understand what you are trying to tell them.

•

I dont like to go on and on about that horse, but the damned animal has given me nothing but trouble.

Ever since my father bought it as a black and then brought it home and the next day it rained and the horse turned light brown.

What we call a tan or a bay, but I dont know why, unless you mean the shitty-coloured bay I saw down your neck of the woods one time.

When my father bought that damned horse he paid too much for him, and he didnt get a good look at his teeth.

I never do that, he told me, makes your friends start thinking of you as a customer.

Anyway, one time I was riding old Sinful and leading that damned bay, and I got to thinking about the circus I saw down your way.

So I slowed old Sinful down and let the bay come up beside her, and then I started easing myself up, really slowly.

Till I was standing on her saddle, with both sets of reins as long as they could get in my right hand.

Then I started timing my little step-jump. I figured you couldnt just walk across, you had to time yourself to the horses' movement.

But just when I took my little whatever, the two horses took their step into Forbes Creek, which cuts down from the Forbes's old place right into our pasture.

And I'm sure he did it on purpose.

That bay jumped sideways just when I was fixing to land light on his bare back, and I think he might have snickered, too.

I landed tail-first in the middle of Forbes Creek, and those two animals took off for parts unknown.

Wound up I had to walk an hour and more to catch them up, me with a soaking wet pair of pants and a lot of creek water up my nose.

•

Mainly what we tried to tell him was how to fit into the world. He was just one of those people who cant do it very well. And no one can tell you how come that happens, as far as I'm concerned. Those people at the school cant tell you, and I cant tell you and the head-shrinkers cant, and the people who write those books, they cant tell you. They can tell you all about how people like that act, but we already know that. They cant tell you how come. They cant tell you whether it has to do with chromosomes and stuff or about how you changed their diapers. They cant tell you anything. You feel like shooting them after a while. Useless.

Seems like on a farm they cant decide what you are, the grownups, I mean.

Naw, you cant do that, you're just a kid, they say when you want to take the truck out for a run, like just up the concession road.

But when it comes to working they figure you're qualified all right, they figure working hard all day will make a man of you.

I wonder if canning peas all day will make a woman of you, for example.

But there were kid jobs; some of them because they were too persnickity for your old man and the hand, and some of them because they didnt want to get some kind of stuff on their clothes.

Feeding the chickens, that's a kid's job. Getting the cows out of the dugout, that's a kid's job.

But shooting the dog, I think that ought to be a dad's job.

You have to shoot a dog if it gets to be the way Lightning was getting, I can understand that.

But I dont think a kid is the right person to do that.

And Lightning knew damn well what was coming up and why I carried him down to the bottom of the home pasture.

I was just a kid, but I couldnt say that to him.

I shot Lightning in the neck and after a while he didnt blink the flies off his eyes, that's how you tell.

Then I shot myself.

But just in the foot. I suppose if I had been a bigger kid I might have shot myself in the mouth, like my cousin.

If I was a grownup I would have been able to stand it about Lightning, so I wouldnt have had to shoot myself at all

He should have done it himself. He shouldnt have been in such a hurry to make a man of me, that's what I think.

But I'm not about to tell him that.

•

All I know is I had three kids and now I dont have any, and if you think I am going to tell you about the other two you have another think coming.

NADAB

1

In the nineteen sixties a lot of youngish people in this country put on untraditional clothes, things like dashikis and Druid robes and Krishna sheets, whatever, and they started looking for exotic religions or at least nifty new ways to look solemn or entranced. They smiled sweetly and handed you a flower. They ate some kind of off-white stuff you never saw before, had to buy it in Chinatown or a strange new store where the pet shop used to be.

In the entertainment pages of the newspapers there were advertisements for mysterious Asian men who were looking for converts in college towns. There was always a photograph of the leader you never heard of before. He had really long hair that didnt look clean, or hardly any hair at all. You didnt think you'd be able to pronounce his name.

My high school friend Robbie Best quit his job at Eaton's, left his wife at her parents' place, and joined one of those outfits. Shaved his head, put on a sheet and changed his name to Nadab. Robbie Nadab, I guess, but he just called himself Nadab. Maybe Nadab Best. I just kept calling him Robbie, and he didnt make a big issue of it with me, because I was his closest friend.

But pretty soon I wasnt seeing him much. He didnt want to go to the pub any more, and I didnt want to quit going, and I couldnt go across the street and have coffee with him in Eaton's cafeteria now. It got so that I would hear more about him than I would hear from him.

The Bests were church-going people. I dont mean they slapped on pious faces and clean clothes and drove their Cadillac to the huge born-again parking lot. But Robbie used to haul himself out of bed with a hangover and go with them about every second Sunday morning. If I asked him about religion he changed the topic. But he was a Christian, all right. He said God damn it all the time.

But now I heard that he was dancing around clumsily on street corners, down the block from the Jehovahs with their right-wing magazines and the underemployed musicians with their open guitar cases. I figured they put most of the coins in their own guitar cases. And I have never seen anyone buying one of those magazines the Jehovahs hold up.

I went looking for Robbie one day after I had had a particularly greasy hamburger at you-know-where, the one in the financial district. Before that I had had a small number of large beers at the fustian pub in the Dripping Dog Lounge at the Kimberly Hotel. I liked this place because they had no strippers, no music and no happy hour.

It didnt take long to spot Robbie. He was one of about eight skinny orange guys hopping up and down in front of the Steadfast Bank. One of them was banging his fingers on a drum slung from his shoulders, and the rest of them had little brass cymbals they clanged together monotonously. Robbie had stopped wearing glasses. I think he was per-suaded that his new outfit would bring him perfect eyesight.

So he didnt even know who I was when I spoke to him. I wouldnt have said anything at all if I hadnt had the right amount and combination of beer and grease.

"Robbie," I said. What in God's name are you doing, bare feet on the cigarette butts?"

"Hairy Rama," he said.

"What?"

"God's name," he said, jumping up and down, banging his brass.

2

I dont know where Nadab got that name. I know I have never heard it before, and it isnt an Indian name, that's for sure. When he joined us that's the only name he admitted to, whether first or family, I couldnt say.

For some reason we kind of drifted together. I had been in the temple for three years, about average for our group, I'd say. For some reason—no one ever told me to— I became the person who showed him the ropes. When we hit the airport he rode there with me on the bus. When we were preparing the feast at the temple he worked beside me, chopping vegetables.

I was the only person there he ever mentioned his wife to. Here's what he said about her: "I dont want to talk about it."

I thought he was a little strange at first, because of his eagerness. He would listen to a tiny suggestion from me, about how to hold a paring knife, for instance, and nod his head vigorously, and clap his hands together.

"Got it!" he'd say. Loud.

Every day his complexion would seem to get a little darker. Maybe I was seeing things, but I thought his shaved head was a kind of dark blueish around the second week, and then his bare arms, they started looking blue, too. He asked me if I knew where the girl Radha was. I told him to watch what he said out loud.

Then he started on the butter. We got goat butter from a farm that was friendly to us, big tubs of it. He would stick his arm in and get a handful, make a ball of it. He would toss this ball of butter back and forth from hand to hand, dancing around me and the other people in the kitchen. Once he tossed it to me, and I caught it, but I said dont do that again.

"Got it!" he said, catching my toss.

Then he started carving things out of butter. We're here to prepare a feast, I told him. But he just said he was preparing another kind of feast for our souls. I reminded him that he was a relative newcomer.

First he carved an animal of some sort. It was hard to tell, could have been an alligator, could have been a llama.

But he got better at it. I was sprinkling cumin on carrot sticks one day, and he was carving butter. I had got used to this, I guess, and wasnt paying much attention, but he reached around from behind me and held his latest creation in front of my face, a little too close for focus at first. It appeared to be a figure of a chubby boy.

"What the heck is that?" I asked, naturally.

"Our Lord, the eighth avatar of Vishnu," he said.

And he placed the statuette on the table along with his paring knife.

He did that until he got pretty good at carving the butter boy. He was finally able to make an image of the boy dancing and holding a little ball of butter.

Usually one of us would rescue the figure from the table and return it to the tub and squash it. Nadab started making spares and hiding them around the kitchen.

One day he made a figure of Krishna with big wings. That didnt last long. Next he made a figure of Krishna with a fish's tail, like a merman, I guess you'd say. It reminded me of something, maybe a statue I had seen somewhere. To be on the safe side I put it in the tub.

Late that night or really early the next morning I was wakened by a thumping a little too near my head. I opened one eye and then the second. There was Nadab dancing in our end of the room, dancing barefoot around three butter statuettes, one regular boy, one with wings, and one with a fish tail.

"You are just too strange for me," I said.

"Slip slidin' away," he said, dancing.

3

The day he came home from the Krishnas was a day to remember, I can tell you. Well, he didnt exactly come home.

"God damn it, stay out of my way, Sis!" is the first thing he said to me.

He threw his sleeping bag on my living room floor, and slammed the front door against the world. He was wearing tight blue jeans and a teeshirt with a picture of some English guitarist on it.

"God damn assholes," was the opinion he shouted as if through the closed door.

I did not think that it was a good time to ask him, no matter how sweetly, what the matter was in general.

He stomped his way into the kitchen, and rattled open the knife drawer. Several knives fell to the floor and clattered around his sandalled feet.

"God fucking damn it all to hell," he shouted this time, dancing among the bouncing knives.

I fought my impulse to squat down and pick up knives. I also gave very little thought to asking him about Margie.

He picked up the biggest knife there, grabbed the top-knot sticking out of his blueish head, bent down to look into the magnet mirror on the fridge, and started sawing at the hair. He managed to create a red slice on his thumb.

"Aw shit, aw God, aw shit, aw Christ," was his cry. He sawed a little more, leaving a scrabble of hair and blood on his head, and threw the knife into the sink. It spun around and popped back out. He had to step quickly to the side. The knife knocked over a thin glass vase with a rose in it. Water spread across the counter top.

"Oh, great!" I offered.

He collapsed into a chair and started laughing. I stood there with my hands on my rather commodious hips and glared at him and the mess for a moment. Then I got a paper towel and went to work on the water.

He had his thumb in his mouth, trying to keep his blood.

"You look like you did when you were one year old," I said.

He took his thumb out of his mouth and laughed a little more. I handed him a piece of paper towel and he wrapped it around his thumb.

"Oh God," he said.

"I take it that's it for the Krishers," I ventured.

I picked up the kitchen scissors from the floor and got behind him and cut his scrabbly hair down to a brush-cut topknot.

"God damned six-armed dickheads," he expanded.

"What did you do with your sheet?" I enquired.

"Wiped my ass with it and left it as my last piece of art," was his reply.

"Art?" I persisted.

"They've got stupid ideas about art," he said, looking at the red stain coming through the paper towel. "All brass, no butter."

I didnt think I was going to learn much more this way. I could have said the one word, butter, with a question mark, and he would have cursed and said something else I would have had to ask another word about. Is that a sentence? Robbie has always had a way of making it hard to say a sentence.

"Some guy from the temple phoned about fifteen minutes before you came whispering through the door," I said, unwrapping his thumb and reaching for the kitchen bandaids. "He said to tell you someone sat on the one you had hidden in the bathroom, whatever that means."

Robbie stood up. His eyes were filled with sadness and glee.

"Lord love a duck," he said, and took me in his arms. First time he ever did that.

4

After he was finished with the Krishnas, Robbie installed himself at Alma's place, so what Alma had, basically, was a third kid and still no husband. None of our business, this late in the day, of course. But I still think of them as our kids. They're not kids, of course, but they are ours. Alma has presented us with two grandchildren, and Robbie has presented us with quite a few bills. At least Margie is staying at her own parents' place and not with us.

But he is our son. Roger has asked me once in a while if I could prove it, but he's only kidding. Or so I keep telling myself.

So now Robbie was plunked down on Alma's living room couch, and from all I hear he spent a lot of time there. Eating and sleeping have always been Robbie's strong suits. At least before and after the Krishna stuff. I saw his crew dancing on Denman Street once, and that was the most energy I had seen Robbie expending since he was about thirteen years old, when he dropped out of little league hockey.

Except for the Sundays. Roger and I always go to church on Sunday, and there was a time when we took Alma and little Robbie. But Alma got married when she was sixteen, if you know what I mean, and Robbie went to a community college for a year and a half.

Dont get me wrong, Roger and I arent your born-agains or anything like that. We've never talked about religion during the week. We've always figured the week was for working, and Sundays were for church. That's the way it was for Roger's parents and that's the way it was for my parents. In our day that counted for something. In fact I met Roger at a church picnic, back when young people went to those kinds of things.

The first Sunday after Robbie moved in with or maybe you could say moved in *on* Alma, we came home from church, Roger and me, and there was Robbie, up on our roof. At first I figured this was another of his weird things, but no, he had a bunch of black tar shingles and a hammer and he was covering the leaky spots. He stayed up there all day, sweating in the sun, banging on the roof. Didnt even come down for lunch, just asked us to throw a wax-paper sandwich up to him. Bang bang, all day and up till dark, around eight thirty that night.

Next Sunday we came home and he was painting the garage. Same thing. All day, with a half hour off to go and charge some more white paint at the Irly Bird store. I looked out the window and saw him up the ladder, painting with one hand and eating his chicken sandwich with the other.

Next week it was the fences, all white in the setting sun.

Trimmed the hedges, mowed the lawn, cleaned the outside windows, dug a new drain, painted the front porch, cleaned out the fish pond, a barrel of water full of fish for the whole week till the next Sunday.

 My neighbour Trudy said I was a lucky mother, but why didnt he come on Monday to finish the stuff he couldnt get finished on Sunday?

Search me, I told her.

This went on for four months, till we had the spiffiest property on the block. Every Sunday at the fall of darkness, Robbie washed his hands at the outside tap and put his, or rather our, tools away in the garage. No thanks, he would say when we offered him some supper. He always looked worn-out when he walked out of sight up Twenty-fifth.

Alma came over about every third Sunday afternoon, with the grandchildren. We were always glad to see them.

"Does he do any chores around your place?" I asked her once.

"He swept a slug off the back step once," she said, with her usual tired-sounding voice.

5

I felt a little funny coming home from church and seeing him painting the fence or edging the lawn. One time he put sawhorses at the end of the driveway and laid down new asphalt. I felt funny because of the neighbours, if that doesnt sound like a stupid thing to say.

I mean his mother and I are not strict believers in everything the Old Testament says. But if we wanted to bring someone home after church for a little lunch or just a cup of tea, we had to think twice about it. I mean with him out there with his shirt off, sweating away at a pile of fire-place wood or something.

Many's the time his mother and I asked him in for lunch himself during those weeks. But she would wind up making him a chicken sandwich and taking it out to him, while he worked right through Sunday. He would never come around any other day.

It was well into fall when I got into my first bad argument with him. I had gone out to the garage to drain the carburetor on the wife's Chrysler, getting ready to put in antifreeze for the winter, you know.

He was in the garage, replacing a broken window pane.

"Where you going?" he asked.

I told him.

"I'll do her goddamned antifreeze," he said.

It was one of the longest sentences he had spoken since coming out of the Krishners.

"No, I like having something to do," I said.

"But it's Sunday," he said. "I thought you church people kept the sabbath holy."

"It's just your mother's antifreeze," I said, trying to keep this as light as it seemed possible.

"She can shove her antifreeze up her ass, as far as I'm concerned," he said. He almost broke the pane of glass he was holding.

"I dont want you talking like that about your mother," I said.

"You can shove half of the antifreeze up your ass, too," he said. "And the radiator along with it."

Excuse me for repeating what he said. This is the first time I have ever used this kind of language talking to someone outside the family, and I'm only using it to try to explain how terrible this all seemed to me. I'm sure it should have warned me about what was going to happen. But I didnt know how to handle it. All the troubles we'd had with Robbie as a kid, he never talked to us this way.

I walked out of the garage toward the back door. He followed me, yelling so anyone on the block could hear.

"She can shove everything in this goddam garage up her ass!"

I turned to look at him. I think I wanted to make sure he wasnt trying to get past me, at her, or something.

"She can drop dead right now," he shouted, "and you too!"

I went inside and closed the kitchen door. And locked it. I could see him back in the window of the garage, knifing putty around the glass.

"What went on out there?" the wife asked.

"You dont want to know," was all I could tell her.

6

Look, we have a pretty good arrest record, at least on this side of town. Eighteen murders in the whole city last year, and fifteen of the perpetrators inside so far.

But this isnt Erle Stanley Gardner. I mean it is a fact of life that people get away with crime from time to time. Murder in Shaughnessy in nineteen thirty-five, the books are still open. Maid found dead on a rich guy's lawn.

We never close the books on them, but face it—some crimes are easier to solve than others. Guy murders his wife after a night of heavy drinking, see them all the time. No problem. Just have to make sure we get the procedure right.

The Krishna guy? Well, we know a few things. It wasnt drugs. It wasnt sex. It wasnt stolen property. It wasnt a drive-by. It wasnt a gang-related shooting. If it was a gang shooting we would have the guy now. Those punks are so goddamned stupid. Squeal tires all the way up Cambie Street right after doing someone at a restaurant full of witnesses. Gangs wouldnt be caught dead using a .22, anyway.

You want motive, you want opportunity, you want information on the victim's family and enemies. And friends, sure.

The victim was a Caucasian male, hundred and sixty centimetres tall, seventy kilograms in weight, blond hair in a pony tail or whatever the hell they call them, wearing sandals and an orange tablecloth and a pair of Standfields. Unmarried. No criminal record.

Shot with a small-calibre rifle from close range.

I am not holding out on you. You want a story, watch television. They catch them all the time. Blow up a building, run a car off a cliff, sell beer for a few minutes, get the killer.

We dont do stories here.

Okay, yes, we have a few suspects. All of them wearing orange tablecloths. All of them said they knew the victim but not very well. Name? John Arthur Radnicky, formerly of Cloverdale.

I know, the papers said his name was Ram Dass Shastri. That's what all the suspects called him. We go by birth certificates.

You might call it a terrible thing, youth shot in his twentieth year. You should have a drive around with us some Saturday night.

7

I remember seeing him and Alma growing up next door, but I didnt think much about him or her as far as that goes. Not in those days. She went and got herself a temporary husband, but I dont think they were ever married. He went and got a wife, or so I'm told. I never set eyes on her.

But after he got away from the Krish whatevers, I couldnt help noticing him. The first few Sundays he came home to work in the yard and so on, he would take his shirt off. Nice skinny kid, but muscles. Probably from all that dancing on street corners. Maybe that vegetarian food they cook up in their big pots.

I took to looking at him through the kitchen window. Seems like I had a lot of work to do in the kitchen on Sundays. Mornings his parents were off at their church in the Heights, and he was out there sweating in the sun, his hair, you know how it was all shaved off except I guess you'd call it a five-o'clock shadow all over his nice round skull? Me, I usually go for pretty long hair that gets sweaty and sticks to a guy's neck. Well.

 I said to myself, Trudy, if that boy crosses the bound-ary between their yard and this one you've got all the right in the world.

I knew I wouldnt see Ed till supper time. He would be beery and vague, and I would have to hear how close he came to punishing par, as he puts it. Plays golf every Sunday, rain or shine.

I mean if you're a golf widow, Trudy, I said to myself, that's just as good as being a regular widow, at least for Sundays.

I never saw him in his dancing sheet. His mother said she saw him once and that was enough for her.

But I saw his flat belly and it wasnt too long till I showed him mine. Well, mine isnt all that flat, but it's pretty good for my age, which I am not about to tell you. But let me put it this way: when that boy was born I was in high school. And Ed's belly was pretty good in those days too.

I gave up waiting for him to trespass on my yard. I took to waving at him from the kitchen window. I took to wearing stuff I didnt usually wear to operate the sink and its contents.

One day I said to hell with it and came outside to wave at him. From the porch. From the yard. Turned out it was me that did the trespassing.

Remember that old saying, your place or mine? He wanted to try his place, or rather his parents' place. Said he wanted to honour them. I didnt have a clue what he was talking about. But I figured that what I had in mind was going to take longer than any church service, and my own son only came home every second Monday to do his laundry in my machine.

Turned out there was a lot he didnt know, and I got to explore an old ambition I had once had to be a teacher. I taught him about the things you can do with old nylons with runs in them. I showed him all about the carpeted stairs. I myself learned something about a bald young head with stubble on it.

Sometimes when he was completing a lesson he would shout "Harry Krishna!" I'd like to have met that fellow.

8

I guess you could say I started noticing things were going missing when I brought my friend Louis home to show him my golfing trophies. My hole-in-one trophy from Widdershins Golf and Country just wasnt there. You should of seen it. It was the ball I done it with, you know, a Titleist No. 2, set on a kind of brass pedestal and then the usual stuff, a plaque with the information, third hole and all, scratched in, and the base, walnut, probably. Only hole-in-one I ever got, and now the trophy isnt there. Then I look around and there's other trophies gone, like the one I got for most congenial at the Upper Mainland tourney in 'seventy-six. Terrific weekend up there, if you know what I mean, and the golfing was great, too. Well, of course I calls Trudy down and says where the hell are my trophies. She says how should I know, maybe you, meaning me, maybe you sent them out to get bronzed. Always a smart answer from Trudy, you can depend on it. I mean if you cant depend on your wife what can you depend on, know what I mean? So Louis starts in about how he doesnt believe I ever got a hole-in-one, and I says to Trudy, tell the man, and she says she figures it's been years and years since I had two on any hole. Gotta give her credit, she knows a funny line when she hears one. I gave her a shot after, you know? Because Louis is a good friend of mine, and I dont want him thinking I cant handle things on the back nine, get what I'm saying? So I am pretty well pissed off, because I dont know when I'll ever get a hole-in-one again, though last year at the Cow Pie open in Prince George, no, really, that's what they call it, takes place first thing when the snow melts, I nearly got one on their par three sixteenth hole, a hundred and eighty-five yards, little dogleg to the right, but the ball hit and didnt roll at all, just sort of sank a quarter-way into the soft green. I was about two feet from the cup, and lined up just perfect, coulda kicked it in, which of course I would never do in a tournament. A week or two later I come home from the club and my electric razor is missing. Trudy doesnt know a thing about this, either. I'm starting to think, is she selling this stuff to raise money for something, drugs, whatever? But she's got lots of loot. I mean have a look in her closet, full of silk shirts and nasty looking boots. I always used to get her to keep her boots on, know what I'm saying? Used to. Well, you dont have to hear about that. So where the hell is my razor.

Search me, she says, and she's humming away, some Beatles song, at the stove, making short ribs. Whenever she makes short ribs she says the same thing, like here's some ribs just about as short as you know what. A real barrel of laughs, this comedienne, as they say on late-night. A week later it's my English pajamas, just got them last Christmas. Turned a little cool that week and I wanted those English pajamas with their nice thick flannel. Nowhere to be found. Next thing is my .22, had it since high school, for Christ's sake. She's humming at the stove. Hey, bitch, I say, because you might as well know, I triple-bogied the eighteenth that day, are you giving away my stuff even before I'm dead? I thought that was a pretty good one. She turns and looks at me with those eyes that look a bit like spaniel eyes, and I know she's telling the truth. Nope, it's nothing of *yours* I'm giving away, she say. Right then I decided to double back and watch the house instead of heading to the club. But then I figured, what the hell, once I get out on the fairways I dont much give a shit what's happening at home.

9

Hey, my brother-in-law is a creep in a *lot* of ways, a lot of ways, but I dont figure him for a killer. For one thing, he wouldnt shoot some religious freak in a religious freak church or whatever they call them. For another thing, even if he *was* going to off a guy, maybe the guy was trying to sell him a flower, he wouldnt go home and get his gun. He'd hit him with whatever he was carrying in his hand, probably either a golf club or a bottle of beer.

So they found the rifle in his garage? Big deal. Well, it looks bad at first, but when my brother-in-law says the gun went missing a couple weeks ago, I believe him. Trudy, well I asked her, and she just gave me that blank look, like she's my sister and doesnt want to even enter into a conversation with me, not even when it's her husband's funeral.

She blows cigarette smoke at me. Nice.

But what burns my ass is the guy next door, well, at his old man's place, guy called Best, if you can believe it. Says he saw Ed bringing the gun home with his golf clubs that Sunday night. I never liked that kid, even when he was living at home. Used to give me the creeps. Sat out in his back yard reading books when he was about fourteen years old, even in the middle of the summer when there was no school.

Once he built an altar out there. That's right, an altar. Made of this square shiny black stuff, marble or orynx or something. Made a few little steps leading up to it. Used to put food there. Trudy said she saw a dead squirrel on it one time. Road kill, I hope.

This guy, changed his name lately, I mean he was one of those religious freaks for a while, earlier in the year. He says he figures Ed was after him. Now why the hell would Ed be after him? I dont think Ed even knew the guy was back at his old man's. Well, on *Sun*days he was back, that's what Trudy says. Fixing up the place. Trudy says he didnt make an altar this time.

She said a funny thing. Said the body is a temple and that's where we should go to worship. Trudy has always been the weird one in the family.

So Ed, they wont let him out. They say he's too dangerous. There was this time he hit someone on the golf course.

"Why'd you do that?" I asked him during our visit.

"The old fucker said he didnt believe me when I gave myself a five on the third hole," he said.

And he chuckled. He chuckled. I dont think he's very worried about this murder charge. Not worried enough.

Because then this Best jerk said when he was at the church or whatever you call it the dead kid told him he was afraid of Ed. Said Ed threatened to shoot him one time when he was working the golf course with some other guys from his outfit, the dead kid.

Now I know this is a lie, for sure.

"That's a lie for sure," I told Trudy.

Trudy just looked at me. I am her big sister, but she always tries to make me think she's *my* big sister. This has a lot to do with the fact that me and Ed had something going before she started up with him. She thinks we had something going *after*, too, I'm pretty sure.

God damn it, the whole thing pisses me off.

And I'd sure as hell like to know why that Robbie Best or whatsisname now is doing all this to Ed. Lying son of a bitch!

10

Hey, I'm glad the bastard is finally in jail. He killed a friend of mine, didnt he? I'm supposed to feel *sorry* for him? Give me a break.

Anyway, I'm not worried about what you think, and I'm not worried about him, I can tell you that. Only thing I'm worried about is Trudy. She said it's not a good idea for me to be seen over there, at least not till the trial is over and that bastard's gone to the slams for good. But she digs me, I know that, and I can hardly stand it, not being over there.

I said how come we cant meet each other somewhere else, and I figure my sister and her kids have all got to be out of this place at least once in a while.

That Trudy. Did I tell you, I showed her a thing or two, and she says she never had anything like that rush with old Ed. All of those older babes like getting it on with a strong skinny young guy, eh?

Well, when it's all over, I figure I'm going to like it in that house. It's got a water bed if you know what I'm saying, and I'm the kind of guy likes to sleep in till the middle of the afternoon. Got a big projection screen TV, got a sauna off the bathroom and that's right off the bedroom. Get up middle of the afternoon and straight into the sauna. Then straight back into the waterbed. Why not?

Christ, listen to that. I hate thunder, always have, ever since I was a kid. Used to crawl into bed with a flashlight, get under the covers, and read my books. My mother always told me count one hippopotamus after the lightning and you'll know how far away the lightning hit. One mile for every hippopotamus. Shit, that one was less than a mile.

Have you seen their cars? He's got a big Toronado, twin pipes, mud flaps, all that. Just like a kid, never grew up. I heard the only place he drove that thing was to the golf course or the Legion hall. Am I talking in the past tense? Well, tough titty. She's got her 'Stang with a rag top, thing's thirty years old and dirty as hell, but if I get under the hood once a week that baby's going to pass every golf course in sight.

They've apparently got a summer place on one of the islands. I guess I should say *she's* got it. I cant figure out why she doesnt suggest we go over there. I guess it's right, though. I mean it isnt going to do the case any good if I'm seen with the wife of the guy that, like, killed my friend, eh?

Jesus, it's bad enough we get this god-damned storm, oh shit, that one was just up the street, bad enough we got this god-damned storm, and now there's some crazy asshole out there blowing his trumpet. There's some people I'll never understand.

THE CREATURE

When he was a boy, and growing up in a valley town with no traffic lights or curbs, the creature had always been seen in a black cape, legs wide, head down, on the edge of the roof of a tall apartment or office building, rain behind it, though in that little town it hardly ever rained. It rained once just before the orchardists could get the cherries picked without splits in their skin, and once again around the Labour Day weekend. It probably stank, the creature, stank of foul long-dead flesh and strained minerals and the torture of steel. But he had always held his breath hard when it was around. When it stood for a moment, for instance, in his bedroom the night after the day when his only older cousin died. When it looked over the shoulder of the fat soft anaesthetist during that first operation in grade six.

It had no voice at all; it would not speak. It would have been less frightening to a kid if it had spoken, even if it had had a voice that shook out of an echo-chamber, even if it had had an accent like something out of giant dark stony mountain crags in some sort of Europe-Asia snowbound night of unrelenting wind. It did not speak at all, nor make any other sound. You did not see it move from place to place. You did not see it arrive or depart. It was there and then it was not. It was not a skullface. It was not a putrid eyeball fleshface. It did not laugh like an animal.

It was not a hyena, and the kid was not in Africa, and none of his wounds were physical, and he was not in bed. It was very familiar. He had known it long ago, when his memory was intact, when he had not riddled his memory by using it. He had written about it in other shapes, but now that it was here again after all this while, he knew that all that writing was incorrect. Decent, but incorrect.

"You are obsessed with the subject," she had said. "Ever since I first knew you you have been obsessed with it."

"In my writing?"

"In your writing and in your life."

"It is the great subject, I suppose."

"I have never met anyone who spends so much of his time thinking about it," she said.

Very well. He would think about something else. Because now that the old thing was here again for sure, he did not like to think about it, really. It had been one thing to grin as he titled a book after it, but now that it was here again he did not love it. He did not even like it.

She felt the urge to push, and that called for rapid panting, as the course taught her, and you could see the baby turn around, opening the cervix. Earlier, pushing on her tail bone during contractions, I could feel the baby's head in my palm.

Very well, then. He would think about life, the coming of life.

In his memories of childhood, layered with the writing he had done about childhood, the kid was afraid of the creature. He knew it did not exist, not like that, not as a creature, but he was afraid of it. Now he was not afraid of it, but he hated it. He was depressed, he would say, if he had to go for a word like that.

Because it was there. He could not see it, but it was there. It was not just something in his head, either. It was so damned sad, if something about yourself could be sad.

If he could have been in a different place. No, if his life were not about the damned things it is about, he would not have to know about the creature. It was not a creature.

From the time the baby got turned around the right way, things went much faster and the mother was now in control. We were in the delivery room, and I didnt know that it was anything more than just the place for the local injection.

Someone looking from the distance of a few houses down the block might say that he had not really ruined all those lives. So people cried some tears and moved to other cities, and made impossible telephone calls. Maybe some of them would not be living together after all these years. That is the regular business of this neighbourhood.

Finally the doctor put his fingers in and let her push a little, and I heard the lip go over with a wet sound. Then she started pushing, her face going red in her determination, and I was as busy as could be, putting moisture to her mouth, lifting her with my hands.

She probably thought, at times anyway, that he liked it. He did not like it. When it was doing its worst he thought he would do anything to get out of its whereabouts. Figure that one out. Death would be, if you really did it, the sure way of getting away from the problem. There'd be no more dying then. No more slow glide of silk slip up the outside thigh, either.

No, he didnt like it, ever.

He could never understand, or never quite believe those young people when he was young who said that they did not mind death, it was just the idea of being old they didnt like. He had always said that he wanted to live forever, and then that he would like to live as long as he could.

Now he was not sure it was worth it. He had read about clinical depression, or at least heard the term. To tell the truth, he had not read much about depression. But he had heard about it. It was something that often came just before death, sometimes theirs, sometimes yours.

Another young nurse looked at her watch and listened with a stethoscope to the baby's heart. 150. 160. 160. Nurse Olafson said that the highest pulse came when the baby's head was between vertebrae.

The doctor came back from his cigarette and sat with his face in the right place. He looked like a painter on his stool, stopping to reflect over the canvas between contractions.

It did not make a sound but he knew it was there. He did not locate it, not behind him, as in the cartoons, or in any particular direction. He did not know how close it was but it was close. It did not stink. It did not cast a shadow. But he knew it was there. It was present. It was *with him.*

It was worse than any words about it. Therefore he should keep trying to describe it. When he was a kid he would lie awake at night in his room, afraid of what was there. It was not a creature. But everything seemed too close and at the same time too far away. There was a relentless buzzing, or something like a buzzing, grinding, drilling, but not a sound, a drilling presence of something. He would finally have to shout, hoping that shouting would break it. His mother would come and ask him what was the matter, and he would try to tell her.

"It is nothing. There is nothing here," she said.

There was something wrong with his brain. Not his mind. That would be all right because he could deny that. But there was something wrong with his brain. Back then he knew that his mother used to be able to do things but now she could no longer do something, and he was there by himself. Not a grown-up. A kid with a brain you could

compare to last couple of lines of the Rain "Barrel"

not fix or trade. You keep the one you are born with. Well, you could make it romantic.

During the next pushes I can see not only the slit of grey hairy head, but now the whole pelvic floor bulging with the shape of the little head, and everyone is cheering. On the next contraction the doctor is holding the forceps with one hand, elbows up, cotton swabs in there with the newly arriven.

He tended to look back on his childhood as a childhood unlike the ones claimed by his friends. That is, it was spent in a small town surrounded by orchards and hills, where, with topical variations, people lived in families much like those presented in schoolbooks and advertising and later on television. It was not a disturbing childhood then.

Once, though, when he was around ten years old he was out later than usual on a Saturday night. He had probably just been to the movie and now he was down by the river a block below the movie house. He'd never been allowed to swim in the river. He could swim at the village pool or out at the lake, but never in the river. Some people did swim in the river, but they were the same tough kids who smoked in the school lavatories.

He was doing his usual lone sensitive kid act at the edge of the river, now, not hiding, particularly, not spying for certain. Not spying as he always meant to do on the strange people from somewhere else who lived for short periods of time during the summer in the little row of whitewashed shacks down by the river. In that town your standing was represented by the distance you lived from the river. If you lived near the river nobody knew your name, or if they did, it was a name that had been around town for a long time, and so exceptions could be made for history.

Now this Saturday night two people he did not know appeared between the shacks and the river. The river was green and opaque, and it ran swiftly with little folds in the water. Really it was a brown kind of green.

They must have been people, the kind of people, who lived in those shacks. The man was wearing an old purplish-blue suit, and she was wearing a dress and white high-heel shoes. They were holding hands, with their arms touching shoulder to wrist, and walking toward the river. When they got to the river they continued to walk, and he, the kid by the water, unseen or ignored by them, watched. He was always watching things, but he was not often this lucky. Now he did not think it was lucky.

Because they were still walking into the river, and the sides went down quickly, and the water tugged at you quickly, so that your parents did not want you to go into that river. But now here were these two in their clothes in the water. The river was pushing on her dress, lifting its skirt to the turning surface of the water. They continued to walk and now there were just their shoulders and heads and then their heads, and he, the kid, may have turned to look elsewhere for a moment, but if he did, when he turned back again those two people were entirely gone. There might have been a little chance that they had come back out of the water. But no, there was no chance of that. If he had looked away he had not looked away that long. If they had walked back out it would have to be on this side of the river, but it would probably be a long way downstream. So maybe they did come back out.

Anyway, he was not sure of what he had seen. No one in his family did peculiar things, so he was not aware of what a lot of things might be. Was it religion? What was it? Drink? Madness? It was something that was scary and beyond him. But it was something he would grow to know. If he grew up and left this valley he knew he would know what it was. That was even more scary.

The nurse on the right poked in the pit and I looked back to see that tiny wet head coming out between the two big spoons, which are then dropped. I saw the bones rippling apart in the head, and before we knew it, out came the

body, comely shape hanging light purple now from the doc-
tor's hand, thick twisty soft cord dangling—his call's for
you—"It's a girl!" all the female voices say, as they often do,
I suppose.

"Oh Baby!" said its mother.

Love was blazing out of all my senses, to both figures
now on the gurney. Then I was laughing. Then I remem-
bered that in all that hurry of images there were two that
one had better remember. Immediately on coming out the
little creature being turned, though she did not know it,
upside down, made a tiny cry. And before that, the most
beautiful thing, its little head, amazingly little head, turned
by itself, toward its mother's left thigh. Its mother just pushed
her out!

He had learned a lot of things since getting out of the
Valley. Some of them were about mortality and some were
not. But then eventually all of them were about mortality.
Every morning when he woke he said either aloud or in his
head, "Another seven hours closer to the grave."

"Time is qualitative," a woman said to him once.

"Everything you have ever done?"

"Yes?"

"Doesnt matter what quality it was. It *was*. It's gone.
Irretrievable."

"You are not the kind of man I want to spend my
quality time with," she said. And she didnt.

The thoughts he had every day had made him this sort
of person: if he saw an ant on the sidewalk he went out of
his path to avoid stepping on it. Still, he ate slippery
bubbling hamburgers, the brown fat running off his wrists.

When he was a very young man he had always said,
even to himself, that he would die before he was thirty.
Then he said he would die when he was thirty. That was
romance. He skulked around in a soiled raincoat and
ankle-high black running shoes. He did this while other
people we wearing things with buckles on them. Three-
voice folk singing groups were popular.

*The last things to remain purple were her feet. She lay
there with her eyes wide open. I saw her whole chin
trembling. It must have been shock. They were squirting her
and wiping her and putting drops into her eyes, and
listening over and over to her heart.*

*I was original and sophisticated in my oral response to
the event.*

"Oh, wow!" I said.

He never for a moment thought that the creature
would depart, would despair of making any headway here.

He got up from the scarred and lopsided chair at his
desk and went into the kitchen to get a cup of coffee, he
hoped, from the newest in a long line of imported coffee
machines. His daughter was sitting at the kitchen table,
fingers in the hair at the sides of her cranium, elbows on
the tabletop at either side of the fat book she was bent
over.

"That's what we like to see," he said, looking through
the sink for a decent coffee cup. "Honest study."

She was nineteen years old. In reply to his habitual
remark she read from the fat book.

"How gladly would I meet/ Mortality, my sentence,
and be earth/ Insensible! how glad would lay me down/ As
in my mother's lap!"

"You havent got that close to your mother in half a
dozen years," he said.

"I was reading from literature," she said, lifting her
face now. It was beautiful and at the same time deeply
familiar. Her upper lip curled back a little, and moist teeth
showed. "Paradise Lost," she said.

"Of course."

"Book Ten."

"Who is saying that?"

"We all are."

She had been hinting suicidal feelings at him since she
was fifteen. Now she was a university student. That made it

more difficult. In literature there is lots of suicide, and university students are very fond of it. They dont know about the creature, but they know about suicide in literature and around the table.

"Do you ever feel," he said, "as if there is someone nearby but you cant tell where he is, and he makes you very discouraged?"

"Yeah, you, Dad."

"Thanks. No, I mean it. A creature."

"You're weird, Dad. Whacko. Creatures, eh?"

"The last things to remain purple were the feet," he said.

"Get out of my face, Dad. I have some fatal thinking to do."

Indoors or outdoors, it didnt matter. The creature was not affected by weather or environment or time of day or night.

What did it feel like, exactly? Other people were always asking what things are "like," and that made some sense, because we all have to gauge new experiences against old ones. People also wanted you to put out some abstract words, as if feelings are more expressible in abstract terms than objects are. What did it feel like, approximately?

Disappointment. I mean you thought you were going to escape, and as in the dream it caught you before your last step to freedom. Heaviness. Sad. I have said that before. Sad. As if for yourself from somewhere outside. Something like the paralysis of shock. You can move, make the usual moves, but how can you, how do you?

see Joyce's Dubliners

There is the bunny. When the hawk has been chasing him, and he has figured out that he is not, in the end, going to get away, he stops and resigns himself, hunches still, and perhaps, people in the country say, dies before the hawk can use his talons and beak. The hawk has always been there, but just now decided to move in. He is the bunny's creature.

But look at bunnies, how fast they make more of them.

My daughter, my daughter. When I said that phrase I felt new at it, as if I had won the right to use it now. There was a kind of easy resignation in joining all the people called Dad. Okay, I will not fight and holler against that business, and I will say my daughter.

She was on the deteriorating sundeck of the house I or we had bought, yes, but I am not thinking of that weakness, that instance right now. I should be, because I had given him a place to stand and look in through the window. She was in her green walker, a kind of chair set in the middle of a table with rollers at the bottoms of its legs. She zoomed back and forth on the sundeck in the sun, saying "Da da da da," which was her word for every emotion.

I was mowing the square lawn in the little back yard. When I bumped the rusty mower against the trunk of the apple tree a thousand blossoms fell down on me. For a second, the place smelled sweet.

DISCOLOURED METAL

"It's a complex fate, being an American,
and one of the responsibilities it entails
is fighting against a superstitious valua-
tion of Europe."

—Henry James

The DC7B, the brochure from the pocket on the back of
the next seat declared, is the newest of the non-jet airliners,
and we were very lucky indeed to be riding over the polar
route in a DC7B. How slowly we rode, and with how wan
a face, and after eighteen hours of bent leg and sore eye
we indeed did arrive in Europe, albeit northern Germany.

Dont get me wrong, we did not snub northern Germany.
But you know, an inexperienced yet southern-valleyed
young fellow, well, Mediterranean swim suits, palm trees,
wind blowing them inside out—

Northern Germany explains the earlier scene at the
Calgary International Airport and Bar, huge throngs of
German Albertan peasants full of memory, and their blond

skinny children. The men were wearing blue straw fedoras and double-breasted suits of ironed blue. The women were broad as a pantry door, every one, their gold teeth and bare faces shining in the light rain and the confusion of the coming flight.

Amongst them Berenice, and our kiss at the glass door, half a tear sliding over the globe of her eye—I finally blew a kiss from the dramatic screen actor hero step into the plane, the way you could in those days. At last into a confusion of rain, and somewhere she could see me from the panelled glass of the air terminal. What a word. It was a nice start, Canadian. This was the first day it had rained in Calgary in nearly a year. We three had no raincoats to take to the Rhine, to Sussex.

Anyway, this is what I remember of the trip. And the very bad thing in the middle, which we had eventually to stop discussing.

read from the DC7B brochure

Knowing the external loads on the plane structure, calculations are made of th   sses imposed on each part, bolt and rivet. What a pla   a dangling modifier. Most structures are highly redun   and calculations can only be made with difficulty. Where doubt may exist as to the actual value of stresses or the path taken by loads, recourse is made to structural testing.

Well, I was glad to hear that.

Elaborate jigs are required to hold the structure and allow proper loading and observation of results. A major portion of the time and expense of development of a modern airplane is spent in the structural testing program. As a result, any commercial plane which conforms to the official criterion of strength and has been certified by the airworthiness authorities of the government can, if operated sensibly, carry passengers with complete safety.

And everybody remembers to do everything. Remembers for her life.

Oh yes sir, I had been in a DC7B before, and I now looked out again at long heavy engines of discoloured metal hanging from the front of the wing. Up we all went so slowly, the cabin criss-crossed by unfretted German voices and wailing Teutonic babies.

There was a bony man of about seventy years across the aisle. It was his first trip in an airplane, back to old steamship Germany, over all. He wore round Kafka eyeglasses, but he was unaware of the Kafka book in the blue and white flight bag in front of his neighbour's feet. Hanging from his neck was an old pair of fieldglasses from World War One, poor skinny corporal in the mud, and an old bellows camera squeezed up shut. On his sharp old knees a wonderful new German-minted tape recorder packed with transistors. He did not speak English, so he ignored the warning not to use the tape recorder. Merrily he switched it on to record the roar and voices of his first ascent in this winged silver. Up and away, away.

So when one is able finally to dry one's hands on one's shirt front and light up a off cigarette, the old guy across the aisle says r ps one's shoulder and points at the NO SMO

"Not lit," I said, poi ign with my Black Cat that already tasted of a, naust. Old familiar taste this side of the aisle. Memory in a nose, a lung.

"Oh, not yet," the old fellow thought he agreed.

And he appeared to be satisfied. He waited for breakfast, because his wife looked as if she cooked a lot. But it is lunch, not breakfast that was brought to them, and that confusion was a sign for me now, sitting here in a Düsseldorf hotel without sleep for some days, I do not know how many because the times have been a changing if anything. It was late night in Düsseldorf, and in Canada, a sprawl of continent, Berenice was walking the terriers in the warm afternoon sun, or is it raining still?

I had a tired cortex in that dull light.

But the plane did its grind northward and east, and I was off on wimpled wing toward new countries. Before this I had been in three North American lands. I wager that I will

*New literary
toritory to mark
etc.*

refer to them, necessary memory in whatever this enscribing is. New territory to mark, off. That is a modest obsession I have. People bear with it.

The old guy across the aisle asked how high they were all flying. 15,000 feet. "Oh yes, fifty thousand feet," he said, so it made no difference. He thought we were all above Greenland. It was all snow.

The first meal was miserable because this was not Boom American Airlines—it was Pacific Western, young lonely trips to Yukon. We were to be contented with limp sandwiches. All right. A bun. A cup of coffee. Champagne made in British Columbia, last year. Whee. We.

Because of which there were soon lines of broad peasant women in wide skirts waiting for the door that says Lavatory, that is wh᾿ ' to have to call it in elementary schoo¹ ᾿e locked door till someone pointeᵈ ᾿ᵈ, and I noticed that there were ᾿nging from the ledges over tl here Canadian babies were w .n their mouths a few miles ab ι the third class buses in Mexic᷑ ᷑nd pots of lard on the overheaᴜ ᷑n print dresses, farmer husbands w᷑ ᷑ld teeth and home- made haircuts. Flying ι᷑ ᷑nere is a Europe inside Europe. Inside memory and human meat.

The first stewardess arrived again, blonde, beautiful if you like, and surly. I always fall in love with airline stewardesses there in the sunlight above the clouds, with God at the ailerons. Below were the flat frozen rivers of Northern Manitoba this middle of May flight. I eyed the stewardess from behind Time magazine, a story all about college professors dedicated to teaching instead of flying around in airplanes, honest.

Beside me were two more professors or whatever they were, fliers, Tony and Lorna. My legs were too long but theirs looked just right. On airplanes and buses, for those

94

few long hours, I always wished that I were little and short instead of six-foot four and handsome. How would I sleep? What do you think? I took off my suede boots and there were holes in my socks, toes sticking through. Stewardess will see. Pull and push on end of sock occasionally.

The Vancouver Province was there, and it informed me sitting faced northeast that the Western Hockey League final, for I cared then about such things, was tied at three games apiece between V̶ ̶ ̶ ̶ ̶ ̶ ̶r and Portland and it struck me that I ̶ ̶ ̶ the seventh and last game t·̶ ̶ ̶ ̶ ̶ ̶ ̶ rope before, hadnt th ̶ ̶ ̶ ̶ ̶ ̶ ember. I wish I ̶ ̶ ̶ ̶ ̶ ̶ ̶ ts like this, ̶ ̶ ̶ ̶ ̶ en I wc

"̶

l
C ̶ ̶ n
th ̶ ̶ e
snc

"1. said
Tony, \

"No th.

It was a c. ̶ ̶ .ow they got around the rules . ̶ ̶ .nternational Film Forum, Calgary branch. Ḧaṟḏ ṯo believe those wide farm folks with their sunburnt wrists ever went to films. Cinema fans? Where are we, I wondered. I looked at their faces and thought the Germanic farmer is man furthest removed from godhood. That was why the women needed horned helmets.

As we all together approached Iceland there was still a little thin light in the sky, no real darkness this far north, and then the sun came flying up in the northeast.

"Like a garnet," I said.

"Like poet blood "

"Like a cc

Last ·   red sun

cor   way

r   it

te   en

have   u pick

up impre   off again.

    "Iceland i   portion of the

earth's surface." Pliny Miles.

"So we who have come
As trippers North

cigar‹
erbia.
· yellc

.dow.

.he busy morn.

aybe, words. C

.es not look 1

bags are p

...nd its other...
...ank the very good c
..d have and so we tried

someone must have told us
the loading gate, and we th
; at last, this drag at the end c
was just toward more wai·
with rippled glass windc
'o learn that it wc·
through the lc·

..ered around the usual airplane ь.
..ıe, then waited for the roars and grind a.
_ward welcomed us aboard in his informal wa)
"You'll find that there are two toilets. One is iı.
.ıt of the airplane and one is in the back—er, rear."
"I wonder whether he's been on an airplane before,
. aid.
"The DC7B is fitted out with the latest in safety equipment," said the steward on the public address speaker.
"You will find a list of safety procedures in the pocket on
the back of the seat in front of you."
There werent any.
And the cooling system didnt work. It got warmer anc
 ̄armer, which pleased some of the women for a while ·
st. I was down to my thin teeshirt, sweltering above ۱
ds. The pilot or someone turned off the lights iɾ
 ̃t to make it marginally cooler.
 ̃oman mentioned to the affable steward tʰ
in the roof and something like wˮ
 ̃ʿward, resourcefulness radⁱˮ
' ˸ʿf from a nⁿⁿˡ

...opped again to refuel at Keflavik, and ...
...re in the little survivalist coffee shop. It was .
...iting as it had been six weeks ago. Partly this was
because we now had ahead of us the longer and more
northerly lap of the flight, more than eleven hours to
Calgary.

Grind, grind, the horror, the horror, as that literary
chap said. All Europe went into the making of this return.
The horror can sometimes be ameliorated somewhat by the
meals that mark the stations of the crossing. But somehow
on this trip they have cleverly contrived to avoid giving us
the comfort of regular meals—they are soon rid of us, and
they know we want only to get home, the holiday over at
last. Shortly after we got on in Düsseldorf, at 13:30, we had
lunch, and that augured well. But at about 20:00 Europe
time, we had donnaconna sandwiches, and then at 02:00
Europe time, which must have been some awful early
evening Calgary time, we had breakfast! What about dinner,
my poor heart enquired, not from hunger but from a kind
of westering anxiety.

However, all good things have eventually to grind to
an end, and even this flight did. Over the Canadian Arctic I
sat with the sweat sticking me hopelessly to my seat and
observed the line-up of large women waiting for the toilet
...y all wanted to come out of the cubicle looking ur
... pretty before meeting their families and frien...

...w in number as well as ...

ground our agonies were not over. The orderly process of vaccination check, passport check, baggage check, was thrown into a turmoil as the members of the "International Film Forum" refused to follow instructions, and instead milled around in their own habitual way, the large bodies bumping me back and forth among my bags and typewriter. I was surrounded by blue straw fedoras and yellow buckle shoes and brightly rouged cheeks. I longed for the sight of the open prairie and my dear thin wife. But she was in Banff, because her theatre group was doing Bertolt Brecht's Saint Joan of the Stockyards. Homecoming. G'wan.

But I got a ride home, and finally lugged my Europe bags into the familiar apartment. There the dogs jumped all over me, and my first act was to lift their small turds from the Calgary Herald on the kitchen floor, and drop them into the bathroom toilet bowl. Then I took a shower, and waited. Then I just waited. And hours later when I heard the rustling at the door I was there, and I opened it for her.

THE RYERSON SPLIT

In 1966 I took a deep breath and moved east, to London, Ontario. I was at the beginning of my writing career, and London was close to Toronto, where the publishers and broadcasters were. My first novel had been accepted by McClelland & Stewart, I had been on a few television programs (yes, in those days Canadian television was interested in literature), and now I had a story in a fiction anthology published by one of the country's biggest Toronto publishers, Ryerson Press.

The anthology was *Modern Canadian Stories*. My story was at the back because I was so young. The editors were Giose Rimanelli and Roberto Ruberto. Other stories were by people even I had heard of—Morley Callaghan and Hugh Garner and Margaret Laurence. I really felt as if I were going places. I didnt feel too badly about spending ten dollars on a pair of stretch-material slightly bell-bottomed pants I had bought in Düsseldorf on my six-dollar-a-day trip to Europe in the summer.

Things could hardly be more exciting. Ryerson Press threw a reception for the anthology in some hotel meeting room right in the middle of probably storied literary Toronto.

People told me that this was a rare event, because Ryerson was the United Church and they didnt usually look kindly on the idea of literary bunfights with alcoholic drinks. I didnt know then and I dont know now whether these people were serious or whether they were just eluding the western fellow with their practiced irony. Anyway, I could remember the summer poetry festival at UBC in 1963. There Ryerson had provided a half-hour's worth of Canadian wine or something, and Jack Spicer and I had liberated a couple of bottles and carried them across some flowerbeds to a well-lit parking lot.

Anyway, here I was three and a half years later, a minor but promising literary figure in a room in Toronto, watching writers who obviously knew each other talk to each other. Thank goodness, I thought, that Earle Birney and Phyllis Webb were there. I knew them both from Vancouver. Earle had been extremely kind to Angela and me here in our first year of the east, throwing a party for us, and introducing me to literary types. Phyllis was working for the CBC, and she had included me in both television and radio productions.

The editors were there, being extremely Italian in their suits. I saw Morley Callaghan, who looked tremendously old, which was to be expected by 1966. He had a red face and was wearing a whiplash cushion around his neck. Hugh Garner also had a red face. He was sitting at a table of little sandwiches and pickles, drinking alcohol and telling stories fairly loudly in a raspy voice. Boy, literary figures, I thought to myself.

The party had just begun. Nevertheless I dropped a napkin on the floor. When I bent to pick it up my German pants stopped stretching and ripped from beginning to middle to end. It was a story I didnt want to hear. I hadnt even had a second drink yet, those nice high drinks in those nice hotel glasses. I hadnt eaten any free food yet. I hadnt had a talk with any writers or even Barbara Amiel yet. Damn, I said to my writerly self.

I couldnt leave this early, I thought. I got myself a plate full of little sandwiches and pickles and sat down on my rip with the white shorts inside, and talked for a while with Phyllis Webb. That was okay, but I was getting more and more nervous. I told Earle Birney about my problem. He said he would lend me a pair of his pants. But my own pants were black and stretchy and skin tight. What would Earle's probably baggy pants with short legs look like? I said no thank you, not because I didnt want Earle's pants, but because I was enraged at my bad western boy luck.

My first Toronto literary reception.

No one from the Toronto *Telegram* had even got to me yet. Who knew when Ryerson would spring for alcohol again?

I wish now that I had worn Earle's pants. I wish I had just borrowed a safety pin.

As it was I resolved to pick my Toronto career up again when given another chance. For now I would just have to get my 1954 Chevrolet, parked seven blocks away where the closest free parking was, that is behind Coach House Press, and head for the 401 to London. The cold wind and probably some of the wind-driven snow found its way to my nether smile. I was stamping on the snow-drifted sidewalks.

I had only one drink in me. I could drive the 401 as fast as the snow would let me. It was two and a half hours to London, in the Ontario dark. I listened to the radio and then I listened to the tires on the highway. My sense of humour did not show up.

Twenty miles short of London there was a sudden bang, and then a continued metallic noise. The car slowed down, and I thought I might have to park there beside the road, in the dark, under the invisible cloud bank that was hiding the winter stars. But whatever it was allowed me to drive slowly along the shoulder of the highway until I got to a garage. There I heard that I had experienced that event spoken of so much in company I used to keep—I had thrown a rod. I did not then nor do I now know what that means.

Except that I had to get a ride into London and then think of what I was going to do with that Chevrolet parked twenty miles toward literary Toronto. The guy in the garage did not ask me about the rip in my trousers. Maybe it wasnt noticeable. Maybe he wasnt Italian. I wondered whether Rimanelli and Ruberto knew what throwing a rod was.

THE FRENCH EAST INDIA COMPANY

Tell me the truth. Have you ever heard of Joseph-François Dupleix?

Sounds like a place to live, you say?

My sentiments, exactly. But I know a lot about Joseph-François Dupleix now. There was a time when I knew about as much as you do.

Let's go back to that time. I heard a thumping of feet on the hall stairs, and an occasional thump on the wall. So after a while I got the energy to look out the window. We live on the second floor, just about the bottom of the hill, Yew Street. Not a nice neighbourhood. Not a heavy drug and break-in neighbourhood. Just lots of scruffy people going by, but little old ladies too, walking Maltese Terriers with rhinestone hairclips.

There's a neighbourhood pub two blocks away, so there are always lots of cars parked with tickets under their windshield wipers. Once I looked out our living room window and saw a guy, had another guy against the hood of a long Lincoln, he was bouncing against him but they had all their clothes on, far as I could see. I mean that is the sort of thing makes it a less than perfectly desirable neighbourhood.

Once saw a woman with an artificial leg, shining in the sun, this was in August. She was struggling up the hill, Yew Street is pretty steep here. I always try to park my car facing downhill in case of battery failure.

She was struggling up hill, her metal leg glinting, and these two boys, couldnt have been older than about eight. One of them sticks his face in her face and the other one kicks her metal leg out from under her.

That's why you dont see pictures of this street in the city magazines they throw on front porches up in Kerrisdale.

But as I say, once in a while you see the other stuff. A single mother and her little daughter clutching plastic toys, headed for the beach a block and a bit away.

Joseph-François Dupleix wouldnt, however, have been caught dead on this street, winter or summer.

Which gets me back to the thumping. I opened the hall door, pretending I was looking for a delivery, and caught a glimpse of a big box going around the corner up the stairs to the third floor.

I went back in and perched on the window seat. Had to move a pile of Tommy Steele records. You dont want to know.

Out our main door he comes and heads to the U-Haul trailer across the street, parked illegally. I knew it.

There was a young skinny woman in the car, an old orangish-red Datsun, doesnt matter. The guy was young and skinny, too. He opened her door, and started to talk angry, it looked like. She got out, and they started yanking on a really big box.

I almost got up to go and help them. Then I came to my senses and settled down. They just dropped the carton once, or rather he did. She laughed at him, but she helped him get the carton to our main door.

This time the hall thumping went on a good time.

110

I would have something interesting to tell my wife June when she came home from the foundry. She hates new developments.

Works as a secretary at the foundry. Been there for years and years. Before I knew her.

There's a reason I was home and she was at work that day. I work irregular hours, fishing. Sometimes I'm out for two weeks at a time. Other times I'm at home for a while. When I'm at home I work on the family tree, the photo albums, things like that.

Nothing like Dewey Tugnut and his obsession.

I watched them unload the whole trailer. Didnt see much in the way of personal belongings except for those crates. I figured the furniture was coming in a van.

He got in the Datsun and took off with the empty trailer. She was standing just outside our main door, right in front of the tiled rectangle that spelled out the words THE SARRASINE. All the apartment buildings in this part of town have twelve-cylinder names.

I could see that she was holding a book in her left hand, which hung at the end of her limp arm. She was spending just the right amount of strength to hold the book from dropping. This book was my excuse, at least to myself.

In a trice, whatever that is, I was down there beside her, having casually strolled from the doorway, an invisible toothpick between my front teeth.

"Hello, there," I said, all the William Holden I could get in my voice. "What you reading?"

She turned up a sad thin face, and I saw light blue eyes that didnt belong with her dark hair, I thought. Then she held up the book. It was *Running in the Family* by a fellow with an odd name.

"Just moving in, eh?" I Holdened.

"Again," she said. If you have read John Steinbeck's more lugubrious pieces you know what she looked like when she said that. She should have been wearing a bedraggled Okie dress with spots. Lugubrious. Nice word. There's two fancy words I use whenever I can. Lugubrious and bestirred.

She was wearing tight blue jeans, high-top basketball shoes and a sweat shirt with no words on it. That would just about make up for anything.

"My name's Dean," I said. It wasnt, but I was trying to encourage people to call me that. You will have no trouble finding out my real name.

"Janine," she said.

"We rime," I said.

Nothing, she said.

I had been trying to get let's have a coffee into my voice, but it didnt work with Janine. Our first conversation was at an end.

I thought it would be a smart thing to do to get that book and read it, or maybe be seen holding it. I bought it at the little book shop on Fourth Avenue. But I havent read it yet. Cant remember the author's name. Sounds foreign.

I soon found out that they were moving in right above us, Janine and her husband. That was where the thumping next originated. I figured they were going to get their rugs or carpets when the van arrived.

It was pretty quiet at night when I started up talking with June. We were in bed, just settling down. She had the wires in her ears, and didnt like taking to them out to listen to me. She was listening to a cassette tape about reducing the size of her ass. I was for that, but I also wanted to talk about the new neighbours, the way people do.

"You should have heard all the thumping today," I said. "They're moving in right upstairs from us."

"The museum," she said. "I know."

She started to put the wires back in her ears. I stopped her arm with husband fingers.

"What are you talking about, museum?" I asked.

"He's opening his museum," she said. "Dont you keep

track of what's going on in your own building? You're home all day, arent you? Or arent you?"

She was alluding to the subject of another tape she used sometimes.

"He's opening a museum?"

"Dewey Tugnut," she said.

"Who?"

"Janine's husband," she said.

And this time she was going to put in the wires, period.

Lucky for Dewey Tugnut the landlord lives on another continent west of here, and the caretaker doesnt care about anything but loud parties and pets.

What I mean about lucky is Dewey had a hand-painted sign, but it looked pretty near professional, in his front window. Big word MUSEUM. Slightly smaller words THE LIFE AND TRAVELS OF JOSEPH-FRANÇOIS DUPLEIX.

"Who the hell," I asked June, "is Joseph-Frankie Duplex?"

"Dupleix," she said, simple as as can be. "He is one of the many many people you have never heard of. Never became a star in the World Wrestling Foundation."

"Federation," I said.

A low blow. She always takes any chance she can to belittle my interest in WWF wrestling. What the world is watching, it says on television, Saturday night. Also Saturday afternoon. Quite often during the week, actually.

Anyway, I checked the spelling of this Dupleix fellow and looked him up in our encyclopedia. We got it a book at a time from the supermarket where we get our ground beef and spaghetti.

Dupleix isnt in the encyclopedia. Not ours, anyway.

But you know, I always tell June, look, the guys in the WWF, what's the difference between them and your Greek gods, for instance. All right, I'll drop it.

In the weekly newspaper there was an advertisement

for the Joseph-François Dupleix museum. Special interest to Canadians, it said.

I ran into Dewey on Fourth Avenue. He had a stapler in one hand and a bunch of paper sheets in the other. He was stapling advertisements for the museum on every hoarding and wooden pole around.

"How you doing?" I asked. I'm what you call a past master at starting conversations and friendships.

He looked as if he was afraid I was a cop or a soldier for the Czar. But he said hello, sort of.

"How's the museum business?" I asked, smooth as silk.

"It'll pick up."

Sclat! went the stapler.

I kind of fell in with his trek down Fourth, stopping when he stopped to staple a page. I offered him a cigarette but he just gave a sad shake of his head.

"Does it hassle you?" he finally asked.

"What?"

Good, we were going. I dont know why I was so anxious to get a conversation happening. Maybe I felt as if he needed one.

"The museum, over your head, so to speak."

"Hasnt bothered me yet," I said, getting jolly and friendly with my voice. "Hasnt exactly been a stampede up and down those stairs."

If I had been hoping to get a smile out of him, I had misjudged my man, as they say.

"I just need the right combination of advertising," said Dewey.

"And what?"

"And National self-awareness."

"You working for the government?" I asked. Still trying to get jolly. It still didnt work.

"No," he said. "I cant get a cent out of the government."

"Who can?" I asked.

"Yeah, the bastards."

Sclat!

I was gluing a heel on one of June's sandals and looking out the window at the street, when I saw Janine struggling up the hill with a great big picture frame in her hands and leaning on her forehead. She must have just got off the Macdonald bus—how, I dont know. I quit gluing and hit the stairs.

"Let me help you carry this sucker," I said, employing that age-old masculine gesture of relieving the frail of their weight.

I know what I am doing. And saying.

She did not curtsey. She did not bat her eyelids. She did not say why I'm obliged to you, kind sir.

She did say thanks, as quietly and quickly as is humanly possible.

When we got to the apartment building, she opened the door while I caught my breath on THE SARRASINE. It was a bugger getting that big heavy ornate frame up those stairs, three flights.

I am in favour of museums on ground floors.

Their door had a simple sign on it, just the word MUSEUM, in ten-centimetre letters. And the number 11 above it.

She held this door open for me too, this time with the hint of a smile on the side of her mouth. First smile I had got off either of them. I guess you had to carry a 25-kilogram picture frame up three flights to get that.

But she had a little sweat in the straight-back hair of her temples. If you are not affected by that, you're a hopeless case.

There I was, in the museum, or rather just inside the door. The museum started, as I could see, in their hall, some pictures on the hall wall. I couldnt see into any of the rooms, really. Their apartment was just like ours, four rooms in a big square, with a little bathroom at an angle off the kitchen.

I put the big picture frame down. It was painted that kind of grey-gold that is supposed to mean hoitsy-toitsy, lots of swirls and garlands and so on, wooden with grey-gold paint. I leaned it against the wall and looked at it for the first time.

It was a fake copy of an engraving, or maybe it was real, who knows? This was a museum, after all. And it looked as if the Tugnuts spent all their money on museum stuff rather than food.

It was an engraving of the head of a guy with a curly white wig on. It came down way past his ears. He had white cloth tied high around his neck, with some frills showing in the open front part of a high collar, the usual eighteenth-century stuff, I guess. His head was turned so that he was looking to his right.

He looked fairly young as dressed up toffs go. But he had a bit of a second chin.

This was Joseph-François, I figured, Dupleix.

"I guess this will be a prominent part of your display," I said.

"Yes." Sounded like a mouse.

"Heavy."

Now she actually spoke. But it sounded as if she was trying to be a museum guide, not quite making it because she was after all just a thin young woman, probably from a small ranching community.

"It is an engraving by Marie Champion de Cernel, after a portrait by Sergent."

"I hope he got a promotion. It's pretty good," I said.

That sort of thing didnt work any better on her than it did on her husband.

Anyway, I had a look around the museum. It used up two of their four rooms. There were glass cases with documents, scenes from India on the walls, a few sculptures, a male mannikin in eighteenth-century duds, a sword and a dagger, all the sort of thing you see in museums in small towns in Serbia, only smaller.

I wanted to pick her up and take her away from all this.

I felt sorry for him, too. Dont get me wrong. June gets me wrong enough, as it is.

I went out fishing for a couple weeks, and I have to admit that we did pretty well. My share would pay the rent for another six months, and we could have lamb chops with baked potatoes, my favourite meal. We hardly ever ate salmon, in case you might be wondering.

When I got back I discussed a lot of things with June and she discussed a lot of things with me, and then we took a rest and I asked her about the museum.

"I dont think there's been a single person go up there," she said.

"Any married ones?" I asked, and regretted it right away. Not only did the subject get dropped, but June was not in the mood for any more discussing.

During the following week I managed to run into both of the Tugnuts a few times. From Dewey I learned that the museum hadnt caught on. From Janine I learned that it hadnt caught on in its last location, either. That was in their apartment in White Rock.

I didnt have any words to return, so I just made a noise halfway between a hum and a throat clearing.

Then he asked me to lend him twenty dollars. I gave it to him, because I knew he was going to spend it on food. For them.

I took to going up and visiting the museum from time to time. They wouldnt take my $2.50 at the door, so in my head I just subtracted it from the twenty dollars every time.

Then one day Dewey gave me back my twenty dollars, all in two-dollar bills.

Joseph-François Dupleix came within a sword-blade of making the whole of India and surrounding countries French instead of English. He is one of the greatest almosts in history. That's why no one knows about him.

I tried to get June to go upstairs and look around. I told her I would pay her $2.50. She said with the bozos at the foundry and me with my family tree and old jukebox records she sees enough museums to last her for a lifetime.

"I know the real reason you go up there, anyway," she said.

"Oh Judas Priest," I replied.

Come to think of it, I dont get into very many good conversations with anyone. I often end up saying Judas Priest to June, and I can go for three days on the boat without saying more than a dozen words and half of them are unprintable.

But one day I got lucky you might say with Dewey. Ran into him on Fourth, and we went into Ruby's for a coffee.

I didnt ask him how the museum was going. I knew that. I had been telling my friends at the Cecil that they ought to give it a look, and I was pretty embarrassed about that. I didnt know whether I would feel worse if they didnt come or if they did come, I mean right upstairs from our place.

I shouldnt have got my shirt in a knot. No one came.

I got some of Dewey's ads and gave them to June to tack up around the foundry. She might have just dumped them on the way in. I never asked.

Dewey would have just sat there stirring and sipping his coffee and breaking his blueberry muffin into smaller and smaller pieces if I hadnt started.

"So what does that mean in your ad, about special interest to Canadians?"

"Well, bilingualism," he said.

"Bilingualism?"

"Biculturalism."

By the bloody sheets of my aunt Deirdre, this was making me impatient. But I dont know, I felt bad for the guy.

"What has Joseph-Somebody Duplex got to do with bilingualism?" I persisted.

"In the early part of the eighteenth century there was such a thing as French India. We always think of India as British India before it was Indian India, but there was French India too."

"I know, I've looked at the displays in the museum," I said.

"There was even Portuguese India," he said.

"Biculturalism?" I suggested. "Joseph D.?"

He was picking out the blueberries, a messy job, and piling them all together on one side of his plate. I shouldnt have cared if no one ever went to his museum. I should have called up the landlord long distance, and the licensing office at city hall, and got him shut down.

But no. I felt bad for him, etc.

"Dupleix was the governor general of French India," said Dewey, as if he was talking about his father.

"I know. With the help of the French fleet he took Madras from the British. Siss Boom Baw."

Dewey looked awful. I was sorry for being so impatient. Or loud, I guess.

"He was betrayed by the French East India Company, and he was abandoned by the French government after the treaty," he said, in a very quiet monotone.

"Like Quebec?"

"India could have been bilingual," said Dewey.

"Dewey, are you French? Is Tugnut a French name?"

"No," he said. "I'm a Canadian."

"Dont look at me," I said. "I'm from B.C."

A day later I loaned him twenty-five bucks. What could I do?

Where they got their money from I didnt know. I never saw either of them going to work. The orange Datsun hardly ever moved from its spot across the street.

Maybe they were on welfare. Maybe he was what they

call a remittance man. No, he didnt have an English accent. And they didnt get any government backing for the museum.

One day, just after Dewey got back from somewhere, maybe tracking down a book about the Treaty of Aix-la-Chapelle, I get that right now, someone came to look at the museum.

This was your average idle youth. You know what they look like these days. Plastic mesh baseball hat on backward over long lank hair, cheap leather jacket, tight black jeans, untied high-top basketball shoes, long thin nose, look of ignorance rounded off by a high school education.

Kind of lad made you wish he was your son, know what I mean?

He was up there for about ten minutes, tops. Down he came, two steps at a time. I was standing on The Sarrasine when he came banging out the glass door, six feet tall, a hand's span wide.

"Hey," I said.

"Hay's for horses," he said.

Not very bright, maybe, but kind of traditional.

"What's your hurry?" I questioned.

"Call that a fucking museum!" he exclaimed.

"There's some interesting stuff up there." I said with a period.

I wondered why I had even started this conversation.

"I got a dollar back, anyways," he said. I think it was at this point that he had a finger in one of his nostrils.

"Not satisfied?"

"Why the fuck do they say it's of special interest to fucking Canadians? That's what I'd like to know."

He was talking as if he figured just because I was standing on The Sarrasine I had a certain control over the building and grounds.

"Bilingualism," I said.

"Huh?" he meditated.

"Biculturalism."

"Fucking pea soups," he said, as he began to slap his Air Nikes down the sidewalk hill.

I didnt think it would be a great idea to go up there right away. I waited till I saw Dewey headed for the bus stop down at the bottom of Yew.

I felt my heart getting a bit zippy as I went up the stairs. I figured it must be the climb rather than Janine.

But I would have to test it later, when she was out and her husband was tending the museum, go briskly up the stairs, see if my heart could take it.

The whole place smelled of fish. It turned out that Dewey had joined the Greeks at Kits Beach, two blocks down the hill, where they stretch out little nets and catch smelts during the evening high tide.

You can get about fifteen of those things in a medium cast iron fry pan. With lots of garlic they arent bad.

"Looks like I'm not the only fisherman in the building," I said.

"You're the only one that gets paid for it," said Janine.

You'll understand if I dont tell you all the feelings and thoughts that were going through me around then.

"I noticed you had a visitor to the display," I said. "He sounded pretty pissed off about something when he left."

Janine found things that needed doing. She moved a little statuette of an Indian elephant about five centimetres.

"We gave him part of his money back," she said over her shoulder.

"That was nice." I dont know why I could not get it through my head that there was no jollying the Tugnuts.

"He saw everything, or everything he wanted to see. We couldnt just give it all back."

Neither of us knew much about the museum business.

"Your first customer, and he's unsatisfied."

"We dont have customers," she said, still not looking at me. "They are museum goers."

"Patrons, I think you call them."

"Yes. We are not selling something."

I walked around her and looked at her face. She had a little pimple on her chin, with drying makeup on it. I felt like holding her.

If you understand what I am talking about, you would have, too.

"So what was this dickhead angry about?" I asked.

"Oh, he started complaining about everything. How small the place was, more than a dollar a room, he said."

"Sounds like a bargain to me."

"He complained about the sign. Wanted to know what was so special for Canadians. So Dewey started talking to him in French."

"Dewey speaks French?"

"No, but he just spoke in French. Just said a lot of things with French words instead of English words."

"And the guy took a dollar back?"

"I gave it to him. He said—"

Oh sure.

"I can guess," I said.

"He said I was the only thing worth looking at in the whole place."

Now there, right on her face, and in the posture of her upper body, was the most difficult expression to read. If it was the last quarter of a basketball game it could go either way.

Well, Joseph-François Dupleix was not in our super-market encyclopedia, but I did find him in the downtown library. When there is no fishing, there is still reading.

Dupleix made a kind of interesting riches-to-rags story, from governor general of all French India to a guy trying to sue his former benefactors for spending money.

Here's what he wrote three days before he died: "My services are treated as fables, my demand is denounced as ridiculous; I am treated as the vilest of mankind; I am in the most deplorable indigence."

That sounds just like the last days of the man this city was named after.

Dupleix died in November of 1763, in Paris. At least he got to finish it in what they call the city of light.

But here's something I didnt much like.

While Dupleix was suing his old company, and writing his *Mémoire contre la compagnie des Indes avec les pièces justificatives,* his wife Jeanne Albert died in the next room.

I began to wonder if Dewey Tugnut had once enjoyed power and riches.

Then I slapped myself on the side of the head. No, you idiot. That's just the point.

I mean if there is still a point in people's stories.

I figured out that the dickhead with the backward baseball cap must live in the neighbourhood, because while looking out our window I would sometimes see him slouching up the street or slapping his huge court shoes down it.

Once I saw him standing in the doorway of the apartment across the street, looking up at the third floor of our building.

I made a point to ask Dewey if he had fire insurance.

I had nothing to go on. It was just the way this gink looked. He probably had a tattoo between his thumb and forefinger.

Next time I saw him he was wearing a teeshirt version of the Union Jack. These were not all that uncommon around Kits that year, but something clicked in my over-large head anyway. I was into my shoes and out the door before you could say Peewee Reese.

He was half a landing ahead of me, taking the steps two at a time. I followed him up. There he was at the open door, handing two dollars and change to Janine.

There was no sign of Dewey.

What was I supposed to do? I handed her some

123

money too. I dont know how much. I was out of breath.

Here we were, the only two paying guests of the Joseph-François Dupleix Museum.

He didnt have a baseball cap on. His hair was pulled back and tied with a piece of light blue ribbon. He was wearing dark brown corduroys. But his feet were still in very large hoop star shoes with the laces undone and the tongues looking rude.

The English flag on his chest could have been a coincidence.

He was standing beside the glass case filled with the War of the Austrian Succession, but he was not paying attention to anything in 1744. His eyes looked as if someone had recently kicked him in the groin, and they were looking at Janine.

I will admit this once, and then we will forget it. His eyes looked the way mine felt like from inside.

I moved a step closer to the imaginary line drawn between them.

Janine wasnt much of a museum guide. She should have been going through some kind of patter, even a two-room patter. But she was just as quiet as always, Mrs Jeanne Albert Tugnut.

Well, *someone* had to say something.

"Is that English flag just a coincidence?" I asked the guy.

He rubbed his chin, the way guys with beards are always rubbing their beards. He had a tattoo between his thumb and forefinger.

"It's a *tee*shirt," he said.

We had moved a step each closer to one another, the way men will. I did not in my wildest dreams imagine that I seemed as menacing as he did.

"Joseph-François Dupleix was born in 1697 at Landrecies, France," said Janine.

I was surprised again by her light blue eyes.

Is that light blue hair ribbon just a coincidence, I wondered.

"Let's not have any trouble," I said.

"There wont be any trouble if you just get the fuck out," he said.

What was I going to do? Go downstairs and listen through the ceiling?

I thought he was just going to take a step toward her, or reach for the big picture on the wall, or something. I took and step *and* reached.

Then I felt like a hard-boiled detective in a Los Angeles novel. They are always getting knocked into cranium sleep too.

I must have needed that sleep, because in the following moments there was a lot of noise in those two rooms and it didnt wake me up. It didnt even penetrate my dream, which was all about being in Asia with Blue Eyes. Eventually I woke up because someone was applying very cold water to my face. When my eyes opened I saw Dewey Tugnut's thin nose about a nose-length away. I bestirred myself. That caused an impressive pain in my head-bone. I was feeling lugubrious.

But I gritted my teeth, glad that I still had them, and got myself the dignity of a sitting position on the floor.

I saw Janine sitting on the side of a chair in the corner near the front window. She was sitting on the side of the chair because like everything else in the two rooms, it was lying on its side. A lot of things were somewhat broken. There were triangles of glass on the floor. The Joseph-François Tugnut Museum had been properly trashed.

"Here, drink what's left of this water," said Dewey.

It tasted a little like metal, but I drank it.

"That guy's got a problem," I said.

"He's got the same problem as the rest of us," said Dewey.

Janine was crying or had been. Her small upper body was rising and falling as she appeared to fight for breath.

"He made a hell of a mess of your apartment," I said.

Dewey looked at me for a few seconds out of his any spare change eyes.

"I thought you were an educated man," he said.

"I'm a fisherman," I countered.

Dewey picked up a broken picture frame and started to pick the shards of glass out of it.

"That dumb asshole didnt do it," he told me. "She did."

DESIRE AND THE UNNAMED NARRATOR

Margaret Atwood's second novel, *Surfacing*, has since its publication in 1972, been adopted as a kind of tract or holy book by an astonishing variety of special interest groups that choose to operate inside the field of literary criticism. In Canada the intellectual nationalists have seen it as a warning against the autoamericanization of the Canadian middle class. In the United States, especially, it is most often seen as one of the most important texts in feminist fiction. Ecologists have noted the conflict between mysterious forest and the techno-waste of the city. In more recent years it has been picked up by deconstructionists, Bahktinists, post-Freudians and even the new wave of social-realists. One of these last-mentioned, Victor Krukow, in the Spring 1985 issue of *New Century*, takes special note of the depredations visited upon society by the inability of any of the four principal characters to break out of their enculturated individualisms:

> Even the title given to the unfortunate movie
> being made by the two men, "Random

Samples," indicates the decrepitude of late bourgeois North America, in which any kind of planning, social or esthetic, is forsworn in favor of the power given to bloodless technology, and the undisciplined consumerism of human beings who look wide-eyed for whatever "nature" might offer in its outdoor supermarket.

(pp.23-24)

It is no wonder, then, that more than two decades after the publication of the novel, it is only the casual reader picking up the paperback in the airport bookstore who has the opportunity to see with her own eyes and imagination the first element of the book in question. Yet that element is inescapably there in the opening paragraph of the book. It might be called, if we must use any critical jargon at all, narrativity. It is the often-overlooked quality that makes any story successful, the not-quite-palpable something that allows a reader, trained or not, to feel as if he or she is in the presence of a real person acting out a real experience.

One of the particulars of such an experience is, of course, the character about whom the reader comes to care. The other is something variously called setting, place, referential environment, etc. In the first paragraph of *Surfacing* the place is perhaps the most traditional in Western literature—the road along which a character or characters, representing whatever it is that the author or his culture wants those characters to represent, must travel. Yet among the dozens of articles devoted to an exegesis of Atwood's picaresque, not one has taken any fruitful notice of that image. Not one has attempted a discussion of the pattern that sees the inaugural automobile replaced by a power-boat, a kind of automobile adapted for a watery road, itself to be replaced by the canoe, the boat deprived of its engine, and at the same time of its technologized noise.

That first paragraph makes brief mention of "sea-planes," and this sets up a secondary pattern for the ensuing narrative, a succession of references to various modes of travel. These include, of course, the "American" power-boats, the police launch, and passenger jets high in the sky above the seemingly remote Quebec woods.

But one does not have to be a meticulous reader to notice that the narrator's important recollections of her childhood are filled with references to modes of travel, from her father's recklessly-driven car, to her brother's dreamed-of rocket-ships, to the "trains shunting back and forth" (p.55), a Sunday treat for the people with whom the pretty little narrator used to go to church.

"The pleasure of the text," Roland Barthes said in his book of that title, "is that moment when my body pursues its own ideas—for my body does not have the same ideas I do" (p.17). That is a power in narrative fiction that is not recognized by those commentators who seize *Surfacing* for their purposes regarding nationalism, feminism, deconstructionism, etc. No memory is as rich and persuasive as the memory of childhood travel; this is because it is a somatic memory. In most childhood travel the subject recalls a kind of pleasant drifting, perhaps the comfort of a blanket or the upholstery of the vehicle. The child was carried along, let us say through the northern woods, with her brain relaxed into the alpha state. So every time the narrator recalls her father's car, even though he may have been a frightening driver, she experiences, for a while, a kind of fugitive comfort.

That is why it is so important that the book begin with a car trip into the north, this time a ten-year-old car in, let us say, 1970 carrying four young people north of the cities. "I'm in the back seat with the packsacks; this one, Joe, is sitting beside me chewing gum and holding my hand," reports the narrator on the second page of text. It is quite important that she be in the back seat. That is where she and her brother always were in their trips in their father's car. And that is where by tradition the more daring of the two couples sits when four teenagers go out for some driving and automotive necking. Joe is holding her hand, yes. But soon he will allow his large hand to fall to the inside of her thigh. And why not? She is lovely and a little distracted at the outset of this voyage into her childhood.

And she is to become what all the city boys in the novel are always manhandling. Atwood left a typically obscure and transparent clue to her purpose in *Survival*, the famous critical text that was published in the same year as was *Surfacing*: "Nature as woman keeps *surfacing* as a metaphor all over Canadian literature" (p.200, emphasis mine). But we have generally seen such a metaphor as created by the male author, as observed by the male narrator. Here in Atwood's second novel we encounter a complication of that system. The female author and the female narrator, one would expect, are bound to present the reader with, if not an entirely different nature, at least a different metaphorizing of the relationship between nature and woman.

That certainly complicates the issue of desire in the reading act. Roland Barthes sees the text as the erotic agency or lineaments of desire: "lost in the midst of a text (not *behind* it, like a *deus ex machina*) there is always the other, the author." And "in the text, in a way, I *desire* the author: I need his [given that Barthes was homosexual, we may substitute "her" here] figure . . . as he needs mine" (*The Pleasure of the Text*, 27). Julia Kristeva returns the reader's attention from the lost author to the materiality of the text itself. In *Desire in Language* she presents the act of reading as an erotic encounter with the tapestry of signifiers themselves. Thus while Barthes may experience a neural-sexual meeting of minds with Margaret Atwood (or the more shadowy figure called "the author") should he read *Surfacing*, Kristeva's reader is more likely to experience a *jouissance* aroused by the author's fictional objects.

Take for instance the narrator's memory of herself as a girl who dreamt of going to Sunday School, "like everyone else." She fixes on the costume: "itchy white stockings and a hat and gloves." In other words, a girl dressed as a woman. One would not be blamed for wondering how those white stockings were held up. One might just want to reach in there and see. Perhaps one could smooth out the itch. Desire in language, as it formulates critical discourse about the arts, in this case, literature, knows no boundaries to curiosity. Was it cool or warm in there? Let us say mid-thigh.

But pleasure of the text, and desire for the signifier do not prepare a simple case of lusting for an admittedly luscious narrator. It is at the very heart of narrative. Barthes again:

> Death of the Father would deprive literature of many of its pleasures. If there is no longer a Father, why tell stories? Doesn't every narrative lead back to Oedipus? Isn't storytelling always a way of searching for one's origin, speaking one's conflicts with the Law, entering into the dialectic of tenderness and hatred? Today, we dismiss Oedipus and narrative at one and the same time: we no longer love, we no longer fear, we no longer narrate. As fiction, Oedipus was at least good for something: to make good novels, to tell good stories. . . .
>
> (*PT*, 47)

Atwood's narrator is, of course, in search for her father. She wants to find him alive, or failing that, at least to find him. Barthes would say that the finding of the father will ensure the survival of the narrative. But what does Kristeva say about fathers and love and story? Let us look at her essay, "The Father, Love, and Banishment":

> *To love* is to survive paternal meaning. It
> demands that one travel far to discover the
> futile but exciting presence of a waste-
> object: a man or woman, fallen off the father,
> taking the place of his protection . . . . This
> act of loving and its incumbent writing
> spring from the Death of the Father—from
> the Death of the third person . . . .
>
> (*DL*, 150)

Surfacing is, of course, an aggressively first-person
novel, the first and third parts in the first-person sports-
commentary tense.

So: Barthes has narrative dependent upon the life of
the father, and Kristeva has writing emerging from the
death of the father. Atwood's narrator, when her story is
almost entire, manages to find some space between Barthes
and Kristeva. In what may be an hallucinatory episode and
may be an apocalyptic moment, she sees some kind of
being in the old garden of her parents' place in the woods.
At first she imagines that it is her father. Then it appears to
be a "thing" seen by people who have become bushed.
Then "I see now that although it isn't my father it is what
my father has become. I knew he wasn't dead" (p.187).

The important thing is that this creature cannot be
easily assigned a metaphorical purpose within the designs
of feminist or nationalist criticism. But it is absolutely
necessary to the narrative. Here the mysterious impanation
makes us more certain that in the narrator we are seeing a
real person living a moment in a real life. We feel certain
that we can see her, the light of the sun in the northern
forest falling between leaves and onto her face and body.
And what of that body? It receives a great deal of attention
through the text. The narrator imagines losing pieces of it.
She imagines an abortion. She mentions her skin
continuously. She manages often to view her body as if
seeing it from another's point of view. It is that body that

makes us think that we are watching a real woman. It is the constant reference to that body that arouses our Kristevan desire.

Let us turn our attention to one of the key passages of the book, the scene in which the narrator, having made her way free of her three companions, dives repeatedly from her canoe, finally to find her father's corpse (for Barthes the end of narrative; for Kristeva the beginning of writing). We do not know, for once, what the narrator is wearing. All we hear is that she removes her sweatshirt. The day prior to this one she had tried to set out, in her bathing suit, in her canoe, but had been held back by the unsettling scene in which the movie-making men force Anna to strip naked.

Presumably the narrator's nakedness here will redress the effect of that scene—nakedness combined with an escape from the men with their camera, speaks for the ascendency (and eventual surfacing) of nature rather than for the degradation of the city and its experience-deferring machines.

She removes, in any case, her sweatshirt, and dives carefully from her canoe into the water at the base of the rock bluff where her father's Indian rock painting should be found. Over and over she dives, each time to surface from the cool lake, its water flowing from her arched back, from her thrust-forward breasts. The sun splashes too on her bare wet skin, and follows the course of bright beaded water as it rolls along the surface of her young body.

Now she kneels (p.141) facing backwards with both knees on the stern seat, then puts a naked foot on each gunwale and stands up slowly. Her wet hair is plastered to her neck and shoulder. The last of the sparkling water shimmers on her tense balancing body. Drops of gleaming moisture fall from her sleek bush. Then she bends her knees and straightens, the canoe teetering like a spring-board.

We remember the importance of the canoe as image, as the last in a line of vehicles, as the transportation that brings the nude narrator closest to both her father's dive and her own. It is in that canoe that I want to remain for a moment, to consider one more subject. First I remove my shirt and hand it to her, to use as a towel. As she raises it with both hands to rub her hair dry, her breasts rise again into the sunlight. What was I to do? I leaned forward and touched the nearest nipple with my tongue. Only then did I wonder what her response might be. But not for long. She pushed me from the canoe, and in the suddenness of the movement she and the canoe both overturned in the sun-dappled water.

We must distinguish between figuration and representation. The latter attempts an imitation of nature; if there is a woman in the text she is a print of a woman in real life. Figuration, on the other hand, arouses our erotic or other responses in just the way a figure in real life would. The bliss of reading depends on immediate response, not an understanding that one is being reminded of responses in life. It would be a mistake to consider the unnamed narrator of *Surfacing*, for example, a representation of nature. She is nature, a figure of nature as well as a figure in fiction. There is no term, other than "line," that is so universal in its applications to all the arts, as the term "figure."

The narrator's figure attracted me immediately, and came to be my favourite image as I thought back on the story. When I saw her squatting in her parents' abandoned garden, her faded blue jeans worn shiny and her shirttails tied in a knot high on her midriff, I could no longer stay in the cabin. She must have heard my steps on the little twigs and last-year's leaves behind her, but she pretended not to. She continued to pull miniature carrots out of the earth as I closed on her, and when I placed my hand on the cool base of her spine, a shiver coursed its way through her whole body.

She stood, her back still to me, and walked out of the garden and into the woods. I followed, ignorant of whether

I were making noise or not, my attention fixed on the marvelous shape of the backside in blue jeans in front of me. As soon as we were inside the sacred coolness of the forest, I stepped up close and put my arms around her from behind. She leaned back into me and let her head recline against my shoulder blade. My hands found their way up the front of her blouse, till they stopped at the undersides of her breasts, that lovely weight. I pressed myself against her bum.

"Ah," she said. Then "ah."

I spoke to her, describing her beauty, declaring my rapture brought on by being in the woods, telling her of my need, boasting my knowledge of Canadian fiction.

Canadian fiction is about terror and death in the forest, about fear and loneliness in the forest of a protagonist's psyche. Terror and death and insanity. A fall from the mountain. Chowder for a bear. A bump in the snow.

"In Canadian fiction," I said, "the human protagonist is alienated from the nature he sees all round him. Nature is a threat rather than a solace. If you go into the woods today you'd better go in disguise."

Anne Murray's "The Teddybears' picnic"

She began to laugh, and it seemed to me that her laughter ran among the trees in every direction, as all I could see was the inside of a thigh moving slowly past my face.

According to Kristeva, "The imprint of an archaic moment, the threshold of space, the 'chora' as primitive stability absorbing anaclitic facilitation, produces laughter" (*DL*, 283).

She had felt protected by her parents in these northern woods, protected and virginal. Now she was leaning on me, but leaning all her weight on me, around me, surrounding me. She laughed as she thrust and thrust again, and my hands were now on that firm thrusting backside, but I could not laugh with her.

"Come up to the cabin," she said after a while. "I'll make some tea."

"I love you," I said. The short sentence barely croaked from my throat.

"I am looking for a father," she said.

"I desire you."

"A father and myself."

I felt as I had felt before, that I was in the presence of a real person acting out a real experience. The artificial quarrel between art and life was either at an end or set aside for the moment.

In the cabin the space was tight and there were five of us. As she made her way between me and the wooden table, having thrown the old tea into the yard, her hip touched mine for a half-second, and I could smell mushrooms and ferns.

She knew the art of making tea in the north. She knew where the Indian rock paintings were. She knew far better than I how to do what she did to me. She was an artist with many arts. She knew how to write all this too, how to make us see, as readers, how through the myriad layering of art she resurrects the father. Then how she lets the father go again, forever this time.

The Probable Event

They met for a mid-day breakfast every Wednesday at Daphne's Lunch, a diner where the waitresses always said they were out of the Special. She was a realist writer who specialized in short stories about being the daughter of a father or the mother of a son. He called himself a fabulist, whatever that was supposed to mean. He wrote stories in which people suddenly find out that they can fly, or dogs can speak ironically.

They both looked forward, after the weekend was done, to their mid-day breakfast every Wednesday. It was not that they shared, at these meetings, their problems and delights regarding writing. If they ever talked about it, it was by accident, as a background to something else. They were both married, but they didnt discuss their marriages, either. Actually, she was usually separated. Sometimes she would let one of her ex-husbands into the house for a while, but usually they were long gone. She generally shared the house with her two sons and a boarder or two. College lads, she preferred.

So what did they talk about? Well, they made a lot of jokes, or if not jokes, witty repartee. They had known each other since university days, thirty years ago. He liked really stupid puns, and she did too, though hers were usually somehow connected with song and movie titles from their youthful days, or wild liberties taken with word-derivations.

"This week I read a nineteenth-century novel about a society lady who threw it all over and made a desperate marriage with a Caribbean produce manager," she said one Wednesday.

"What was the title of this novel?" he asked, affecting diffidence.

"*Bride and Breadfruitist,*" she said, and took his last piece of toast.

They would eat the Great Breakfast All Day, or whatever was substituted for the Special, and then they would sit for another hour while Ray or one of the waitresses brought more coffee. Often they would be brain-dazzled by coffee when they went their separate ways.

It was hard to say why they did this most Wednesdays. It would be impossible to show that it did their writing any good. There was no erotic component to their friendship. Once, twenty years before, she had got quite drunk at a party and undone all the buttons on his shirt and pushed him into a closet full of hanging coats. But he never did decide whether she had known quite who he was at the time. She was not overly pretty and his bulbous nose kept him from being a collar ad kid. In terms of the spoken language, neither of them gained anything much from their meetings at Daphne's.

But they loved their Wednesdays. If they had to miss one because either of them was going somewhere to give a lecture, the following Wednesday loomed even more valuable. It was a strange business. The people in Daphne's Lunch knew about their ten-year-old tradition, and the comic rituals attending their observations.

They did a lot of smiling and laughing during their weekly meal. Even if things were particularly glum at home, the first smile would begin when the second person arrived at the back booth in Daphne's.

"Saw a classic movie this weekend, about a motorist who grew old and died, waiting for the traffic light to change," he would aver.

"Would I recognize the name of this gripping cinematic tale?" she would enquire, still good-naturedly.

"*Forever Amber*," he would say, and add a clash of cymbals.

That was not an example of their wit. It was an agreed upon exchange that was totally without merit of any sort. That was why it was spoken.

But he knew that for all their shared memories and language, she saw their friendship in a way that he did not. She figured that he could see it her way, but that for his own reasons, he chose not to.

She thought that human beings acted the way they do because of their upbringing and environment, and that their characters or personalities are responsible for the way they bring up their children and create *their* environment.

Many people think that way; there's nothing out of order in thinking that way. There are therapists all over town who depend on that idea, and they are sincerely trying to get their clients to understand it.

Another way of trying to understand it her way was to look back as honestly as possible on your own life and nearby lives and to write a report on what you see. If you can make a nice English sentence you can become a writer who gets serious attention from critics and loyalty from intelligent people at earlier stages in their lives.

He agreed that there had to be some kind of cause and effect system alive in the world, and in fact was smart enough to keep his fingers away from hot stove elements and that sort of thing. He even admitted that there might be a relationship between human environment and human behaviour. But when it came to putting down English words and making stories of them, he thought that trying to make up something he had never seen was more interesting than getting a better look at something he had experienced.

So what about the fact that they mainly talked about their pasts?

I suppose you could say that she was comfortable in it, that these talks or word sessions were a relaxed form of what she did in her novels. But what were they for him? Maybe, when they werent talking about the past, the discontinuous wordplay, no matter how unsuccessful, was necessary to the maintenance of his viewpoint. But why didnt he just relax and let his talk be different from his imagining prose?

It didnt look as if any of these questions would ever get answered in these weekly sessions at the diner. But they kept coming. Maybe it had absolutely nothing to do with the fact that they were both novelists. They had met at university, where neither knew that the other wanted to be a writer. So it went.

Until one morning in July.

Or mid-day, really. They were having Great Breakfast All Day this week, two eggs over easy, three strips of bacon for him, three little dark sausages with HP Sauce for her, hash browns, a slice of orange, and toast, with marmalade for him and dark jam for her. The coffee would keep coming.

"Look at Ray," she said, and her body language, or rather head and face language said not to make it too obvious.

"Looks normal to me," he said, and wiped some egg yolk off her plate with his toast.

"Look at his eyes," she persisted.

"What should I be looking for?"

"Suicide. Murder. Assault with a deadly weapon."

He looked at Ray's eyes. Now Ray was always affable at work, always playing the affable host, really. His eyes, though, were hard to remember. How did they usually look? In any case, right now they did look a little odd. They were flat across the top and semi-circular on the bottom. They were looking the wrong way. The irises and pupils were in front, all right, but the eyes seemed to be looking back inside. No, eyes wouldnt work that way.

"Afh," he said. "Nafh."

She put jam on both sides of her half-slice of toast. It was her custom. If he had tried it he would have got jam, or marmalade, on his watch band.

"When was the last time you saw Daphne?" she asked.

"I havent seen Daphne in months," he said. "I was just saying last week, in case you dont remember, that this place ought to be rechristened Ray's Neighbourhood Bar."

"It's not a bar."

"*Malheureusement.*"

She held her coffee cup in the fingers of both hands, her elbows on the table, rim of the cup to her lips. She was letting his mind sift.

This was something different from their usual weekly foolery, maybe. He looked at Ray some more. Ray always walked with his head forward and down a little, as if the rafters were too low, but today his head was really forward, really low. Something like a vulture, if you can imagine a tortured vulture.

"Not tortured," he said.

"What?"

"I was just correcting myself."

"Revising, you mean."

"We are not talking about fiction or writing or stories or literature."

"Is that so?"

He would have liked to get back to their usual line of prattle, away from the possibility of diagnosing people. But there was something of a warning in her facial expression, or her presence among the cigarette smoke, bacon fumes and human body heat in the air there.

"It's just past the beginning of the month," he said. "Maybe June was not a good month at the till."

"And maybe baby frogs do rain down from the sky," she said.

"Now you're talkin'."

They drank their coffee and reverted to their usual manner of dialogue for the remainder of the hour.

All that week he sat down intending to write a story about Henry Hudson discovering that the Indians of the Six Nations had a baseball league. Henry Hudson did not know what the Savages were doing, but he suspected that it was religion and set about trying to put a stop to it.

But he didnt really get far into that story. He spent a good deal more time teaching dangling modifiers at Augean Community College.

She wrote twenty-five pages of her new novel that week. It was about the embarrassment and hurt pride she had suffered during a supposedly romantic but really sexual liaison with the son of an old friend. She wrote out of the furnace of revenge, and the writing, as they say, went very well.

In the middle of the week, they met at Daphne's Lunch, and this time they were in time for the Special, or rather the special that was substituted for the Special. Mulligatawny soup and a Reuben sandwich. Good. He would put a bit of HP Sauce in the soup. She would open the sandwich and dab in some mustard.

"I cant write three or four pages at a time since I quit smoking," he said. "Quitting smoking is ruinous to the health of my posthumous reputation."

"Bull," she said, "shit."

Ray served them himself. He spoke the words one would use in normal good-natured hostmanship, but they were words only. His usual manufactured bonhomie was not there. His eyes were flat across the top and rounded beneath, and they seemed to be looking far into the past. His middling short black and white hair stuck out sideways, like a crown of thorns.

When Ray had gone up to the front of the diner to ring up something on the cash register, the silence at their table became something to get rid of. He got up and fetched the HP Sauce from another table. He grunted as he got up, such a grunt being a serviceable bridge between significant silence and habitual conversation.

"Still no sign of Daphne," she said while he shook and shook the bottle. "What are the possibilities?"

"They are innumerable."

"On the contrary, they are few in number, one usually finds. She may have left him for a real estate genius."

"Someone could have been coming back from the future and time-travelled right into the space she was occupying. Did you ever think of that?"

"May have had a disfiguring accident, or paralyzed herself while trying to commit suicide," she said.

He wiped his Reuben fingers on a paper napkin.

"A goose could have hit the windshield of her car. She could have swerved off and struck an oak tree. Could have heard a rain of acorns just before slipping into a comma."

"That's coma."

"Semi-colon," he said, by way of compromise.

Ray arrived with a spout of coffee and they murmured their thanks. Usually they talked quite loudly in Daphne's, figuring that the other regulars were interested in their wordplay. But today they were speaking more quietly, like conspirators in a potting shed.

Ray put the coffee pot back on the warmer and went to the front of the diner. She turned her head and they both observed Ray. She tilted her head back to look through her glasses. He looked over the tops of his. Ray's profile appeared noble in a domesticated sort of way. He looked distracted and sad. No one feels comfortable in the presence of a sad diner operator. No one feels like singing.

No one else in the room seemed to notice Ray's sadness. At least no one asked him about it. All in all it seemed like a normal Wednesday as far as the demeanor of the other customers was concerned.

"Why dont you have a nice piece of that Banana Creme pie I can see in that glass display case?" he enquired, liquid sugar in his voice.

"You shut up, Smarty," she said. "You try that every week, and have you ever seen me have a piece of pie?"

"Sure," he said.

"That was your birthday. I was having it for you."

And so they went their ways for another week. During that week she got a phone call that was partly importunate and partly apologetic. It was the Canadian Broadcasting Corporation. Some people wanted her to write a fifteen-minute treatment of the history of fiction in the city, and they wanted it for broadcast in two days. She put her novel aside for a day and wrote a humdinger of a radio piece.

He heard it on the radio Sunday afternoon. He thought it was very nice, not only because it mentioned him as part of the ongoing reaction against realism, but because the sentences were so good. He had the radio on on Sunday because he had made himself a new rule, not to write stories or novels on weekends. Weekends would be for attacking his drawer full of unanswered letters. At the moment he was ten months behind.

He *told* himself it was a rule, but really it was just that he found things going awfully slowly anyway, and he thought that if he gave himself two days off he would be able to spring at the story with a burst of energy and invention on Monday morning.

After all, as some twit of a prairie reviewer said in some low circulation newspaper, it must be easy to churn out the stuff if you can just make everything up. No need to check against the facts. Just let those ambulances fall from the sky.

Is that so? What about memory, he would have asked, if he had ever sunk so low as to reply to a reviewer, what about the memory writers? They've got twenty novels and two hundred short stories in their memory banks, and who knows how many others in their diaries and notebooks. Dont you think that transferring all that onto hard copy is easier than trying to think stuff up?

In other words the work, as they used to say in Hemingway books, was not going well.

A couple of years ago they would have asked one another at Daphne's, "How's the book coming?" Now they were more likely to discuss the interpretive problems they faced in reading one of the new comic strips in the *Moon*.

"His eyes look worse every week," she said.

It was true. The straight lines that used to be the top edges of Ray's eyes were now sagging, and the sag in the bottom edge of each eye had become a deep droop. He shuffled as he walked now, bringing their lentil soup and shepherd's pie, this week's substitution for the Special. His characteristic wisecracking had disappeared a few weeks before. Now he didnt even say hello when he put the food down in front of them.

"Ah poop, with Ray like that I dont know how long I will want to come to Daphne's. If it wasnt for getting to see you, remaining ember of my life, I dont think I would drop in here at all."

"His skin is dead white," she said. "It looks as if he didnt comb his remaining hair this morning."

"When my kid was smaller and didnt have her own ideas about such things, I used to bring her here for lunch, or Saturday burgers."

"I'm really worried about him," she said, turning to look at Ray, who was using a wet dish towel to wipe the same spot on the counter in front of the coffee pots, over and over.

"She always found a new and novel way to coerce me into buying her a milkshake, even in the days when we were still making sure her diet was healthy."

"You cant say new *and* novel," she said, returning to her soup.

"At least the food is still good," he said.

"Just be glad he isnt cooking. Just hope nothing happens to Maurice."

Maurice Wong was the short order cook at Daphne's Lunch. They used to joke with him that one day he would own the place. Maurice showed them that he knew how to make a smile, but he didnt understand the way these people talked with one another a few feet from his serving window. Now that they were talking about Ray, he couldnt hear them because they were talking for themselves, not the little community at Daphne's.

"What are you writing now?" she asked.

He stopped his spoon halfway to his mouth and glared at her.

"Oops," she said.

They fell to their task, the lentil soup, the shepherd's pie.

There was one hell of a noise. Crash. Bang. Splanngang. Riiiiip. Smash.

Tinkle. Clatter.

It didnt sound like that, much. But then think back on any sudden loud and scary noise you have heard, and you will see that you cannot write down words that will sound like it. Hear, I guess, not see.

There were broken white dishes and broken clear glasses all over the place. There were people on the floor, and at least one of them was bleeding from a leg. There was soup on the wall. The table closest to the front counter had a long deep gouge in the blue formica.

People were saying "What" and "Jesus" as they got up and felt each other for damage. Many of them were rather old, and had to be reassured that they were not going to be hauled off to the hospital.

"Jesus! A gas main exploded!" she shouted.

Her hands were clearing imaginary glass fragments from her clothes. Her eyes were wild, darting through fallen red hair.

"No," he said.

"*Something* exploded! The Shell station!"

He pointed kitty-corner across the street. The Shell station was operating, business as usual.

"Well, Jesus Jesus, Jesus!" she persisted. "A bakelite, what do you call them, a carmelite."

"A mcteorite? Moldavite?"

"A meterorite. Dozens fall to earth every day."

He considered picking the pieces of wood and plaster off his food and resuming work on the substitute special. But he gave up on the notion.

"It was internal combustion," she said.

"You mean spontaneous combustion? As in that Dickens novel we studied in grad school?"

"Spontaneous combustion. Count the customers. Look for empty shoes."

"Smoke coming out of them?"

She sat down on top of the table, next to her upside down soup bowl. From that position she could see her reflection in the undamaged mirror on the opposite wall. Her hands pushed her heavy hair up and dropped it nicely into place.

He liked it when women did that. But now he had other things to look at. He was bent over, looking at the floor, or rather the wall down by the floor. His finger found a hole in the wall a few centimetres above the moulding. He stood up and went to the gouge in the front table. Then he went back to the hole. He sighted back toward the gouge. And beyond. The plate glass window looked something like a dense spider web, about a metre across at the widest part. There were holes in it too.

Then he found another hole, in the wine-coloured padding of a booth. He sighted back toward the window again.

"What are you doing?" she asked. It would be fair to say that there was some impatience or annoyance in her voice.

"Geometry," he said.

Other people were at last asking each other whether they were all right. The old man with the wound had his trouser leg pushed up. There was a red streak across his rather fat calf.

When he was asked exactly where he had been sitting he was eager to demonstrate.

"Now what are you doing?" she asked.

"Corroboration," he said. He was down on his hands and knees beside the old man's feet. He got the old man to stand up again and then sighted back at the window.

Ray had not said a word to anyone. Neither did he go around checking for damage. He was standing in front of the cash register. Not stiff. Moving his head enough to see what people were doing. His eyes looked as if he had bought them cheap.

"I cant believe this is happening," she said.

"Happened," he said.

"Wha?"

"Happened. It's happened. Already happened. Now we find out what. Etcetera."

"I cant believe it," she said. "I cant believe it."

By the time the police car and its two large-behinded young policemen arrived, he was gone somewhere, so she had to listen to Ray's short replies to their questions, and then hear the questions asked of her.

"I dont know," she said. "It was just like some big explosion or something, right out of the blue."

One of the young policemen asked her another question.

"It was like, I dont know, the world you see just flying to pieces right in front of your eyes," she said.

Another question.

"I cant remember exactly," she said. "We were just talking about Ray and how sad he was looking, when all at once there was this noise and things flying around. It just didnt make any sense at all. I didnt know what was happening."

148

Now he was back, talking with the other policeman. He took the policeman to the hole just above the moulding, then pointed back at the broken window. He took the policeman outside and pointed across the street. The policeman said something, and they walked over there.

Ray was now sweeping up broken glass.

She started to pick things up, the spilled dishes, bits of wood. She was going to help clean up, but then she just couldnt. She had to sit down.

He was back, explaining something to the two policemen up front. Most of the old people and other customers were gone now. A few clustered on the sidewalk in front of the door. She sat and noticed that she had been shaking but now was hardly shaking at all.

"We can go now," he said. He was standing beside her. He leaned over her and picked up his umbrella. "Let's walk over to the park."

They walked over to the park. He did not put his arm around her. He didnt even take her hand. They had been in graduate school together two decades ago. That was the basis of their relationship.

They walked across the little league baseball diamond, from third base to first base. They sat down on the home team's bench behind the chicken wire.

"What were you doing across the street?" she asked.

"More geometry," he said. "I followed the line of sight from the bullet holes to the front window. Then it was simply a little triangulation."

"Is that what Ray's involved in?"

"Ho ho."

She pressed his arm. That was something new.

"Well," he said, "I followed the lines and wound up on the roof of the laundromat across the street. I found four brass shells. The cop said they were .30-.30s."

"Holy shit," she said.

"That's sort of what they looked like, lying there."

They got up and walked some more. He didnt put his arm around her but he walked closer to her, and sometimes his coat brushed against hers. They walked around the lawn-bowling green.

"You surprise me," she said. "Checking those bullets and tracing them back to their source."

"Cause and effect," he said.

They walked back across the soccer field. They were walking as close together as it was possible to walk without holding one another.

"We could have been—" she said.

"Daw daw daw *daw*."

"Killed," she said.

"I will admit that possibility. In fact I am surprised no one in Daphne's was at least seriously injured."

They reached the main street and stood where they knew they would turn from each other to go their separate ways home.

"I guess we're both going to write about this," she said.

He peered at her over his glasses, looking for something to do before replying.

"Do we talk with one another about our writing now?"

"We could be dead," she said. "Without ever doing it."

"Doing it?"

"Talking about our writing, you fool."

"Oh. Are we dragging this out in terms of dialogue because we dont want to go home so soon after being almost dead?"

"Of course," she said. "Want to go for a coffee?"

"Not to Daphne's," he said.

They went to a little cappuccino place up the street. She ordered a cappuccino and he asked for an ordinary coffee.

"I wonder whether we *will* both write about it," he said. "I can see you doing it. The two writers are in the coffee shop, not mentioning anything about writing, but carrying on their traditional Wednesday afternoon lunch ritual."

"Thursday."

"Thursday?"

"That's how we do it," she said. "Change unimportant details. I'll give her short salt-and-pepper hair, and so on."

"I dont think you should ever write a story about a story-writer," he said.

"I have heard that before," she said. "But as you know, I have had quite a lot of success doing it. Readers like to identify with writers in stories because they all think they could be writers too."

She ran her forefinger around the lip of her cup, and poked it into her mouth.

"Why dont you think you should write about writers?" she said.

He held his cup before his chin, ready to put it to his lips to punctuate the end of his sentence.

"Writers' lives are so dull. Nothing ever happens to them. If you ever wrote about real writers you'd be tempted to invent some sort of violent action in order to give them something to do."

THE STUMP

I can see him now, as if I were in that house and watching him from some invisible vantage. Human eyes in a fly on the wall. He shakes his abundant flaxen locks, and rises from the swivel chair in front of the old beaten typewriter with the Spanish keyboard. He is wearing no shirt, and his narrow hairless trunk rises out of his blue jeans like that white German asparagus prized by people who wait for it in cities with airports all over western Europe.

His name is Robert Kroetsch, a poet with a jittery mind, never married because his metabolism is too quick. When he was a whiplash boy, growing up in the little orchard town of Lawrence, B.C., he imagined himself a science fiction writer, a science fiction writer so successful and famous that he would be invited to join the first crew of earthmen bound for a second planet.

But he has inexplicably fallen into poetry. Maybe poetry was sitting around waiting for someone with a pulse as fast as his, for this quick lad who could not grow a whisker on his long narrow chin. His first few poems had fallen somewhere into the crack between typewriter and magazine, but eventually his burning veins produced a breath that worked its way under a lot of people's collars, and in the eighth decade of the twentieth century he became the most famous poet in the land.

Now he was trying to dodge some imaginary shrapnel, and write a poem that would save his life.

He was not a kid any more, but he could not put a centimetre of suet on his back. He could not slow his heartbeat. The birds recognized him, and stared into his house through the wide window in back. They watched this creature stuck inside, who should be pulsing and windruffled on a branch of the cherry tree.

But he was stuck inside all right, and that is what this story is all about. That house on the sweetest street in Nanaimo is the subject of all this care.

I wish you could see it, it is that important. What people do, in a tale we tell each other, or the life we see developing incomprehensibly around us, is shaped by the contours of the place they are doing it in. It is environment if you are a social worker, setting if you are a playwright, landscape if you are a gardener.

If they put a little square box around each infant tomato, the adult tomatoes will grow square bodies, and will thus pack nicely into a bigger box. If you abandon a baby boy to be brought up by wolves, he will be a wolf boy, and howl at the full moon, wont he?

So do you remember the times you have read a novel, and then when you saw the movie you were disappointed because they had not got the house or the street or the farm or something the way it had laid itself out in your reading mind? Sure. The horsemen turned and rode the wrong way once outside the gate. Oh, is that what plane trees look like? In the movie Catherine Barkley has dark hair. Really.

Are you old enough to remember detective novels and cowboy novels as reprinted by Dell drugstore paperbacks? On the back cover the detective books had maps, an aerial view of the house where the murder took place, with the roof removed. The cowboy books had maps of the whole valley, showing the big ranch and the road to town and the mesa and so on, the box canyon, remember? I think it was Dell books. Maybe Popular Library. Dell, I think. Remember the detective novels had a keyhole with an eye looking through it on the front cover. I dont recall what westerns had.

Anyway, remember how you used to read through that book and notice your picture of the place differing from the map on the back cover? You would try to keep it the way it was shown, but soon the earth would be rolling away under your eyes, and the bartender was fat, even when the book said he was lanky.

I have been thinking for a while about what I said, how skinny Robert Kroetsch became the most famous poet in the land near the end of the twentieth century. I said that, didnt I? Something like that. So I'm thinking. There was some poet alive in the seventeenth century, say John Donne, and here we are still reading him now. Can you imagine someone reading a twentieth-century poet three centuries from now? I think people have a hard time imagining that the world will last that much longer than they do. I know I do. I think Robert Kroetsch does. One of his poems starts: "I wonder, by my trough, how I lived airing our love,/ and how my teeming brain will gleem/ down past my time."

That, though, is neither here nor there. I am thinking of Nanaimo, of the Nanaimo that appears in lanky Kroetsch's short poems, and the one in which I am imagining him at his desk. It is an outdoor desk, by the way, fashioned from the lowest metre of the trunk of a huge tree that once towered over his bluff-side property.

For you people on the prairie, a bluff is not, here on the west coast, a little copse of trees on the bald-headed, but rather a kind of cliff made of soil, something a suicidal horseman might leap his pony from.

You see? Even when I explain it, the southern Saskatchewan reader is still going to have a clump of willows in mind when he sees the word "bluff," or maybe a clump of those scraggly things called prairie oaks.

All right, I said earlier that he rose from a swivel chair, and I implied, perhaps, that he was inside his cedar-shake house on Vancouver Island. Nanaimo used to be a coal town and now it is a motorcycle-magazine town. Kroetsch lives there because he was brought up in the Okanagan Valley, which is more or less the opposite of Vancouver Island. Here he is now in Nanaimo, trying to finish a poem that will prolong his life. Actually, he isnt so much trying to finish it as he is trying to get the middle of it going. He always writes his poems in three sections—beginning, middle and end. He has finished the beginning. He wrote that indoors. But the middle wouldnt come this morning. He moved to his almost natural outdoor desk and tried for a middle. No luck. He was stymied, you would say. Up he stood. He ran his cigarette-stained fingers through his flaxen hair.

"Stuck in the middle," he said.

He murmured.

If you want, he breathed.

If he can finish this poem, and that includes rendering a boffo ending, such is his esthetic, he will have finished a book of poems called *The Stump*. He will be able then to proffer this book to his publisher in Toronto, Marty DiSalvo, who will publish it without question, because he has never before published a poet so successful. Even Doreen Seaweed the west coast shawoman never reached the public with such an impact.

And as soon as *The Stump* is published, Kroetsch's forlorn lost loved one will read it. She will understand the clues he has left about his house in Nanaimo, the whereabouts of the weapon, the note, the schedule. She will get across the country, if she is living across the country, or she will hie down from the Skeena Valley if that is where she has her tent. She will get there in time, and she will save his life.

"DiSalvo has never seen such a relevant manuscript," said Robert, sitting down again, staring at the Underwood.

He decided it was time for lunch. He could find his way to the refrigerator with his eyes closed, which he did. He reached inside, with his eyes closed, and brought out the first thing his hand closed around. It was a carton, or most of one, of pink grapefruit juice. That was lunch, then. He drank it all, and opened the carton and stood it on the sinkboard. Later he would empty his ashtrays into it and chuck it into the garbage can.

She has never been in this house. She has to pick up the clues in his poem *and* imagine the place. Poetry books do not have maps on the back covers. In the sixties a lot of them had maps on the front covers, because an American poet named Charles Olson had a map on the front cover of his first widely-distributed book.

Usually blond Bob doesnt or didnt have anything resembling writer's block. He had once written twelve sonnets in a day. He loves sonnets. He loves the way they resemble a small house, with a bigger room for cooking in and a smaller room for sleeping in. He likes to put a sonnet to bed. He loves the couplet at the last. He feels like a shoemaker with the polishing rag covering his hand during the voila.

Now regarding *this* house. In poetry it was perhaps not usually so serious a thing as in a novel, this problem of seeing the place. On the next island over there is a woman novelist who wants you to see exactly the kitchen she sees, exactly the wharf she looks at through her kitchen window. But poetry, in poetry you are directing people more to words than to floorplans, isnt that true? More to the inside of the ear than the furniture in the living room.

"The deep recesses of her odorous dwelling/ Were stored with magic treasures—sounds of air,/ Which had the power all spirits of compelling,/ Folded in cells of crystal silence there." There's Shelley and the kitchen he gives to the Witch of Atlas. It is filled with sounds, and isnt that what poetry is made of?

But Robert Kroetsch was not Shelley. He was not any poet in the great tradition. He had come to poetry from the odorous Okanagan Valley, with a deep duty, he thought, to change things. For over a decade he had been trying to make readers see what was in front of his eyes.

He wanted to make the stain on the table before his eyes unconditionally present to his reader. He was bedevilled by absence.

When he was a kid playing guns they didnt shoot real bullets. Billy the Kid didnt shoot real bullets. Billy the Kid is a present they give you when you are young. When he read the many biographies of Billy the Kid, he always tried to imagine the ranch exactly, no matter how the authors described it. Once he went to New Mexico and it was noisy with low-flying black air force jets

Once in a poem he seemed to break into the lyric, or maybe break out through the lyric, with anger, with impatience. He declared that he wished he could present an actual orange to his reader and watch the reader peel it and get juice on his thumb knuckle, and so on. It is one of his best poems ever. I have just spent an hour looking for it, and couldnt find it. But I know I have it there somewhere, in that pile of Kroetsch's poetry books.

I went to a lecture about Kroetsch's poetry one time. A professor from Kingston said that the orange was a symbol of Irish Protestantism and explained Kroetsch's political stance. He brought in the House of Orange and the Orange Free State, and California and Florida and Walt Disney. He said that Kroetsch's poem was about his desire to return this country to monarchy and strict order.

It was a pretty good lecture. I didnt believe a word of it.

But to return to the poet sitting in front of his patio table. He had raised the stakes. He had decided to put his mimetic powers to the test. The last poem in *The Stump* would be a treasure map, except that the treasure would not be a pot of gold. It would be the body of the poet. If the woman in question figures out the poem and then figures out the map, she will find that body warm. If not, someone else will eventually find it cold.

"My poetry is my life," the poet said in his first ever national interview.

But what if that intended reader should happen to miss Kroetsch's poem? How long a time is he giving himself after the publication of his book, after it finally appears in the nearest town to that place she lives in such a long way, perhaps, north? Do poetry books find their way up there? Of course, with a poet like Kroetsch and a reader like her, that book, *The Stump*, will find its way into her hands, and there will be enough time to find the warm thin blond somewhere on his property.

But if she does happen to miss that poem—what if she is reading the book and somehow doesnt get to that poem, or decides to skip it? Will she read this story? How will I see that she gets it? I dont even know who she is or where she lives, up north there somewhere. Will time run out on me, on her? On the poet?

And if I can get this published in the right place, and she happens to read it in time, so what? I have not read Kroetsch's poem. Yes, but if I did read it, I would not imagine the house and yard the same way she imagines it, much less the way the poet imagined it. But let's worry about place later. What about time?

Well, actually, that problem is pretty well taken care of, when you stop to think about it. Time will not run out. This is not a football game. It is a fiction. Fiction has its own time, and the perpetrator of the fiction is in charge of it, and this life-saving prose is after all a fiction.

So wait, if these are fictions, this story of mine, and the one she will, one hopes, read, and the poem-puzzle he will write when he gets over his block, what have these to do with saving lives? Lives, or at least the lives in question here, exist outside the stories. The stories are there to make life interesting in one's idle moments.

It seems to me that there are two approaches I can make to helping the poet help the reader save his life, which he need not, remember, put on the line this way. Poetry is my death, he might as well say, if the signifier is really more interesting than the signified, as the hippest critics have been saying about his recent work.

Two approaches. I could fix it so that he gets over his writer's block and produces a poem of almost eyeball-wracking clarity and nerve-exacting detail. A poem that any somewhat intelligent reader with a patient heart could follow to its breathing climax. I could tell about his smacking his forehead, say, with the palm of his left hand, the one he writes with, and sitting himself down at the stump and writing without blot for hours, producing the first long poem of his life, so to speak. I could turn pages into poem:

> At one o'clock on equinox a shadow from that fir
> Fell on the floor and up the wall and reached
> Into the open drawer of spoons. There your eye
> Would find one error, one misapplication of doubt,
> One silver item that belongs beyond this wall . . .

And so on.

Or I could write a story about the gaunt poet at his outdoor table, feverishly yet quietly laying down unheard runes. In the story I could describe his domicile to its smallest detail, fix every mote so carefully that when you, I mean she, when she reads the poem she will have an exact duplicate of the real building, the real rooms clear in her head.

If I can get the story written by the time he gets the poem written, and if I can see that it gets into print and distribution as quickly as his book does, I might be able to save his life. I do not know who this particular woman reader is, not exactly. But if I can make the story somehow glamorous as well as precise, I will reach a great number of potential life-savers. As Kroetsch would say, that would be sweet. That would make writing worth living for. Too often it has seemed worth dying for.

So I have to make a glamorous and precise story, and I have to write it in such a way that the magazine with the widest circulation in the country will want to print it. Why dont I just go to Kroetsch's place and watch him for day after day, until I see what he has in mind, and just stop him, just make him go on living? Even without her. Even without her there is a reason to live and a reason to write. If she wants to leave everything and go up north, why not let her? Or if it is not up north she went to, if she went to Nova Scotia. And especially—what if she went to Tokyo? What if she is browsing in the glove section of a Seibu store right now? In Japan they dont read stories or poems by Canadian writers from Nanaimo or White Rock. Oops.

Well, I cant think about that. I have a poet's life to save. I had better just get to inventing, I mean describing his house exactly, so that any reader could find her way around in it. And not worry about metaphors, for instance. We still dont know what he has in mind regarding his physical person. He hasnt finished the middle of the poem yet, much less the denouement.

I'd have to say that the chances arent great.

But that skinny baby-faced hay-haired lad is the best poet in the country. You have to do what you can.

Here goes.

The kitchen is painted a kind of Granny Smith green. But before you get to the kitchen, there's the walkway that goes from the front gate around the side of the house overlooking the ferry terminal. The front gate is made of old waterlogged and crumbling four-by-fours, probably cut before World War II. They are nearly black, and smooth from decades of rain. There is no actual gate, just these two posts, about waist high to an average woman. You have to picture two posts that are not any longer parallel as they rise from the earth. Their tops, where their heads would be if they were people, lean away from each other a little, say ten degrees off the parallel. If you are entering the yard between these posts you are facing just about north, perhaps ten degrees off true north. If you are looking straight in front of you, you will be seeing at about seven metres (though it will look different depending on whether there is fog or overbright sunlight and overdark shadow) an old rusted screen partly covered with a grape vine. If we are nearing the equinox, as we are while I write this, there will be many clusters of Concord grapes that have reached nearly their optimum size but are still uniformly green. Let us say that at this angle you can see twenty bunches of grapes, though the number will not register in your consciousness.

I hope you are seeing this right. You've got to be picturing it exactly the way I am imagining it, I mean looking at it. My life, or rather I mean his life depends on it.

Maybe two-thirds of the rusty screen is covered by the grape vine, obviously a very old vine for these parts. One time an old lady came by and said "I remember that grape vine from when I was a little girl." If not two-thirds, certainly sixty percent. In the summer time no one can see into that porch, but then there is never anyone on it. That is why we are looking at the walkway around the side of the house, because the back door, the kitchen door, is the only one used by anyone. Now the grass is usually long and obscuring half the walkway, or making it, let us say, narrower than it need be. But what is the walkway itself composed of? Let's see.

[handwritten margin note: an endless chain of description is something all writers face.]

162

FRED AND PAULINE

"How did I get so old?" he asked her, uneasily conscious that he was probably quoting some literary jape that shouldnt have been there in the first place.

"I am getting old just as fast as you are," she said. If she had been peeling apples at the time she would have kept her head down, looking at the long long apple skin as it fell unbroken from the Roman Beauty.

"I suppose there is some possibility in that," he allowed. "But with you it doesnt matter so much because you never promised not to get old. Besides which, I am four years older than you are in the first place. And in the second place, women live nine years longer than men do, for obvious reasons."

She did not rise to that Royal Coachman.

"Five years older," she said instead.

He pulled his belly in. It made him look a little better. His chest rose and stuck out under his chin. But it was hard on the back and so forth.

"Well," he said "what about Fred Wah, for instance. He doesnt get older. Or if he does, it is just one little part of him every five years or so. In general he looks like a kid. Except the older he gets the more Oriental he looks. But there he goes again. Oriental people dont look as old as Honkies when they get old."

He was fretting away. She liked that better than his more genuine unhappiness, the kind that makes one wake up sweating on a night that does not deserve such a response.

In his fancy she was now paring the fourth large apple. When he was a young fellow he liked it when it was time to pick the Roman Beauties. Last apples of the Fall, and they were large, filled up your nine-cent box really quick.

"Well, Pauline is not Oriental, except by marriage," she said.

"Very good. I will pretend when the time comes that I invented that one."

"What else is new? And Pauline is young enough to go skiing down glaciers, to jump into ice-cold lake water, to zip through a thesis."

"Some zip," he interpolated. "It took her over twenty years."

"Exactly. Now she is a student with a brand-new degree. That makes her young, younger than all of us."

He marvelled, not for the first time, at her logic. It was unanswerable, so he returned to his other activity, the failure to write and complete a poem. The frustration caused by this activity was making him grow old faster than he would have liked to. Actually any rate was faster than he would have liked to.

He ground his freshly sharpened pencil-point into the ashtray that was no longer an ashtray because they had quit smoking. It was years and years after Fred and Pauline had quit smoking, but now it was three months ago. He threw the useless yellow pencil onto the table, where it bounced once and skittered to the kitchen floor. She eyed him. He would pick it up later. He had better. This was a

164

conversation they did not have to have out loud. Grow old with me, the best is yet to be.

"I can no longer finish a poem," he said.

He felt as if he could not really describe to her the way in which writing a poem is like paring an apple. If you can do it all in one continuous motion it will be very satisfactory.

"That is probably why Fred looks so much younger than you," she said. "Have you ever seen a poem of Fred's that looks as if it is finished? Have you ever heard him talk about finishing a poem? Or reading a poem that sounds as if it is finished, that comes to a conclusion with some kind of obvious, oh what do you call it in music?"

"Cadence."

"Yes, that Beethoven thing. Da dum."

"Well," he said. "I always thought it was because he couldnt."

"What?"

"Couldnt finish a poem."

He knew he had stepped into it. The situation was obvious. He wished it were twenty years ago and he were having a cigarette with Pauline.

"Could not—"

"Could not, and would not—"

"And would not, exactly. They are the same thing if you are writing poems the way you said you were a quarter of a century ago."

"Let's go and see Fred and Pauline this weekend," he said.

"As long as you do not seek their advice in finishing your poem," she said. The apples were all done.

"No, I just want to see whether they have any new lines in their faces, any age spots on the backs of their hands," he said.

"Maybe you should stick to writing stories, anyway," she said, drying her hands for some reason.

That was a relief, because that was what he thought

he would like to do, anyway.

"Yes, where I can make up people like Fred and Pauline, and make them any age I want to. I think I will just put a touch of white in Pauline's hair."

Feller at the Sunsplash

There was a lot of noise in the open square of the old market in Victoria. It was a summer's day, there were billions of American tourists in town, and this was a place where the heritage people felt a lot of pride. It looked like about as old as you can get on the west coast, and at the same time it looked like the kind of place where no Winnebago rider would be afraid to browse for a frozen yogurt cone.

The noise was coming from a band that was warming up some giant electronic speakers in the square. It was the middle of a long August weekend called Victoria Sunsplash, a combination of Black music and hip poetry, and the brainchild of one Hope Anderson, Black poet and semi-professional music promoter.

Yesterday Taj Mahal and his guitar and bongo had mellowed lots of listeners out in the buttery evening sun; and then in the twilight Amiri Baraka woke them up to their own bulging eyes and quivering ears as he laid down the fiercest lines of poetry ever heard in staid Empress Victoria. One was grateful to be there.

Today there will be a family of drummers from Senegal and a famous singing prince from the record jackets; but there is also a sign in the window of the sports store in the corner of the market square. The sign says that Bob Feller will be there to sign autographs.

You have to understand that 1948 was the greatest year in the history of human civilization, and that one of the most important things to happen in 1948 was that at last Bob Feller would get his chance to pitch in the world series.

In 1948 if you were talking about singing you said Sinatra. If you were talking about hitting you probably said DiMaggio. But if the subject was pitching you started and ended all discussions with the phrase "Bob Feller."

Bob Feller did get his chance to start in a world series game. In fact his Cleveland Indians beat the Boston Braves four games to two, and Feller started in the two games the Indians lost. Those losses, especially the loss in the opening game, formed the material for the sad heart sports story of 1948.

Feller should have won that first game. He pitched a two-hitter, and lost 1-0 to Johnny Sain, the best pitcher in the National League. Moreover the one run that crossed the plate had no business being there, and the proof was on hundreds of sports pages the following day and all the next winter. It is one of the most famous photographs in sports, Lou Boudreau laying the tag on the shoulder of Phil Masi, out by a foot and a half on Feller's great pickoff in the eighth inning. But National League umpire Bill Stewart called Masi safe, and he scored on the second Brave hit of the game.

It was a terrible shame. I was not a Cleveland fan. In fact in 1948 the Indians beat my cherished Red Sox in the first American League playoff. But this was Feller's twelfth season. His best four years he had given to the U.S. Navy during World War II. He was supposed to pitch in the 1954 World Series, but the Indians lost four straight, and Al

Lopez felt that he could not afford to give the old guy his last chance.

Inside the sports store Mr Feller was sitting at a card table around near the back. There werent any customers around. Everyone was outside catching the free concert. But this was the kid who had come up to the majors at the age of seventeen and struck out 76 batters in the 62 innings he pitched that first year! Sitting at that card table he looked about the way he had looked during his last season, hair combed straight back with water, face that looked as if it had never left Van Meter, Iowa.

I walked right up and said hello, or rather not hello but some other word, as if there werent any formality to be got over. I am not good at talking to famous people. They scare the hell out of me. But then this great pitcher was up here in Victoria, Canada, and what would he think?

I put my hands about nine inches apart.

"Masi was out by this much," I said.

"It was twice that," he replied, quickly.

possibly relates to theme of the exageration of memory throughout the text.

SPREAD EAGLE

OTTAWA **(Staff)**—"Strange things are done in the midnight sun," wrote Robert W. Service of the gold rush era in the Far North.

And his words are still true, for at Dawson City this weekend they finally got instructions to bury an old Alaskan sourdough and Spanish American War veteran whose mortal remains had been waiting for burial for 68 days.

"Well, heh, I'll tell ya," said Eagle Claw Billy, the second oldest prospector in the district. "If it was up to me I'd be awful careful figgerin out the cost. That's the way old Nathan would of wanted it. I seen him buyin raisins by the raisin afore he went out on a summer's prospectin."

The midnight sun glinted off the old man's round spectacles as he drank the draft beer the younger man had bought for him. The younger man was a romantic and somewhat nationalistic poet of about forty-five, bound for his Governor General's award and Canadian content.

"What do you mean by cost?" asked the young poet.

The day the old prospector died last December the temperature was 56 below. Last Friday it had soared to 65 above. The sourdough's old friend, Jack "Highpockets" Butterworth, a well-known character in Dawson City, telegraphed Conservative MP Erik Nielsen an urgent plea: "For goodness sake, do something fast."

Eagle Claw Billy put his empty glass down on the table and signalled with his eyes to the poet, who signalled with his poised fingers to the waiter for another round.

"Yeh, I'll tell ya. Cost. That means a lot up here in this country. Lot of people figger a prospector is tryin to hit it big. Matter of fact it's just like any other job. You want to make a decent month's wages, only out of the ground. That is, when you can dig into the ground."

"I mean about burying him, the cost," said the young forty-five-year-old poet.

"Diggin or breakin," said Eagle Claw Billy, foam on his grey whiskers.

As soon as he got the telegram Mr. Nielsen called Northern Affairs Deputy Minister E.A. Cote.

Mr. Nielsen explained that, as he understood the story, the old sourdough remained unburied because of administration differences and tieups between the commissioner of the Yukon, the government of the state of Alaska and the several federal departments of the Canadian government that would be involved.

"Digging or breaking? What?"

"Yep. Cost. Figger it'll cost more to break his arms and legs or dig a wider grave? Maybe dig one in a spraddle shape," said Eagle Claw Billy.

"Spraddle? What? More beer, waiter."

"Arms and legs out wide. Dig a grave in the shape of a spraddle. Cross, kinda," said Eagle C. Billy.

Immediately Mr. Cote sent a message to Yukon Commissioner Gordon Cameron to "investigate and report."

Saturday the commissioner reported.

Commissioner Cameron explained one of the facts of life about the Far North. He pointed out that it was not unusual in the Yukon in winter to leave bodies above ground. To do otherwise would be difficult because of the deep penetration of the frost that made the soil hard as concrete and grave digging difficult, if not impossible.

"Spraddle?" asked the determined poet.

"The way they found him," said Eagle Claw Billy. "Reminds me of the time they found two of them together, froze together, him on top of her. Decided to pry them apart like you do with froze fish, only with tire irons. Worked too, except for a little botherin-type trouble."

"What?"

"Just a little thing, you might say, heh."

"Trouble?"

"Miss Chance," said E.C. Billy.

"Mischance? What? Beer?"

"Thankee. Miss Chance, lady's name. Got them pried apart, all right, only they lost a little bit offen him and added a little bit to her. Broke it right off inside. How they ever got froze like that nobody ever could figger. Spose to keep a man warm in the middle of December. Miss Chance, I guess, that's all there was to it."

"I'll be a son of a bitch," said the young poet.

"Moren likely," said Eagle Claw Billy.

But there was another complicating factor.

The old sourdough died last December, but it was not until "some weeks later," said the commissioner's report, that he had been found "spread-eagled in the snow" and frozen stiff as an icicle.

"Aint likely to bury him like that, though," said Eagle Claw, ostentatiously holding his empty glass upside down. The young forty-five year old poet thought about his Canada Council grant and bought some more beer.

"Not likely?" he asked.

"One thing he couldnt stand was Easter. All them missionaries gettin the Indians and Eskimos all riled up and drinkin. Just when he wanted to get his supplies and stuff ready for the season."

"Easter?"

"Imagine, him layin in the ground with his arms stuck out like that, like on a cross. Spread Eagle."

"Spread—"

"Name of the Indian found him in the snow. Old Spread Eagle hated him, sorta. Spread Eagle is a Christian. Crosstian, the old fucker always called him. Spread Eagle hated him all right, figgered he was playin around with his Eskimo wife."

"I thought the Indians didnt like the Eskimos," said the poet.

"This Indian works for the government, I forget which one, and he's a Christian. Pretty wife, too."

The public administrator at Dawson City had taken the case in hand Feb. 8. On Feb. 10 he commissioned an undertaker to take care of the burial for $160, the customary fee in such cases. On March 8, the undertaker replied that since this could be "no ordinary burial," it could not be done for the flat fee of $160.

Instead the old sourdough (still presumably spread-eagled) "must be straightened out before we can bury him." With this extra attention the fee would be $200.

"Just about ten dollars a limb," remarked E. Claw Billy.

"Them's the breaks," said the young forty-five year old poet.

"Yer a pretty sharp young fucker, aint ya?" said E.C.

There the matter rested for a few days.

Then as the temperatures climbed came the urgent message from "Highpockets" to the Yukon M.P. Orders went out for fast action and no haggling.

The old man was finally laid to rest yesterday.

"Amen to that," said Eagle Claw Billy.

"Amen?"

"Thought I heard somebody say two more beers," said Eagle Claw Billy.

October 1, 1961

Do you remember those death threats Roger Maris was getting in August and September of 1961? There he was, wearing the Babe's pinstripes, and he wasnt even Mickey Mantle. At least Mickey Mantle was a Yankee from the word go. Maris was a Cleveland Indian first, of all things, and he was never going to hit .300. Mantle was chasing Maris all summer, and one thing was for certain: as a couple they were going to knock off Ruth and Gehrig.

But Mantle didnt get any death threats.

Even I got some death threats. One of them is coming true right here on this foldaway couch.

Do you remember those death threats Roger Maris was getting? Did you think they were all from fans of the Babe? Old timers who didnt want anyone to get 61 home runs, even with the schedule expanded to 162 games?

For those who dont know what I am talking about, here are the bare details, though why I should bother, I dont know. Babe Ruth's record of sixty home runs in 1927 was the favourite myth in baseball. Ty Cobb's lifetime batting average of .367 was harder to do. Joe DiMaggio's

56-game hitting streak is not likely to be topped, as they say. But Babe Ruth's sixty dingers gave the biggest galoots in the game a yearly target to assault. A few guys had got into the fifties. Trivialists liked to point out that the second-best total was Ruth's 59 in 1921.

Then along came 1961. It was as if the last two digits called for some kind of disrespect toward the Bambino. Two things happened in 1961 to break a lot of hearts, or at least to leave the sour taste of ambiguity in baseball fans' mouths.

In 1961 the American League of baseball added two teams. Until then each team played 154 games a season, 22 against each of the other seven teams. In 1961 they would have to play 162 games, 18 against each of their nine opponents.

In 1961, Roger Maris and Mickey Mantle staged a home run race that had every newspaper in the western hemisphere providing a graph on the front page every playing day. By mid-August it was clear that Roger Maris at least was going to hit more than sixty home runs. The commissioner of baseball said that if Maris didnt have 61 by the 154th game, the Babe's record was still there. After 154 games Maris had 59 homers. In the last eight games he got two more. They put an asterisk after the number wherever it was reprinted.

But those 61 homers were still there. And as the years went by the asterisk disappeared, along with other records by the Babe, such as his 714 lifetime homers. Sixty-one years after Maris's meretricious heroics the asterisk was not even remembered. And for sixty-one years no other big leaguer was ever able to hit more than sixty homers, no matter how many games there were to a season. I know. I was born in 1961, and I was in the stadium in Toronto on the October day when Coral Godard hit his sixty-first homer.

That was seven games from the end of the season. In those seven games big hairy Godard marched to the plate thirty-three times. He struck out twenty times. He was walked once. He was hit with a pitch once, a wonderful piece of ironic bravery by a rookie left-hander who had gone to Godard's high school ten years after the hairy person more or less graduated. Once he got the ball on the fat part of the bat, but this was to centre field in the plastic Miami ball park, and it was pulled down on the Cubaturf warning track.

In his last time at bat in the last game, when the divisional results had been settled for three days, the large first-baseman hit a foul ball that passed the pole at mid-height and probably reached the Gulf Stream. On the following pitch he swung his lamino-club so hard that idlers in both dugouts involuntarily flinched. But he caught only the top third of the ball. The Miami infield dawdled and posed and lobbed a man out. The season was over, and so was the pursuit.

Coral Godard had sixty-one poppers, just like Roger Maris. He had no asterisk. The Toronto sportswriters started what they supposed would be a traditional journalistic remark, noting that Godard had achieved the highest total in the twenty-first century.

The total would do a lot for Godard's already inflated salary. But the pelf was offset by the remarks he would hear all winter and well into the following season. People felt that they had to comment upon that last week, with those thirty-three trips to the platter. At least Roger got two long balls in his last week, they would point out, and he had nothing but an old-fashioned bat made from a mountain tree.

A typical bad day would be May second in Cleveland. Standing three metres off the bag at first, Godard had acquired the skill of singling out sentences and near-sentences from the thin roar of the usual light assemblage of Indians fans. If you were there and had his ability, this is some of what you might have heard:

"You couldnt carry Roger Maris's jockstrap, ya bum!"

"He cant carry his own jockstrap!"

"Yer a choke artist, ya big hairy creepoid!"

"Roger woulda hit a hundred homers if he was alive now!"

"He woulda hit seventy-five when he was seventy-five, ya jerkoff!"

"*Belle montre et peu de rapport!*"

"Shaddup, Frenchie!"

"Hey, Coral, yer sister . . . " [etc.]

You will have noted that abuse from the grandstand did not evolve much as major league baseball stepped across the century line for the second time.

Godard, and even most of the sportswriters in the American League thought the razzing and threats would begin to fade away as the season proceeded into the hot months, especially if he had, say, twenty homers in June. But on June twentieth in Baltimore someone left a dead cat with a pinstriped baseball uniform at the door of his hotel room. There was a number three on the back of the little uniform. In Detroit later that week Morgana IV the kissing bandit ran out to first base in the home half and kicked the great hairy firstbaseman in the slats.

In August Coral had seven home runs and twenty-five runs batted in. The Jays's psychologist advised Grand Cayman Island, where the team's spring training facility could be set up for rest and recuperation. Coral was opposed to the idea. Then in Kansas City someone took a shot at him. He left for the Caribbean the next morning. The paper sent me down with him. I thought I would stay for a few days, file a couple stories about how the big fellow was filling his days, and coincidentally pick up a few rays. I had not imagined how hot it gets on Grand Cayman in August. I decided to leave after three days. So did Coral.

As we were on the same plane, I thought I would play my hunch, and go wherever he was going. He took a connector flight from Atlanta to St. Louis. St. Louis hasnt been in the American League since 1953. This was getting pretty interesting, especially because it was obvious that I was going to follow him everywhere I could. First he tried to shake me, but when he found me sitting on his lap in a taxi, he just laughed, and then sighed and then said:

"The season cant get any worse than this," and away we went.

To see a voodoo queen. To see a Washington University physics professor. Maybe not quite a professor. Sort of a graduate assistant. She was gorgeous, a St. Louis honey blonde, but you dont want to hear about that. It certainly didnt seem to matter to Coral Godard, not at first.

Now I am not a science reporter, and I dont expect that twenty-first-century physics is going to make much sense to a fuddy-duddy reader in the twentieth century (remember, I used to live there), so I will not spend a hundred pages on the plans and specs of the Deutero-Tempus machine, patent pending. In fact, I still cant believe that's what that lady graduate assistant called it. I think she was razzing me with a midwest sense of humour. Who knows? She said she was from *East* St. Louis, and you might know what they are like over there.

How did Coral know about Lorraine Knight? Hey, how did your favourite NFL lineman know about Dr. Needle? If there is something illegal but helpful, your professional athlete will hear about it. If there is a new gadget on any university campus on the continent, there will be two people wanting to know what it is capable of: the contract lawyer from the Pentagon, and a veteran ballplayer who needs an edge.

I think Lorraine had a liking for a man with curly black hair on his back. Either that or she had a romantic notion about the relationship between science and the human heart. She thought the Pentagon and most of the Scientific Community was a little short in the heart. Whatever the case, she said that the Deutero-Tempus could put a human being back into any year in the last hundred and ten. She was working on longer range stuff, while there were hardly any professors at Washington University who would even believe a decade. Most of those physics professors didnt even have straight hair on the tops of their heads.

I stuck with Coral as much as I could, but there were times over the following week when I lost track of him *and* Lorraine Knight. She was apparently a lot nicer to him than the fans in either Cleveland or Toronto. She told me later that she faced a tough conflict when Godard volunteered to be her first sixty-two year voyager.

You see, she had to explain to her ballplayer that time-travel is so far a one-way trip.

I say this despite the strange logic of narrating this tale in the past tense about events that will not happen until another fifty-nine years have transpired.

Be that as it may.

In the old movies people like Danny Kaye were always zipping back to more scenic times, and then zooming back home in the present. But put your head to this: if you are going to send me back to Chicago in 1882, for instance, you just have to send me back over the tracks the world has made since then. But how are you going to send me into the future? There arent any tracks.

That is not the real scientific explanation, but it is close as you can get in a journalist's language.

"She says she wants me to take a short trip first," Coral told me in the bar at the Mark Twain Hilton.

We sports writers are often cast in the role of straight men. That might explain why so many of us evolve smart-ass writing styles.

"What does that mean?" I asked.

"She says I should go back one year. Then I could look her up and we could get together and have some fun for a year before I head out."

"Head out?" I asked.

"That's the technical language for going back through space in the Duteous Tempo," he said. A lot of ball players

180

couldnt have got that far without saying "you-know" at least once.

"One," I said. "That is not quite the right name for the gizmo. Two. There isnt any technical language for all that yet. Cripes!"

That's what I said. Cripes. In the twenty-first century.

"Be that as it may. I told her I thought she was a very nice person as well as a great scientist, but."

"But?" I asked.

"But I have to get back to 1961. Before the end of the season."

"What are you going to do that for?" I asked. "You cant come back, you know."

"I know. I think I can handle living in the 1960s. As long as I stay away from my family. I think I could even manage to handle living in Toronto in the seventies and eighties. But."

"But," I said.

"But the main reason is I have to do Something about Roger Maris."

"Tell me about Something."

"I think I might let him get sixty. Maybe fifty-nine."

Have you ever read any novels about time travel? They always bring up this basic problem: what if the time traveller does something to mess up history? What if the gink from the future sees the lamp beside the cow and takes it away, and there's no great Chicago fire? I wrote a story about that a long time ago when I was still wondering what kind of writer I was going to be. I had a historian from Northwestern University go back and torch Mrs O'Malley's barn after all. He felt terrible about all the suffering he caused, but there are certain higher principles, which means greater dangers. He went back to his job a hundred years later at Northwestern. I didnt know real time travel would have to be one-way.

To tell you the truth, there were times I wished I were inventing this story instead of covering it.

One morning I went over to Frankenstein Knight's condo and they werent there. So I went to the laboratory and he wasnt there. But she was. There was a scent of eucalyptus in the air, used to be my favourite smell.

"Gone?" I enquired.

"Gone," she said. Her demeanor was ambiguous as you can get. She was deprived of Coral but she had sent Godard along the tracks.

"How do you know he didnt go to 1927?" I asked.

"Check the encyclopedia," she said.

I went back to Toronto and tried to re-enter normal life, if talking to naked men in a dressing room after they've been getting all sweaty playing a boy's game in front of thousands of people eating junk food can be called normal life. I guess you might call me and my colleagues the historians of popular life. I shared a desktop at the Toronto *Star* instead of Northwestern University.

Yes, you know what I was thinking. But I needed some time to think *about* it. I figured I had all season anyway. I could even cover the Jays if they made it into the late-Fall Classic. Coral Godard might be following Roger Maris around the league in 1961, but if I was going to go back I could go whenever I wanted to. Time was something we didnt know everything about, but I knew that much. If you are going to travel to Minneapolis, you can get there from Vancouver or Miami or Keokuk. If you are going to September 1961, you can get there from today or next Tuesday or a year from now.

Yep, I had time pretty well figured out. Then I woke up one night on a littered floor, surrounded by lockers, and I couldnt remember how I got there. A doctor who usually looked at the bare bodies of much younger men told me something I hadnt thought of regarding how much time I had.

"If you're one of those newspaper guys who have a novel in the desk drawer, get busy on it," he said.

I like a guy with that kind of an attitude. Reminds me of the guy I thought I would make of myself.

So you know why I went back to St. Louis.

"Why havent you sprung your success on the world?" I asked.

There was still a part of me that thought she had Coral hidden away in her bedroom closet, or in a shallow grave on the banks of the Mississippi. I thought maybe Coral had decided to live somewhere up a river in Paraguay, with some refugee Nembutal dealers.

And I know this much about science: whenever there is a landmark invention or discovery, there are usually hundreds of people involved. Whenever the Nobel prizes in physics or medicine are announced, they name several guys in white coats at Berkeley and Manchester. Whenever it is a single maverick you have to be a little suspicious.

On the other hand, she told me, there were those two men who did nuclear fusion in a pot of heavy water at room temperature.

"I still dont know whether he is there in 1961," she said. "The message he was going to send hasnt arrived. He might have been spread out and sent all over the time map, for all I know."

I, of course, transferred that notion to myself. I could not imagine my molecules sprayed all over the last half of the twentieth century.

"What was the sign?"

"He was going to jump out on the field and greet Roger Maris when he hit his sixtieth whatchamacallit," she said.

That's what he told *her*, but I thought I knew a little better.

"Send me to spring training, 1961," I said. "I'll send you a sign. I've been thinking about this: if I arrive safely in 1961, I'll talk to somebody in the printing trade who needs a few dollars. That's the year Allen Ginsberg's

Kaddish and other poems came out. Lot of people still think it's his best book."

"I know less about old poetry than I know about base-ball," she said, with a little patronizing impatience.

"Take my word for it. If I make it, you can have a look at page 38 of the first edition of *Kaddish*. If the second line still says 'or will we find Zoroastrian temples flowering on Neptune?' I didnt make it. If it says 'be' instead of 'we,' that will be the misprint I paid for.

"Why did it have to be something about ancient poetry?"

"I didnt think I could influence Kruschchev about the Berlin Wall."

"Why would you want to go back there when you cant return?"

"A guy in expensive shoes told me I'm not going to see the 2023 season, anyway. So I figured I would like to watch Mantle and Maris slug it out. And I want to get reacquainted with baseball on natural grass."

Here is something we should all know about scientists. They deal with objects and forces and energies they tell us are objectively observable, though one of their own tribe told us a century ago that that was a myth. But in the middle of all this impersonalism they are as vain as opera singers and novelists. You can get them in their vanity.

So I played that card. I loaded myself down with little valuable things I could trade for the local currency, and miss Svengali Knight turned the dial.

Later, or should I say earlier? Anyway, on the day that Maris hit number 33 off Bill Monbouquette in Yankee Stadium, I had this thought: if I could talk her into sending me after the large hairy one, somebody else could talk her into sending him after me. The hit man always looks over his shoulder for *his* hit man.

Of course you people would never know the full ram-ification of these pursuits. If a contract killing occurs you see it as a newspaper crime with an unknown motive. Then you are stuck with the new history. As far as you are concerned, if I failed in my quest Roger Maris never did hit his sixty-first.

If that is the case, I just had to leave this letter, to let you know that at one time he did. Maybe it never got into your *Official Encyclopedia of Baseball*, A. S. Barnes & Co., 1970, but it could have if I had succeeded. (Is this foreshadowing or backshadowing?)

Of course you will be justified in disbelieving all this. Roger Maris got an asterisk for *tying* Ruth, you can say.

Unless you are reading this in 2022, and thinking this confirms where I went when I disappeared.

A blast from the past, I suppose you might say. A present meant for the future.

September 27, 1961 in New York City. Who would want to be anywhere else, any other time? It was certainly a baseball writer's dream to be there. I guess I was the only person in town for whom the dream was edged with a bone-scraping nightmare. I dont know whether Roger Maris got any sleep last night, and I dont know where Coral Godard spent the night, but I can report to you that I sat up all night smoking cigarettes because in September of 1961 you could not get in New York City what I was accustomed to employ to get through a bad night.

The night before, Baltimore's young Johnny Fisher had offered Maris a fastball at the knees, and Maris had shown his appreciation with a high drive that curled around the right field foul pole for his sixtieth homer. I saw this from a seat I had bought the rights to from a gent in the parking lot. It felt rather nice to be in the paying seats instead of the press box. But I could not sit back and relax, glug beer, joke with my neighbours, the special grace of the baseball park. I was scanning the crowd for Godard. I didnt see him till the home run. Ruthian clout, I caught myself saying in my head.

Most of the crowd of sixty-two thousand people yelled their heads off, delirious that they were here to see this historic dinger. A few thousand of the older fans booed or remained seated, getting out their asterisks during the ten minutes it took to get the game started again. I stood up, mainly so that I could see. As Maris circled the bases, the Yankees in their milky white pinstripes rushed out to greet him. Some of them did. It would be interesting to look back at whatever photographs there are, to see which Yankees were still in the dugout. John Blanchard was out there first because he had been the on-deck hitter. Yogi Berra was there. Hector Lopez was there with his enormous toothy smile. He jumped on Maris and demanded to be carried to the dugout, but he was pulled off by Whitey Ford.

Coral Godard was there. Or almost there. All at once we thousands could see a new dark blue blazer among the pinstripes. Then we could see a number of New York's Finest in leather jackets, converging on the suit and leaving the field for the ball players. I dont know exactly what Coral had planned for that moment, but I was grateful for the foresight of the people who run the House that Ruth Built.

In all the noise and turmoil I was out of my seat and headed for the exit. I figured I wouldnt run into much traffic headed that way, and I banked on the cops' deciding they just had to get that hairy and over-excited fan outside the stadium rather than cuffing him and hauling him to the slams. Yes. I found Coral outside section 12, trying to rub a mark off the toe of a brand-new loafer.

"Was that just the signal, or did you have more in mind?" I asked.

"If I'da had a gun they wouldnt have just left me here, would they?"

"Dont play dumb, Godard. You could kill a gorilla with your bare but furry hands. If they still have gorillas in 1961."

He looked at me hard, under the shadow of his single head-wide eyebrow. He emanated protein. He was strength personified, or maybe beastified. I wasnt afraid of him. But I was getting confused about history.

"I gotta stop him," he said at last, having reached as complex a conclusion as we were likely to see.

"Okay," I said. "Let me ride with you again."

"You try and stop me, and you'll wind up in the same basement," he advised.

I had to start thinking on my feet, and while sitting in the cab. I had to think about how to stop this creep from killing Roger Maris, and I had to think about the ramifications regarding time and space, which simple people in the twentieth century thought were aspects of each other. In the world of physics Albert Einstein had been the Bambino, but someone was going to come along and hit sixty-one in that league, too. I was thinking as fast as I could, and I was not about to take the time to think about how Coral Godard managed to get the address of Roger Maris's apartment. I will only say that a guy who can find Houdini Knight's laboratory in St. Louis should be able to find an outfielder's abode.

I thought and I thought. Coral didnt interrupt me: he was trying to think too, I guess. When we got out of the cab on that darkened corner in Greenville, Coral was going to kill the home run leader of the American League. But by the time he was banging on the front door with his fist or his head—I forget which—we had a deal. This is the sentence with which I ended my persuasive argument:

"There's more than one kind of time travel."

Which meant this: there were three letters in a green metal box in the office of an editor of the New York News—or was it the New York Times?—written by your humble servant, who had the advantage of knowing which New York newspapers would still exists in 2021. One letter instructed a sequence of editors on what to do with the other two letters. The other two letters were addressed to the president of Washington University in St. Louis and to the commissioner of baseball. Those letters are there right now. They are part of the reason for my writing this story.

In other words I got it through Coral's well-armoured cranium that his great venture would come to nothing if it was proven that he had been alone in breaking Ruth's record only due to an act of homicide. He would, I said, receive the asterisk that would have gone to Maris.

 You can see the problems in tense created by the combination of narrative, speech, and time-travel.

Roger did not look like a front-page athlete. He did not even look like the Roger who had slapped homers all through spring training. He had lost a lot of hair, and his skin had gone grey. There was some kind of colourful disorder spreading on the skin of his lower arms. He stooped. He seemed unable to lift the long revolver he was carrying when he came to the door of his green-sided bungalow. It was three in the morning. Roger Maris was not going to sign an autograph.

Coral reacted to the armament by rushing his predecessor, driving him against all the furniture in the living room. Luckily there was no one else in the house, or if there had been they had departed by the back door or window at the first sign of athleticism.

Coral banged Roger several times. He socked him once on the nose and once on each eye.

"Why the deuce are you doing this, man?" might be a paraphrase of the only question Roger could get out. But his words did stop the knuckle man from the future.

"He doesnt want you to hit sixty-one home runs," I said.

"He's got company," said Maris, between energetic gasps. "That's why I'm living in this nowhere dump."

He opened the door a little wider and spit some blood mixed with sputum outside.

Then he agreed to the deal. This deal, like all realistic

pacts, would disappoint all three of us a bit, but make the times we were living in habitable.

The hard part was going to be persuading the New York Yankees. The second hardest part was going to be fooling or placating the home plate umpires. The surprisingly easy part was going to be making Coral Godard look like Roger Maris. He wasnt that much bigger, maybe a little more muscular around the chest and shoulders. A lot of the difference faded when we shaved a kilogram of hair off his arms and the middle of his long eyebrow.

Anyway, it worked, more or less, or you wouldnt need this story now. You might remember that there were suspicious stories at the time, but they were chalked up to the circus atmosphere of the homer hunt. The ball player the reporters saw after the game was Roger Maris, a man with two black eyes. The outfielder the Bronx beer swillers saw in the wide green was Roger Maris, an oddly bent figure in pinstripes. Yogi Berra and Mickey Mantle and Bobby Richardson ducked interviews all that week. Coral Godard was a twentieth-century major league purloined letter.

He went to the plate at Yankee Stadium twenty-three times over the next four and a half games. Although it was illegal according to the rules of baseball, he was wearing the same number on his back as that on the back of his teammate in the dark tunnel behind the dugout. Have a look at pictures of Bill "Moose" Skowron during those tense nights: his facial expression can not be attributed to the pennant race. There wasnt any pennant race. Bill really thought he could solve Maris's dilemma by socking the interloper in the front of the head. Organized baseball, or at least a local contingent of it, kept the wrappers on him. It's only for five nights at the most, Bill, they said.

Coral struck out and grounded out and lined to the first-baseman. He could not reach the Orioles pitchers and then he could not handle the Red Sox pitchers. Once he got within fifteen feet of the warning track in centre field, no mean feat at Yankee Stadium. Roger Maris stood in the dark tunnel, smoking Chesterfield cigarettes and wishing he were in the game offensively. On the plus side you might say that it was a good thing that Coral didnt reach base very often. There was no guarantee that a Boston infielder might not spill the baked beans.

But thank goodness, as millions of unknowing fans said, for Tracy Stallard, a name that will live forever in the annals of the game. On October 1, 1961, the last day of the season, Tracy finally dealt Coral Maris a knee-high fastball, and the shorn one lifted it magesterially into the upper deck of the next borough. Babe Ruth had hit his sixtieth on the last day of the 1927 season, off Washington's left-hander Tom Zachary, right here at Yankee Stadium. Coral rounded the bases, got jumped on by twenty-eight people in Yankee uniforms, including one with the duplicate number on his back, as you can ascertain by looking at a photograph in *Sport Pictorial*, and then left big-league base-ball for forty-five years.

He was not, as he told me in athletese, completely satisfied. He would be condemned, through some portion of the twenty-first century, to sharing the major league home run record, but at least he will have been the only person ever to have hit a sixty-first home run.

"Who knows? Maybe you would have hit sixty-*three* home runs if you had stayed around for the 2023 season," I said. I admit that I was sporting a grin that showed just the tips of my teeth.

He stared at me with the rudimentary beginnings of emotion on his face. He hadnt thought of that.

After he left that game, I was hoping that Maris would pop number sixty-two in his last at-bat. But he grounded to second on a pitch he should have taken for ball four. Aint that always the way?

•

The Yankees won the World Series easily, in five games over the Cincinnati Reds. Maris hit a homer in the third game. I watched it on a rudimentary black and white television. I dont think Coral was interested. Then, as always happens when the world series is over, a winter loomed, and the reality of the workplace reasserted itself. As I did not have a workplace I had to find myself some fake I.D. and hit the concrete. It didnt take as long as I had feared. I landed a sports page job in White Plains, mainly horseraces and track meets. I didnt tell them about the little visitor inside my middle regions. But it's a couple years later now, and they are going to learn. I havent been able to get out of this foldaway couch for seven days.

So here I am completing the last part of the deal, the part Roger wasnt told about. Coral wanted me to tell the whole story. I am supposed to consign it to a time capsule at the *News*. Coral got the idea from me, of course. His idea was that the time capsule is to be opened the day after he disappears from the Blue Jays in 2022. Well, it appears that I was able to get the story down, but I dont know about the time capsule. Maybe the person who finds this will seal it and deliver it to the *News*.

Coral said to tell every detail and make it realistic. He said that way history would eventually get it right. People would know that Roger Maris never hit a sixty-first homer. All I had to do was tell the story and not leave any loose ends.

BEING AUDITED

"Oh Christ, I'm being audited!"

Yes, I heard that one more and more often.

"Did you hear that Barrie's being audited?"

"They went after fishermen last year and painters the year before. This is the year for writers."

For years and years I just ignored or envied the stories of writers, many of them just hobbyists, as far as I was concerned, who were filing with the income tax people as Authors, and clapping on their berets to loll on beaches and in bistros on the Balearics on the proceeds.

"You should file as an Author."

To hell with that. I am serious. I am interested in writing, not in a career, not in a bank account. I dont know how to roll over a term deposit or how to get the butter on a croissant, anyway.

"You should get an accountant. Look at Dave; he bought his Volkswagen on his tax rebate."

Sometime in those years I started filing my taxes on the long form, claiming a few hundred dollars for paper and stamps and so on, and there were no questions asked.

You can claim a room for your writing office, someone said, or maybe I read it in a magazine I wasnt discounting as an expense. I was living in a small house, so I claimed a deduction of one-fifth of my rent.

Outside my room I could see the rain falling on the yellow leaves tamped into the gutters alongside the sidewalk. Some birds that didnt give a dropping for the south were competing with the filthy pigeons in the parking lot of the hamburger drive-in across the street. My daughter was born, and I really did like changing diapers, though I dont think I admitted this to my wife.

"You should talk to Garry," said my wife.

"Who," I asked with my usual wariness, "is Garry?"

"The tax consultant. I have told you this for three years in a row. You should talk to Garry. He saved thousands of dollars for Miriam. You should at least talk to him, you stupid bugger."

We moved into a bigger house, and though there were a lot more than five rooms I kept claiming a fifth of the mortgage for a deduction, feeling all the while that I was bringing my country and its citizens to ruination because of it. I didnt know that all this while a friend of mine was discounting the costumes he did public poetry readings in. I just sat over my IBM Selectric, piling up the chapters of a novel I would never offer to a publisher because I could not stay interested enough to find out what was going to happen in the last chapters.

But writers ten years younger than I were going to see Garry and telling stories of the wonderment they felt as their rebates arrived in those windowed envelopes. You stupid bugger, said my wife every morning while I pushed some spoon-sized shredded grain into my mouth.

"All right," I said. "Next year for sure."

About another three years later I made my way to Garry's townhouse just the other side of Chinatown. It was a funny street, tarpaper roofs for a while, then rows of alternative architecture. Short birds were pecking at a dead body in the vacant lot across the street. I was a little disappointed in myself, getting older and accepting a world in which personal rewards were becoming as important as the desire to reshape the world's imagination.

Garry was jolly, too big for his suit, and a chain-smoker. He smoked like a busy American, pushing the long butts into a niche in the huge ashtray, grabbing another cigarette out of the open package on the desk. He talked and talked and laughed, and set me totally at ease. His eyes went round and his brows shot up as he told me we could rewrite my tax returns for the past three or was it four years, and scoop up a rubble of dollars, all legally.

"Have you been writing off your personal library?" he asked, 4H pencil poised.

"I should save all my receipts for books?"

"How big is your personal library?" asked Garry, jabbing a cigarette into its niche with energetic anticipation.

"About the same size as the library at McGill," I said, but I have a better collection of contemporary poetry."

"Have you been claiming depreciation on your impressive library?"

"What? My books are getting more valuable as time goes by," I boasted.

"Ho ho. You have a lot to learn, my boy."

"I dont want to learn," I said.

"Quite right, sir. We are going to make you a tidy bundle. To comfort you on those nights when the muse has abandoned you for fairer but more fleeting climes."

He told me to bring all my records, my old tax returns, the measurement of my house and garage, and my wife the next time I came.

"You stupid bugger," said my wife, when the check arrived. "You should have done this years ago." She went right to the bank and started a term deposit.

So began my new life as a receipt-keeper. I began to understand why certain people, after we had all pitched in ten bucks to pay for our share of the meal, would pocket the cash and take care of the bill with their credit cards. Now I would sheepishly ask for a receipt from any fly-by-night paperback store, mumbling that my tax-man insisted on it. It became my habit to stuff receipts for anything into my fat wallet. I had to start carrying an Italian shoulderbag to relieve the weight on my ass pocket. I cant remember whether I wrote *it* off.

But all the while I told myself, I *reminded* myself, that I was doing all this to please my wife. I was still the pure youth who went into the writing game because my country needed it, because the young writers in the books I had read before I was a young writer were sensitive people, romantic figures precisely because they were willing to forego the usual pleasures of the up-and-coming, to sit alone late on Saturday night, destroying their hopes for a long life with crushed cigarette packages and instant coffee rings on every exposed sheet of paper.

Meanwhile, year by year my wife studied all the financial sections of the newspapers, and the business magazines, and every brochure she could find in the racks at the banks and trust companies and credit unions that jostle one another for space along 41st Avenue. She started to invest her salary and mine in baffling plans with banky sounding names and even more baffling initials. Conniving with Garry, she tried to persuade me that it was fiscally clever to *borrow even more money* rather than paying off the debts you already had. She routinely took money from one account in one bank and deposited it in another account in the bank across the street, a few minutes before the banks closed for the weekend, shaving a little interest off both of them, she explained to me.

"What do I care about all that?" I said. "My only concern is to make a paragraph that will cause someone to gasp or sigh."

"You'll have to find time to do that later on the week-end," she replied. "Right now you have to come to Vancouver Savings and sign some papers."

I hardly have any time to write as it is, what with teaching and marking papers, and cooking, and weeding, and driving the kids to all those places kids have to go to keep up with their late twentieth century. And you cannot write off the orthodontist or the piano teacher anyway.

But every spring I continued to make my trudge to Garry's tropical bungalow, where he would show me photos of his place in Ireland, and hand him the envelopes filled with receipts. And sometime later I might hear the figure attached to the rebate I had theoretically received from Ottawa. I have never actually seen or touched any of the money. My wife always has some kind of iron-clad reason why it has to be applied to some open wound in the latest term deposit or RRSP or demand loan or daily interest scam.

But all the while the big house around my tax write-off writing room was growing bigger and newer and less convenient. Architects and engineers, carpenters and plumbers and tilers stomped their boots through the rooms and whined their machines outside my nervous and delicate chamber of the lyric dream. I could never look through a casement window without noting that that casement window had not been there a week before. I wondered how the hell my muse was going to recognize the place when she made her next visit from the mount where she and her sisters never had to make renovations.

"Jeeze, I nearly flew right on by," my muse said one year. "When did you get the new paint job on the fence?"

"I think it's a new fence. This year's tax return."

"You needed a new fence? I've been wearing this same diaphanous gown since I helped Percy Shelley write *Prometheus Unbound*."

"Dont ask me about fences. Right now I am having trouble with a poem called *Allophanes*."

"Your usual hassle with structure?"

"Dont talk to me about structure."

"How much do you have invested in this new poem with the suspiciously Greek name?"

"Dont talk to me about investment."

"All right. I'll come and visit you in the wee hours. I have some rounds to make in Kitsilano anyway."

"Thanks."

"But do something about that casement window. John Keats at least took the glazier's name label off his. And as I remember, he wasnt anywhere near as healthy as you are."

I dont remember exactly what year it was that I heard that my byzantine tax returns were going to be audited. I can only tell you this: that it was the year they went after writers. And this: it was the year they took the walls off my house.

Let me explain—though I think I should warn you: this will be a story involving the federal government's concern for human comfort, the international threat of soaring Arab oil prices, and the alacrity with which so-called private enterprise will jump in and make dollars out of joy or distress.

Sometime, a few years ago, while we were living in this house, or a facsimile of it, big ads began to appear in all the Canadian newspapers, urging patriotic Canadians to stuff their house walls with more insulation, to reduce our national dependency on the punitive and capricious pricing policies of OPEC. We would all pull together to make us snug, and cut our fuel bills.

So sincere was Ottawa's care for her parka-garbed children that the government was prepared to make semi-forgiveable loans to house-owners who would shove guck between their exterior walls and their interior ones, and under their roofs. Their favourite recommended substance was a fast-hardening foam called urea-formaldehyde.

"I dont know," I said. "That sounds awful. It sounds poisonous. At least it sounds like a combination of piss and that stuff they kill and preserve laboratory animals with."

"Are you a famous scientist?" enquired my wife the financial wizard.

"You know very well that I am an insufficiently famous writer," I rejoined.

"Well, I am a locally famous investment analyst. And I have all the information at hand. UFFI is the most efficient and easiest-to-install insulation in the world. The government has access to the best of scientific research and advice. Oil prices will go up and up. The foam will be a most sensible investment."

Whenever I hear of some purchase being an "investment" I strain my neck, looking around for a snake-oil drummer.

"We live in Vancouver," I said. "This is where people from the prairies move to get away from Northrop Frye winters. The climate hasnt changed much in the past sixty-five years since the house was built, or even in the six or twelve years since we bought it. We dont have any insulation. We dont even use our fireplaces."

"Come on," said the federal government [this is a rough translation], "if you do not get in on this limited-time offer you will be a bad Canadian, a profligate wastrel and a fool among your peers."

"All right," said my wife.

"Just give me fifteen minutes some time," I beseeched no one in particular. "I think I can write three wonderful sentences."

Minutes were hard to come by for a while. Men in masks were tromping through the house, men outside were drilling holes in the stucco and through the cedar shakes under the stucco, a huge machine in the street was shooting gooey white stuff through a hose and into the holes. Traffic was screeching to a stop to watch these Martians pump security into a citizen's "major investment."

All the birds in the neighbourhood deserted their leafy home.

When it was all done, when the five hundred holes in the wall were patched with something three shades away from the original colour, when our Pacific Rim Japanese

Current winter finally came, we sat patriotically in our various rooms and tried to imagine how warm we felt. The loan we took out to pay for our share of the job was just another debt. At least we didnt have to shell out a couple of hundred dollars for snow tires.

Astute, college-educated readers will have arrived at the opinion by now that the use of the house is symbolic, either of the house of fiction, in Jamesian terms, or as the psyche's image of self in the Freudian sense. That is no lasting comfort to the writer, who has to live somewhere.

A few years went by. In the United States of America newspaper and magazine articles began to appear, telling American and otherwise captured citizens that people who lived in UFFI houses were being poisoned by the walls and roofs. We had noticed that since getting the urea-formalde-hyde envelope we were no longer bothered by insects indoors.

"That formaldehyde really does its job," I said, having given up writing for the afternoon.

"Not funny," said my wife.

"Maybe insects just dont like a place that's so warm in the winter," I offered by way of compromise.

"It's not funny if our daughter's health is being threatened by this stuff," she said.

After a year or so the Canadian government admitted that there might be something wrong with the stuff. The ads started appearing in the newspapers again. The companies that had formed a few years earlier to pump in the foam were now proclaiming themselves experts in removing it. The government said it would, after a lot of hectoring, kick in with a couple of thousand dollars to help patriotic you-know-whats to rip out the guck.

"How much?" I shrilled.

"Well, twenty-seven thousand dollars. We live in a big house," she admitted. "But it will be an investment in our health, and especially our daughter's health."

"Invest! Invest!" I advised.

So the Venusians laid seige where the Martians had scored their fleeting victory. This crew wore even more fearsome masks. Not content to drill circular holes in our unfortunate house, they carried implacable weapons of destruction and attacked the very structure of one's identity.

"The Walls Do Not Fall," I tried to shout over the sounds of battle

"You want to move over a bit?"

The walls fell. The Venusians raked all our possessions into piles in the middle of each of the overly-numerous rooms, and covered them with enormous sheets of thick plastic, securing the latter to the floors.

It was time to retreat.

We moved out of the house, or what was left of it, and went our various ways. My wife domiciled herself in a hotel suite in Richmond, so that she could be close to her college. My daughter and I slept at a succession of friends' houses, on couches, in basement rooms, in a solarium. It went on for weeks that stretched inevitably into months. It meant driving all over the Lower Mainland every day, to my university, to my daughter's school, piano lessons, skating lessons, and so on, to restaurants for breakfast, to the dentist as usual, to distraction in our spare time. My job was getting harder to do. My story was lying somewhere between the paprika and the electric iron under a sheet of plastic which itself was under a drift of sawdust and poisonous foam particles. It was examination and final paper time, and Christmas was coming. I spent my birthday in bed. It was then that for the first time in my life I caught pneumonia.

That's when Miss Chan from the tax department called.

"We want all your receipts and other records from the tax years 1977 to 1981. Have them at this office in three days."

"My house has been torn down. It is full of poisonous dust. The records will be hard to find because they are nailed down in a pile of god knows what under plastic, and there are huge machines and many extra-terrestials all over the place. I have to mark a hundred and twenty papers in three days. And I am in bed with pneumonia for the weekend."

"Well, we have our problems too," said Miss Chan.

"What is your favourite Canadian book, Miss Chan?"

But she had hung up.

It was a tremendously cold weekend in Vancouver. In my back yard the cherry leaves were frozen in packs to the dead lawn, and there were great chunks of broken wood and stucco on the cherry leaves. Semi-feral cats hunkered in the back lane. The sky looked like soiled washcloths frozen solid. Even the voices on the car radio had slowed down.

I picked my chilly way through a hole where a wall had been in my middle age, and crawled under the first in a succession of brittle plastic covers. Thin blood dripped from my nose onto the sad bundles of socks and teeshirts.

Under the sixth plastic sheet, on the fourth day, I found some old receipts in a box along with my 1954 *Baseball Digests*. On the sixth day I coughed for an hour, and my almost-useless fingers closed around some more documents. I gave up looking any more, and drove down to Garry's retreat. It was warm in there.

"Can I just sit here till it's time to pick up my kid?" I asked.

Chuckle chuckle.

He was used to my bravado and hi-jinks. I was serious. I think I fell asleep for a while, in my sheepskin jacket in his easy chair.

"Can I write off the medication and mileage?" I enquired.

Chuckle chuckle.

As it turned out, Garry managed to save me more than I had hoped for. I lost about seven hundred dollars because

I couldnt find the receipt for one plane trip. Oh, and I probably lost about ten years off the end of my life. I could still feel my lungs when I bent over at third base the next summer.

"Next year they'll go after actors and dancers," said one knowledgeable friend and outfielder.

"Once you've been audited and they dont turn you up as a fake, they'll leave you alone," said the catcher. "It might turn out to be to your advantage. Now you can get away with lots of stuff you never dared try before."

"I just want my lungs back," I said, wincing as I swung unsuccessfully at a low outside curve. "I just wish this hadnt started. It wound up costing a hundred and fifty thousand dollars."

"I thought the UFFI-removal was twenty-seven thou."

"My wife figured that since the walls were down for the UFFI anyway, she might as well get a few renovations done."

"Your place will always look like Saigon Alley," said the non-playing husband of the first baseperson.

A few more years passed, probably two, and never more than two days went by in succession that heavy-booted workmen did not tromp the floors, which themselves kept changing, or stumble around the heaps of building materials in the yard, where my wife was supervising artisans and working stiffs whose task it was to rebuild the gardens of Ninevah.

"If Albert arrives, tell him I have just gone to dump my Canada Savings bonds from the Royal into the term deposit at the credit union," she would say.

"Who is Albert?" I would ask.

"I told you. He's the architect who is bringing me the plans for the pergolas."

"What is a pergolas?"

"Plural. Pergolas. Cant stop to explain again. Have to go fix the term deposit."

"What's a term deposit?"

"That's what you signed the papers for last Friday, you stupid bugger."

"What should I make for supper?"

"I dont know what's in the fridge. Surprise me."

It is hard to hammer out a novel while some guy in a plastic baseball hat is hammering out your porch wall. But unless you write stuff and get money for writing it, you arent a tax-deductible writer.

"Are you writing for money?" enquired a tired-looking muse one night in the early autumn.

"Why? Is it against the rules?" I asked, a little testily.

"Well, I dont remember John Keats living in a palace," she said, and I detected for the first time a little—not exactly a sneer, but an expression that suggested that she was thinking she might be wise to put a little distance between us.

"Hey, I had pneumonia last winter. Serious stuff. I can still feel it when I have two cigarettes in a row."

"John Keats didnt get consumption from remodelling his house. When he said 'forlorn,' he wasnt talking about the prime interest rate."

She had me there, and I knew it.

"I throw myself on the mercy of the court," I said.

That got a very small smile from her.

"All right," she said, carefully measured resentment in her feathery voice. "I'll give you one rather nice final chapter."

And she did. When I woke and read it, it was as if I had never written it. It was as if I had wakened and found myself in my grandmother's little house in Penticton, in 1948.

Fall was pretty nice this year. The smell of woodsmoke is not around any more, because the city is even bigger, and people are forbidden to burn summer cuttings and other rubbish out back of the house. But there is still a feel of that old magic in the air. It is different now that one has a tax-writeoff computer and can set it up above-ground. But the leaves are still there, with gleaming chestnuts among them. The American League team won the World Series for the second year in a row, but even that couldnt ruin everything.

Then my wife gave me the news about Miss Chan.

Miss Chan had gone on to better things, probably marriage and a joint bank account. Probably a two-car garage and pay-TV. She had been replaced by a Mr. Wong, who had taken it into his head to familiarize himself with his new position by going over my account.

This was (and probably still is) Mr. Wong's position: George Bowering is not a "serious writer." I have not heard Mr. Wong's definition of the term, because so far I have corresponded with him only through his department's labyrinthine forms and through my consultations with Garry. I do not know what Mr. Wong's favourite Canadian book is. Perhaps by "serious writer" he means someone he has heard of, someone who gets mentioned in *People* magazine, or who sells movie rights for a million razbuckniks.

Anyway, Mr. Wong is not satisfied with Miss Chan's leniency. He says that what I do is a hobby. He says that a writer really has no use for a computer—computers are business machines. I think I know what Mr. Wong took at university. The thought enters now: maybe I failed Mr. Wong in first year English!

Garry told me that Mr. Wong picked the wrong year and the wrong target. Garry rubbed his pencil-filled hands together and chuckled, and said I have nothing to worry about. But I havent been able to contact Garry lately. He is in Ireland. But I have nothing to worry about. I am going to write off the microdisc I am recording this sad story on.

I kind of miss Miss Chan. I sent her a copy of my book, *Kerrisdale Elegies*. I wanted to find out how she thought it stacked up alongside Rilke. But she must be reading it still; I havent heard from her. I guess I will send a copy to Mr. Wong. I wonder whether he thinks that Rilke is a serious writer.

I kind of miss my muse, too. She hasnt been to visit me since I came back from Europe. I thought I saw her one night on the *Kurfürstendam* in West Berlin, but I was hurrying to catch the last subway home to my apartment in Dahlem, so I will never be sure. When I got home from Europe, though, I hardly recognized my house. So I will understand if it takes her a while to find it, too.

The reader will wonder whether there might not have been a more satisfying ending to this story. All right, here goes.

Mr. Wong tried to rise from his chair, but he was exhausted. He fell forward across his desk, his glasses flying off his face at the impact, flipping twice in the air and sliding across the polished linoleum floor.

"You are more serious than anything I could have imagined," he managed to say. "I cant fight Ottawa and you both. Go, go, please, I dont want you to see me like this."

My wife and I and Garry walked arm in arm out into the light drizzle of February in White Rock. Gulls called derisively from the long sandy stretches of low tide. We paid them no mind.

"You were wonderful," she said. "I have not seen you like this since our early days at the Writer's Club."

"I could not have done it without you, you and your financial expertise," I admitted.

She nudged me with the elbow I held to my side.

"Oh, and Garry," I added.

Garry chuckled.

He stood back, chuckling, as my wife and I embraced there in the parking lot next to the beach, the grey sky and the grey water taking on a light tinge of silver.

"I'll pay for the parking," I said.

"This time dont forget to get a receipt, you stupid bugger," she said.

STAIRCASE DESCENDED

I opened my eyes or I open my eyes and thought or think
it was or is morning. That is a terrible sentence to begin
with. I take it back. I open my eyes, usually, and think it
might be morning.

One wants to stay in bed, of course, and to hell with
the time of day. But one is also predisposed to getting out
of bed. For me that is a problem, the first one of the probable day. Here is the problem: when I wake up I am lying
on my right side, knees as close to my chest as possible,
one hand under the pillow or rather my head because the
pillow has fallen to the floor, there is no pillow. The other
hand, who knows? It could be pulled up under my chin.
My knees as close to my chest as possible. When I was
young I could tuck my knees right up against my chest. No
more. But of all the things I cannot make my body do any
more, this business with the knees is the least of my
troubles. I can lift the knees a lot closer than most men or
even women my age, I will wager.

The problem is getting my body out of bed. I do not
mean a slacking of the will. I mean that when I wake,

nearly blind eyes looking at a red blur of unknown numerals, my body is locked in that position I was so careful to describe just a moment ago. And mind you, I am sick and tired of description. If I go on with this I might have some difficulty with description. I might not do it. You will not find me throwing around adjectives, in any case. I hate the god-damned slithery unnecessary corruptive willful Anglo-Saxon self-satisfied secondary stylish things. Ha, just a little joke there, you dont mind? Just fooling.

Trying to get that body out of that bed. It might help if I described the bed, but I wont. The body is locked in place by a small imperfection low down in the vertebraic column. If the body lies in roughly the same position for a given period of time, as for instance when I am asleep, it is next to impossible to change its attitude. For instance I cannot induce it to lie on its back and stretch its legs straight toward the so-called foot of the bed. Nor can I swing the legs over the side of the bed, though my body lies on the edge, not the middle of the bed. It is a medium-wide bed. My father died in it, and there was a woman who used to find room for her body beside mine. In those days my body did not lie in the same position all night.

Many people get out of bed by swinging their legs together, rotating on their buttocks, perhaps, and allowing their trunks to be levered to a vertical position as their heels fall to the floor, where there may be cold wood or gritty linoleum or a warm wool carpet. A warm wool carpet. If there were a warm wool carpet in this room I might sleep on it, and avoid this problem of getting out of the bed. But then the problem of rising to the vertical from the carpet might be even more daunting. I return to the appropriate problem. I wished and I wish that I could rotate and rise, my heels falling on whatever is down there, sometimes it is hard to remember all these things. That is connected to my dislike of description, I am sure. If I find that I cannot remember something that one would never imagine forgetting, anyone's forgetting, one wants to crawl under the covers if he can find them, and go back to sleep, if you can call what I do sleeping.

Not that I dont try the various ways of getting up in the morning. It is impossible, thank goodness, to describe the feeling when one wants to get up but the body will not do it. It is not the same thing as wanting to move your arm when you wake up with your arm asleep over your head. You begin to move your left leg, let us say, and a signal arrives saying that you will soon be in great familiar pain without hope of gaining some movement at its cost. Hopeless. The signal comes from the small place in the lower region of the sacroiliac, you remember that word. It was very popular in radio show jokes in the late forties.

So here is what I do. With extremely small movements I nudge the body closer to the edge of the bed. This nudging is meticulous and painstaking and would seem to be hopeless of success had I not done it on previous occasions. First I might point the big toe on my top, that is left, foot toward the bookcase and move the foot a bit. Then the lower or right shoulder. Then, with the long bony loose-skinned fingers, damned description, of both hands wrapped around the corner of the edge of the mattress, I manage to bounce the round bony ball of my right hip an inch or is it a centimetre over, to the right, that is. You will just have to imagine, if you can summon your faculties better than I can mine, how long this procedure goes on and with what discomfort I must continue it. It makes my body sweat, which is amusing, because my body affords a comparison with the denuded skin of a mature chicken, and one has never seen a chicken perspire, no matter what other discomfitting things one has seen a chicken do. Sweating like that every morning or whenever it is I get out of bed, and yes I finally do, I wish momentarily for a shower. Place of potential disaster. Enough, and more.

Enough. If I do not get at it I will never tell you how I get out of bed and thus solve the first problem of the day. And why bother getting up, you ask. I do not get up. After enough edging and pointing and minute hopping with my frozen shut body I manage to propel myself so far to my right that I achieve the edge and more of the bed. Of course I have not been able to rotate on my hips as we would all like to, but I do turn as I depart the bed, and fall face downward to the floor. There is no stopping me then, not till I come to rest on whatever that surface is. Of course, I always remember if I am jolted enough. It is hardwood, nice dark boards of hardwood. Once they shone, a rich dark brown lateral glint of—no. There is a bang, of course, when I cease falling, and even though I have my hands in position to prevent my face from striking the hardwood, I do land nice and crisp on my knees and elbows, and so the tight grip thus far maintained by the little spot of imperfection in my vertebraic column is slackened just a little. Enough so that in my present position I can begin a careful crawl toward the toilet.

2

Sometimes it is a crawl and sometimes it is more like a creep, a creeping, let us say, to avoid vulgar ambiguity. It would be nice just to stand up and walk or at least hobble to the bathroom, and on the odd occasion I can do just that, if there are enough objects or close enough walls on the route I fall into so that I can support myself on something. There are times when I start by standing up, having pulled myself up the brass leg of the bed, but have to collapse to the hardwood again because the first step or shuffle, let us say, brings a serrated knife blade, this is a fanciful description, you understand, into the small of my back. A small that is the largest thing in my attention at the time. Poor jest, but necessary.

I proceed, embarrassed a little, I mean here is a grown, perhaps, man, on his hands and knees (if it is one of my lucky mornings) crawling out of his bedroom into the hallway and, turning a little to the left, into the bath-room. If you are a man, or if at least a man a little like me, you know that in the morning there is a compulsion you cannot shake. In fact it is often the agent that gets you out of bed in the first place. This is the non-negotiable necessity of passing water. Some people are lucky: they hop out of bed in the morning, perhaps flinging their arms wide of their trunks in a little reminder of elementary school exercises, and hippity hop to the toilet, where they pull it out and piddle away, great creamy suds rising on the sides of the bowl, a 1950s radio song humming in their heads.

While I am crawling toward the bathroom and then across the bathroom to the convenience, fifteen men in my neighbourhood have done just what I outlined above. I crawl past the sink, along the flank of the bathtub, noticing for the hundredth time that one of its clawed feet has a smear of toothpaste on it, and how did that get there, again. It could not, certainly, be the same smear that was there, let us say, last February the 12th. But there I am then at the device. There is a certain principle at work now—the more movement I am capable of, the more I am capable of movement. It is as though the knot in my back is melting. In an hour or so I will be walking like a normal man or a normal man with a body made of shredded wheat, as I once quipped to Marsha, a woman you will never hear about again. Here I am. But there is no question of waiting until I can perambulate. Not that it is not a temptation. Just let the bladder go, let it unblad, I suppose you could say, and relax. Reeelaaax, says the voice in my left ear. That is where the devil sits when he has time, my mother once said. Enough about her. There will be no resorting to "moti-vation" in this account.

There I am. There is no question, then, of pointing Percy at the porcelain. I am committed, you might say if this were more serious, this telling, to telling you the details. The truth is that I could stop right here, and I

I thought he was resisting description [handwritten marginal note]

would not mind. You would probably cheer the abandon-
ment. In fact it is unlikely that you have made it this far. If
you have, please sign your initials right here: . All
right, there I am. I am one hundred and eighty-six centimetres in height on the occasions when I can stand up
fully. I have never been able to measure the toilet bowl in
centimetres, but it is just under fourteen inches in height.
All right, I will just tell you and let's forget it. I kneel full of
gratitude that I am there and hang poor Percy over the hard
white lip. On most occasions he has reached by now the
condition of hangability. But there are mornings on which
he will not retreat from the condition he was found to be in
on my waking. I do not know or have forgotten what those
neighbours of mine do on such an occasion, but I can tell
you what I do. I can tell you but just this once I do not
believe that I will.

Flushed not too far from my embarrassed face, the
toilet is finished for now, and glad I am of it. Now there is
the sink and perhaps the shower. I would like to take a
shower every morning. In fact there was a time a few years
back when I did, and not always alone, I can tell you. What
a ridiculous image, you say. All right then, you will get
urine and atrocious posture instead of soapy euripus. Now
I simply hope that by the time I am ready for the shower I
can stand up in it. There is nothing gratifying about coming
to rest on one's hands and knees in the tub and feeling the
hard water against one's back. But first the sink. I always
feel a little guilty when it comes to the sink. This guilt
reaches, as most do, a long way back, into childhood,
when one's mother warned one about putting one's weight
on the poor sink. Damn. There is something about a bathroom that allows one's mother to sidle into the discussion,
the monologue, yes I know. But you are here, arent you,
you did sign in, didnt you?

All right, I pull myself up the sink, like a sickly
monkey pulling himself up the bars that imprison him
while offering him something to ascend. There you go, a

simile, I think. You will not, if I have my wits about me, see another of those. Bad enough that I fell into this so-called present tense. No, I made a promise to myself not to spend all my precious time talking about this talking. If it is talking. It looks more like writing to me. There I go. Okay, a short paragraph. I decided on paragraphs, with you in mind. You might remember that.

Up the sink I climbed. (That felt good. Not the climbing. I mean the tense.) (This will get out of hand. I really must stop that sort of thing right now, no matter what attractive thoughts come to mind.) By now I can bear this, the simulacrum of standing, while leaning heavily on the basin. I can manage to get the stopper in. I didnt use one for years till I started paying for my own hot water. The taps on. The object is to wash and then debarbarate the face. Now my one hundred and eight-six centimetres give me a new problem, or rather the revisiting of an old problem. I cannot bend to get my face anywhere near the right altitude for laving. I must spread my feet as far apart as possible, rest my bony forearms on the edge of the porcelain, and do the best I can, bobbing my head for a painful half-second, and throwing water and soap toward my cheeks. This goes on. I want to stop but I have to proceed. I want to stop writing or talking or thinking, but you cannot. You cannot stop thinking if you are not a Himalayan anchorite, and what else is there. So, eventually one gets a razor in one's hand and eventually manages to make momentary scrapes at the face. It is a little like reaching for a piece of paper that is just out of reach on the floor on the other side of those monkey bars. If you overextend your shoulder and elbow and wrist for a second before they all snap back into their proper proportions, you can make a little scrape at the whiskers and soap if you have the razor at the correct angle. This is how I shave almost every morning. I have thought of growing a beard but I cannot. I have random hairs on my face, no pattern and certainly no carpet. I used to tell myself that this unmanliness was a sign that I was a forerunner of human beings from the future. I read a lot of science fiction in my youth, and time travel was my favourite narrative device. I was going to say something about that but I cannot remember what it was. Let us say that I have shaved.

Perhaps now I can get into the shower. The main reasons one gets into the shower, or the main reasons I do, are my hair and the cleft between my buttocks. Perhaps I can get into the shower and at least lean against the wall.

3

Now we come to the heart of this story. It is a story, dont you agree? Now we come to what I thought of as the whole of the story. I could probably put this a better way if I started all over again. But then what would you have? Probably a well-rehearsed narrative and therefore something you can not trust. If you think that is literary theory, think again. There is nothing at all literary here, I the least so.

I am now approaching the bottom of the stairs from above. That is, I am descending. Not at all like the royalty those words might make one think of. I am wearing a pair of slippers so old that I cant remember who gave them to me. One never buys one's own slippers any more than one buys one's own after-shave lotion. They, the slippers, have heels that have been crushed under my own for so long that they would appear to someone who has not yet put on his glasses for the day to be made that way. There are plenty of slippers with no heels to them, you know that. You also know by now that I am for some reason slow to get to that heart of the story I promised or at least mentioned. I am also, I must tell you, since I started on this dressing of the narrator, wearing my ratty old bathrobe or is it housecoat. It is an item that falls to a level just below my knees, and is belted at approximately the waist. That is all. Under this piece of drab phlegm-green terry-cloth, I am as naked and as attractive as a hog hanging in the cold room at Peerless Packers.

Ah, say you, ablutions done and staircase descended, he is now going to perform the comfortably familiar ritual of the morning newspaper and fresh egg. That is, ah say you all this, while at the same time saying it looks as if this person is going to force upon me or us a lot more sentences than we need about every moment of his waking and god help us perhaps comatose life. Not so. At least I hope not so: I did not, I will admit, plan on narrating the getting down out of bed and the getting up to the white bowls. How about this: I think that you can depend on my torpor to protect you from a recounting in the familiar present tense of my whole day, one like the next that they are.

No, this is the point at which you encounter not a fresh egg and a minimal daily, but two women at a kitchen table, drinkers of so much coffee that in an hour they will be taking turns at the downstairs toilet, and expenders of more words in that hour than appear in the missing news-paper. It is not really missing, save from this account. Either it is on the front steps where it has been for five hours, or some child, pauper or dog has made off with it again. If there has been a high wind earlier this morning, its pages will be wet to transparency and wrapped around various bushes or weeds in the yard and the neighbour's tall lawn. The neighbour does not read the newspaper. He is a long-haired youth whose occupation seems to be burglary, judging from the peculiar coming and going of packing cases and trailing electrical cords. But you will not be bothered with him again. I do not even know his name, so I can not even withhold that from you.

So to those two women sitting at the kitchen table, the way women will, sprawling a little, no, that is not quite right, their bodies relaxed so much that they seem to be

215

saying with their easeful slouch that they own the space. No, I will never get that right, so I will drop the attempt. One might as well commit a lot of description, or lay out a row of similies. Anyway, there they are, the two of them, total weight, let us say of a hundred and fifty kilograms, maybe less. The prettier one is the neighbour lady, but the other one is smarter. She is the one who is related to me by marriage. She thinks that I am gone, and she has her friend persuaded of that illusion. Sometimes it sounds to me as if she thinks that I am dead and gone; other times it seems as if she is convinced that I am just gone, fled, fallen away. Just disappeared from sight. I do not do everything I could do to persuade her otherwise, but I continue to make small attempts in that direction. Why do people call that a direction? Let it stand. I hardly can myself.

They are having one of their usual discussions. This is what the lady of the house says:

"Each thing itself, then, and its essence are one and the same in no merely accidental way, as is evident both from the preceding arguments and because to *know* each thing, at least, is just to know its essence, so that even by the exhibition of instances it becomes clear that both must be one."

To which her visitor responds:

"Ha ha ha ha. You may be right about that and you may be wrong. You could not prove it by me. All I know is that when my old man wants what he wants and I dont want what he wants, essence, well, essence never enters into it. It might have worked differently for you when your old man was around. Might have been essence all over the place. Ha ha ha ha. Far as I know. Ho ho."

Now the woman who lives in this house never condescends to her friends or any stranger. She just assumes that they enjoy the possibility of entering the conversation, when they get the chance to talk, at a level that will be commensurate, is that a usable word here, with the one she is speaking on. So she will continue (ah, the future tense, which no more covers the future than the present tense the present):

"For it has been already shown that the soul of the incarnate deity is often supposed to transmigrate at death into another incarnation; and if this takes place when the death is a natural one, there seems no reason why it should not take place when the death has been brought about by violence. Certainly the idea that the soul of a dying person may be transmitted to his successor is perfectly familiar to primitive peoples."

"I wish I had known that yesterday when I was at the houseplant sale at Corby's," says her fellow coffee-drinker. "That place was full of primitive people. Oh my!"

At this juncture I decide to try to make my presence known. Luckily, I *have* had a shower this late morning, and that stream of hot, nearly steaming, water on the small of my back makes it possible for me to walk, even on a level surface. I generally start with a significant stare at one of the two women. Sometimes the visitor is not there; on that occasion I stare at my close relative, bending my neck down the way a pigeon does when it is contemplating a puddle but wary of a crowd of human feet. Having inaugurated the stare, I lift my left hand to a level with my left nipple, wrist tucked in to trunk, and wiggle the upward-pointing fingers a little. When you do that, trying to make each digit independent of the others, the middle finger, the longest, usually refrains from wiggling. Nevertheless, I hope that it *appears* to be wiggling because its neighbours are so doing. I do not want to be thought to be disguising a rude gesture, even with the palm facing the wrong way. Not yet, in any case.

"There is an unmistakable indication in the text of Sophocles's tragedy itself that the legend of Oedipus sprang from some primaeval dream-material which had as its content the distressing disturbance of a child's relation to his parents owing to the first stirrings of sexuality."

"Stirrings!" exclaimed the neighbour, "It's too bad you

never had any children before he departed. My boys are stirring all the time. I tell you I hate cleaning up their room. And sometimes I dont feel at all safe myself!"

You could not say the word sexuality to this woman without rousing her. Even sitting still in her chair, forearms on the table between them, she seemed to experience a sea change. Her body seemed to become more rounded, to make rounded areas of shininess in her print dress. Perspiration made her throat glow, and moisture appeared in the edges of hair over her ear. Her mouth would not entirely close when it was relieved of its labor of speech. Moisture shone from her front teeth. Her eyes, which before had been simply brown and cool, now glowed as if all at once connected to the electrical power lying patiently in the wires inside the walls between rooms. The palms of her hands were probably wet. The creases at the backs of her knees were likely sticky. She moved her knees a little farther apart, looking, in all likelihood, for air.

How disappointing. I had intended, as you will have gathered, to spare you that sort of thing. The foregoing description should appear thus:

~~You could not say the word sexuality to this woman without rousing her. Even sitting still in her chair, forearms on the table between them, she seemed to experience a sea change. Her body seemed to become more rounded, to make rounded areas of shininess in her print dress. Perspiration made her throat glow, and moisture appeared in the edges of hair over her ear. Her mouth would not entirely close when it was relieved of its labor of speech. Moisture shone from her front teeth. Her eyes, which before had been simply brown and cool, now glowed as if all at once connected to the electrical power lying patiently in the wires inside the walls between rooms. The palms of her hands were probably wet. The creases at the backs of her knees were likely sticky. She moved her knees a little farther apart, looking, in all likelihood, for air.~~

You think that you know what you would do in this situation? You have that profound confidence? The universe for you is not a maze with possible beasts at the end of any corridor? I congratulate you on your good fortune. I am without envy. I simply wish to express my joy that there is such a fortunate one among us, and therefore maybe many. Joy is likely too exalted a word. What can I put in its place? I suppose we could agree on satisfaction. All right, my satisfaction. But now you must also allow that it is not for me a simple decision to say or do what I do or did in the above circumstance.

I am not stupid: I know that you are objecting to my silence here. Why, you ask, do I not shout at the women to make them notice and indeed acknowledge my existence, and more than that, my presence? And while we are at it, why do I not effect another conducting of the senses; that is, why do I or did I not reach out and touch the woman of my choice here? Why not grasp the neighbour lady's thigh or seize a handful of my matrimonial partner's raven hair and pull it, vertically or horizontally about seven centimetres, or to be more certain, fifteen? I do not know whether I will be able to explain this to you. I know that there must be personalities like mine in the world, personalities that have been shaped more or less like mine over all the years of our growing up, albeit like potatoes growing in rocky soil, some of us being compelled to grow around a rock and never to achieve the shape assigned to the potato in the little golden book of west coast gardening. If you happen to be one of those rare but surely extant personalities, you will understand easily why I did not make those auditory or palpatory attempts at communication. In fact it is probable that I would not have to waste breathe or ink or whatever I am expending in the explanation. You would intuit and agree, you would find the parallel in your meek heart, or behind your meek heart. For the others, probably the majority of you, I can try the outline of an explanation. Probably anyone, of any personality, will have a layer, a striation of my condition, if condition is an appropriate word here, reluctant as I am to admit it.

All right, for you, the majority, I will try this. If I were to reach out and touch or grab or caress or pull, whether the pretty one or the smart one, and if I could feel the touch and the recipient could not, I would be, ontologically speaking, in trouble. If she could feel it and I could not, I would be filled with doubt at best. If neither of us could feel it—that is, if my hand went right through, say, the upper leg of the woman from down the street, it could mean any number of things. It could mean that we are both goners or creatures of the imagination, and if so, whose? It could mean that I am dreaming, or at least that one of us is, or if that is not stretching likelihood too far, both of us are. It could be that we are both figures in a fiction whose perpetrator is not paying sufficient attention at the moment. It could mean that this is the general rule of things and that my long-held opinion that matter comes to rest against the surface of matter is in error. The possibilities are not endless, but the end is too far away for the amount of energy I have to spare for postulating its place. Suffice it to say that I am aware of many possibilities that I do not want to prove or have proven to me.

It would be a simple thing to attempt a casual, accidental-seeming touch, if there were not other hints of my non-existence, at least as far as these women and the dimension they were in was concerned; and here I go into some sort of past tense again. If they acknowledged me by sight, and were not just ignoring me but unaware of my being, I could touch them without any but the normal fears, a knuckle to the temple or whatever. But then the touch would be unnecessary, as this explanation would be were I speaking or writing to people who could easily understand my attitude. But because these people seemed not to be able to notice me (and this is not just a singular instance, you must remember) by sight, there was a good chance that they would not notice me by touch because the latter was impossible. If not a good chance, at least a chance. As it is, at least till the present time, I would rather try another time to make them notice me by sight, just *in case* they were ignoring me out of spite. I want to hold onto the illusion, if it is an illusion, that I exist, for a while.

There was another possible explanation that I was going to offer, but now I feel that it would take a considerable feat of memory and thought to bring it to the surface of my brain, and I would rather return now to the narrative, if you will agree that that is what I departed from. Besides, the explanation, for those of you who do not resemble me in the most particular of my traits, would be overlong. It is likely that I would lose you, either in the sentences or from the room.

In the meantime, if that is not a silly thing to say at the preface of this resumption, I am in that other room, let us call it a living room—requisite number of furniture items, crooked magazines on one of them, and I can see the brace of women through the extra-wide kitchen door, at least it is the kitchen door from my viewpoint. From theirs it is probably the living room door. It is not really a door, but rather a kind of formality for those who like to know that they are passing between rooms, a kind of minimal archway, really a rounding of the corners, a sort of slight decrease in the distance from wall to wall. Through this thing I will call a door simply for the sake of this narrative, which I persist in misnaming, I can see the two women and hear their conversation as suggested above. I mean I dont expect you to believe that I have caught a verbatim series of remarks from one particular morning—I am using the present tense from time to time, after all. Really I just went and selected some likely passages from books of an unmistakably intellectual bent.

Now what I do is to remove my clothes. I cannot remember what I said I was wearing, so I will rely on you to remember, or to go back and look it up. Let us say that I was wearing pajamas, my ratty old striped blue and white ones that I have to hold the pants of up, unless I am wearing my old greenish terry cloth robe. Well, let us say, or I will, that I was at the moment in question wearing all that stuff. And my bedroom slippers, the ones, I remember now, with the squashed down heels. I take all these things off. No I dont. But I undo the belt of my robe, and then I let the pajama bottoms drop. I kick off my bedroom slippers in order to kick off the pajama bottoms that have settled around my feet. Then I can dance.

Here is what the dance looks like. Rather, here is what I imagine the dance to look like; as the dancer I am in no position to observe or reflect on the dance. I hold the skirts of my off-green terry cloth robe in my two hands and lift them sideways, away from my body. Then I contrive to bend my bony legs, knobby, really, they are knobby at the hip, knee, ankle and foot, bend my knobby legs and kick my feet out sideways. All this time I make certain that I am facing the conversation at the kitchen table. I might describe an arc, little part of a semi-circle, there in the adjoining room, but always with the effect of total angular continuity. I dance and dance. I take a chance and kick my bony heel knobs together. My genitals swing back and forth in opposition to my legs. That is, when my legs are kicking left, my genitals are still swinging right. But enough about them. I dont think that my genitals are any funnier or any more an affront than the rest of my white, hairless, smooth, gravity-formed body.

What do I want? Do I want to test the limits of their ability to pretend that I am not there? Am I by now allowing that I might not exist, at least for them, and enjoying a dare otherwise prevented by childhood training in repression and civility? Why dont I approach, why dont I press the advantage that would be granted by proximity? I believe that I have explained that above, at least for those readers or listeners who would benefit by explanation, that is, understand and even, perhaps, sympathize. Now, wouldnt that be grand? Sympathy. I, even were I not after all a literary figure, as I am sure I am for you, one that you may even have grown tired of, would appreciate and welcome sympathy as quickly as the next fellow. But now I was finding it to be as much as I could handle to try for recognition.

How did my audience, if I may beg your indulgence in calling them that for the nonce, react to my terpsichorean antics? After I had exhausted myself, and was sprawled out in what had been her father's favourite easy chair, legs extended in front of me, skirts of my robe falling behind each stringy thigh, this is what I heard them to say:

"Diogenes, another follower of Anaximenes, held that air was the ultimate element of all things, but that nothing could be produced from it without the agency of the divine reason, which permeated it. Anaxagoras was followed by his pupil Archelaus. He, too, asserted that everything in the universe was composed of like particles, which, however, were informed by intelligence. This mind, by causing the conjunction and dissolution of the eternal bodies or particles, was the source of all movements."

"I'd have to think for a while to agree about *all* movements. I got a husband, and you dont know how lucky you are sometimes, and two huge boys, and I cant believe that there is any mind behind their movements, especially when they are coming down the stairs, or when they are picking up knives and forks, when I can convince them to use such elementary tools."

I was exhausted. There was nothing more I could do there. I was certainly not going to go into the kitchen to get coffee or a muffin or even a piece of limp broccoli. I did not want to play ghost, because I might start to believe in my own demise. I did not want to touch one of those people. What if I touched one, and she responded in such a way as to show that she had known I was there all the time? One does not like to entertain the notion that one is that little worthy of remark. I would go upstairs, and then I would decide whether to get dressed and go out, thinking of the near impossibility of donning socks, of bending to stick one over a big toe, and if I did go out I would get a cup of coffee and even a lemon-guck-filled danish pastry. I would go to Daphne's Lunch. Everyone knows me there. They say hello and say my name out loud when I enter the premises. They know enough to let me sit at a banquette even when I am using a table for four, because of my bad back. I am visible there. I do not know the names of any of the waitresses or the regular patrons I see there every time I attend. But we are a community. A community of laggards, perhaps, but a *polis*.

4

Perhaps you will agree that that scene, with the two talkative women and the dancing geezer, was the heart of this story, given that you have already acceded to the notion that this is a story. What, then, will we call the following. The following scene, perhaps a kind of loosening of the knot we have got ourselves tied in, takes place in Daphne's Lunch, where you will not hear saints and thinkers discussed all that often. Oh, once in a while I will quote Heraclitus to some hapless toiler for the minimum wage. But in general, philosophy is not broached there. Until today. Or that day. Let us say today.

   Today I found myself talking with an old gent who seemed to admire his ability to pick a teabag out of its cup and suspend it over its home in such a way that the drips of tea would fall into the centre of the red-brown liquid. No, I *find* myself talking with him. I do not know his name, and I do not think that he knows mine. It is in such circumstances that one may find oneself these days. There is a little ambiguity for you, I mean that sentence. But you knew that, didnt you? All right, I will get on with this tale. Nice day. Nice day. Havent seen such nice weather this time of year in years. Last year we were soaking wet and cold as hell this time of year. This kind of weather is good for your rheumatism. Good for what ails you. You bet.

224

Wouldnt mind being thirty years younger all the same. You bet, I would settle for twenty.

And so on. I know how to tailor my conversation for this crowd. It never strikes me that the guy I am talking with might be tailoring his conversation for this crowd, with me as part of this crowd. Who knows? We might, if we were to meet somewhere else, say one of the conference rooms at the Regency Hotel, have begun a discussion of Anaxagoras and his tradition. Be that as it may, we got onto a discussion of ontology or the like anyway. How we got there from the quite ordinary weather, I do not recall. Or I do not want to write or say it out. Eventually I got most of the lemon-gunk into my mouth and some on my lap, and was in conversation. I could end this account right here, and not make it any the less inconclusive than it is going to be. You will say that you would have liked to be warned of that at least around page four. Well, here is your chance. You can drop it right now, leave the beanery, browse the book store, two blocks east, cross the street, find an uplifting story or a meaningful fiction. Let me suggest the paperback edition of Michael Ondaatje's *Running in the Family*. Even if you dont buy it, you will have avoided the following conversation.

"My wife cant see me."

"You too?"

"She looks right through me."

"They are like that. That is why they are wives."

I let him sip his tea. I allowed the waitress to refill my coffee cup. I had to think about this. How will I relate to this gent who doubtless has a name but one that does not hang in the air between us, a story that will not be instantly convertible into the cliches of figurative language surrounding connubial friction?

"She thinks that I am dead. Or if not that, she is of the opinion that I have in some less mortal way retired from the site of our domicile. She thinks that I am no longer there."

"Sounds just like my wife, bless her departed soul."

Back there, I think, in the heart of the story, I cannot persuade anyone of my existence, much less my propinquity. Now my appearance, in such an habitual location, is unquestioned. I can now not speak the opposite. I cant persuade someone of my absence, my non-being, albeit only in the eyes, or rather out of the eyes and mind of another, or in this case two others, at least.

It strikes me that this gent without the name may think that he is only speaking with a revery, only imagining this conversation, imagining that there is a coffee-drinking fellow with a bad back with whom he is in conversation. It is late morning. Old bones rest and old brains enjoy their little trips.

"Have a look at me," I say.

People dont, as a rule, like to do that in places like Daphne's. They usually let their eyes flit. To the waitress as she turns her back and carries something to the kitchen hole. To the passing balloon outside the window, a kid has been to a celebrating bank. To the widow at another table. She is smoking a cigarette and reading a small paperback novel placed inside a leatherette cover. But this fellow does look now.

"Am I to look at anything in particular?" he says.

"Can you see a scar on my face?"

He looks.

"Yes I can."

"Where is it?"

"Well, there are two. There is a small one right at your hairline above the middle of your forehead, and there is a slightly longer one that runs from the corner of your mouth down at a forty-five degree angle."

It was more like a thirty degree angle, but I let it go.

"Thank you."

All right, I do exist. At least in this circumstance, in this environment, I exist.

"So to you I am visible," I suggest.

"Sure. Unless you are not supposed to be here. If your wife calls I will say I havent seen you, if you want."

"No, no. That's not what I mean. She would never phone this place anyway. Nor would she enter it willingly. She goes to well-lit places where they serve little things on croissants for seven dollars."

All right, I have settled the question of whether he is imagining me. There is still the question about whether I have created him. If he is a product of my imagination, there is not all that much currency in his attestation that he can see me as well as talking with me.

It strikes me that I could just rest comfortably, take everything at face value. But it also strikes me that I am not any better off than I was in the living room of my own house, except that here I am enjoying a second cup of coffee. There I was pretty well convinced of my presence; I was proprioceting quite handily, thank you. But others were not reflecting knowledge and awareness of my corporeal entity. Here I receive outside attestation of my being and presence, but I feel the possibility of uncertainty as to whether I have not generated, mentally, of course, the agent of that corroboration.

I should, perhaps, as they say, have stood in bed.

Maybe I did. But no, I cannot accept that. I can not allow that all that pain of rising for the dubious day was nothing, or for nothing. Or that it will be if I do it. I do not want to spend a life made, from now on and who knows how long till now, entirely of mentation. Of course all you can receive through the agency of this expenditure of words is something that resembles mentation more than it does any more physical and palpable action, if we can speak of action rather than the thing acting as palpable. Maybe I dont even palpate anything any more. Did I just imagine being downstairs and dancing? Am I not now sitting on a reddish banquette at Daphne's, thinking of my hard bed as down that street, up those stairs? Is there anyone reading or hearing this?

Diggers

o descendiendo por las lentas gradas
de un templo, que es innumerable polvo
del planeta y que fue piedra y soberbia

—Borges

One day in May they had an unusually low tide in Puget
Sound. All that water rushing out through the little necks at
the north end left unusual reaches of muddy bottom all
along the sound. In Seattle people went down to the new
water's edge, and found things like nineteenth-century
dimes and various kinds of shoes no longer made. Startled
clams were spouting water at collectors, and some fish,
habituated to an easy spring, had to hump it all at once.
Two Washington State Ferries went aground.

Byron Huss read about this in the morning *Post-Intelligencer* and nodded his head, though there was no
one else in the room. Byron was interested in finding
things. He was a little interested in finding things

underwater, but in general he was a land fellow. This may have been because he was brought up in the Valley. When he was a kid in the Valley he used to walk everywhere he had to go, and while he was walking he kept his head down, on the chance that he might find something.

The first week he was in Seattle he found a folded ten-dollar bill on the street. It smelled like the inside of a woman's purse.

A week ago he had found a golf hat that had been run over once. On the front of it was a representation of a flag, say on the eighteenth hole, and the words Quandong Country Club.

There are always innumerable things lying on the ground, waiting to be spied and picked up. Anyone anywhere could go out for a walk right now and find something worth picking up. But Byron Huss was even more interested in things that are under the surface of the earth.

He sometimes liked to imagine himself walking across the desert floor on the outskirts of Saqqarah, and stumbling over something. When he picks himself up and dusts himself off he looks and sees that he has stumbled over a little triangle of stone, a miniature pyramid. He starts kicking sand away from it and it gets bigger and bigger, but it is still a pyramid. There's no one else around. He digs a trench around the pyramid until it is taller than he is. Then he has to talk to someone, but not too many people, as few government people and foreigners as possible. Luckily he can drive a back hoe and a dump-truck and a bulldozer. He doesnt have to hire very many labourers, and soon he has a pyramid as long around the bottom as a block in New York, and as high as the sky, and at last there's a door . . . .

For a while Byron had a metal detector. Used to walk up and down the sidewalks or rather beside the sidewalks. The beach was hopeless—there were twenty-five guys per hundred feet at five in the morning, forget it. But how many streets are there in Seattle and suburbs?

On the street people either avoid you as if you were a crazy person if you're detecting metal, or they shout happy greetings at you. They shout because they can see that you're wearing earphones.

"Hi! Find anything?"

"Mostly beer can tabs," he always said.

It was true. But sometimes he found an engagement ring. With engagement rings you always put an ad in the paper. Five times out of six no one claims it. Sometimes he would find a wedding ring. With wedding rings you just keep them. They're just about all the same anyway.

But beer can tabs have retired a lot of metal detectors. Even guys who take their metal detectors to the headwaters of Cascade streams find themselves clogged up with beer can tabs. This is America. If you went down to the dock the morning of the record low tide you found a five-inch carpet of beer can tabs on the black seaweedy sand.

So Byron just read about the tide. He knew there'd be thousands of amateur and professional scavengers down there, and also on every beach up the Sound. Some of them would be drinking beer and throwing their tabs into the water.

These days, what with collectors' magazines and all, there were lots of potholers at any interesting site you can name. Someone gets their house bulldozed and there are guys in jeans and logging boots there, with detectors and shovels and screens. Every old ghost town and mining camp in the state has been gone over for a decade. You'd be lucky to find a two-inch triangle of blue glass.

So rather than a lot of semi-hopeless digging in some *site*, Byron would put his thinking cap on. He would meditate on the planet's age. There have been billions of people on the world, dropping things, burying things and then dying before they dig them up, throwing mementos into the dark during an emotional break-up.

A lot of the greatest finds are made by accident. Some old retired fellow digging up his lawn to make a vegetable garden, finds a little strong box with worthless mining stock and valuable gold coins. Someone's putting up an apartment block, digs into an ancient graveyard. Those people used to get buried with their best stuff.

Byron liked the idea of the random. He was into the aleatory. He dug the principle of serendipity.

On weekends he would often get into his old jeep with bare steel brake and clutch pedals, and head off. Sometimes he would stop beside a logging road. Sometimes he would be unobtrusive on the edge of a small town in the Okonogan Valley. Once in a while he would dig his shovel into a river bank because the dirt will just pour out of that hole.

He didnt find much. He found the bones of a small animal and figured it was someone's buried doggie. Once he dug up a silk parachute, all yellowed and clumpy.

But in nine hundred and ninety nine holes out of a thousand all he got was dirt and primary insects.

But that wasnt the point. The point was that all over the world right now there are hundreds and thousands and millions, maybe, of buried things, from cities to silver dollars. There is a pirate's chest just six inches under the surface somewhere, people walking over it every day.

Byron Huss had a nice sun tan. The muscles in his legs were long and powerful and thin. His heart and lungs were in top shape. All this he owed to digging. You see a lot of pot-bellied metal detecting people, but diggers are pretty trim.

Not that he was all that good looking. He was a kind of average looking short guy with army-issue glasses. He had a tattoo on his left shoulder but it was hard to see because of the hair that grew around it. He usually had a shirt on anyway, so no one was likely to see it very often. All in all, Byron Huss was the kind of person you might not really notice on the street or in a crowded elevator. If a policeman, for instance, asked you to describe the people that were on the elevator in question, you might forget all about him.

But out in the trees or in a field of alfalfa, with his short-sleeved shirt and brown shorts for the summer sun, he was noticeable. If you were a woman who came walking down the creek and saw him you might be impressed by his tanned and muscular arms, for instance.

She was carrying a shovel, and wearing a small pack high on her back. She was short, bare-legged, and wearing glasses. Her boots and the work socks visible above them made her tanned legs, though short, quite comely. Her shorts were faded cut-off denims. Her brown hair was tied up and messy and contained a few leaves.

Her blue eyes were magnified just slightly when she looked through her glasses at him and spoke.

"Hi. What are you . . . ? I mean . . . ."

He kicked some dirt into the shallow unpromising hole he had, and replied.

"Oh, hi. I'm, um . . . ."

"Gee, I didnt . . . Is this your place?"

"No, I mean I dig here. I mean . . . I'm digging here, but—"

"It's not your field."

"No. I dont know . . . ."

"What?"

"What?"

"Pardon me?"

"I dont own this place, no."

She sat down, and he put his shovel down pretty close to where she had dropped hers, and they began speaking to each other, a little more successfully, more orderly. He had never spoken to anyone about digging, and she said she hadnt ever met another digger.

By the time they had finished telling each other their stuff it was getting dark.

"Can I give you a ride?" he asked her.

"My four-by-four's just about a mile down the road," she said.

"I'll give you a ride," he said.

Sitting beside him for a mile, she didnt say a word, though he turned off the radio. Then after she had got into her own vehicle and put the key in the ignition, she spoke up.

"My name's Shirley," she said.

"Byron," he said.

"Shirley," she said, and started her engine.

The next Sunday afternoon he was about four feet down and just about ready to start a new hole a few yards up the fence, when he heard her call his name in surprise, just before she came into sight between a couple of gooseberry bushes.

She was wearing a Seattle Mariners baseball cap, and looked as cute as hell in it. She was carrying her shovel the way a U.S. Marine carries his assault rifle, and her face had dirt on it.

"Any luck?" she asked, the potholer's greeting.

"Nah, not a bottle top."

When a potholer gets asked the traditional potholer's greeting question, he always denies that he has had any luck all year. If he gets really intimate with the other potholer, he might start confessing his fortune, if he has had any.

Byron Huss was not fortunate. But then he was a metaphysical rather than a scientific digger.

And here she was again—Shirley. Shirley what? Well, here she was. What were the odds on running into her two Sundays in a row? They were over a hundred miles east of Seattle's most easterly suburb.

Boy, if he could dig that well against the same odds, he'd be more than satisfied. Still, he found himself being glad they'd run into each other.

"What about you?" he asked.

"Not a nail," she said.

"You look like you've been working pretty hard. Up by the alluvial fan?"

234

She rubbed the back of her wrist against her cheek. She licked the white underside of her forearm and rubbed at where she thought there was dirt smeared on her face. He saw sweat in her shirt's underarm as she lifted her elbow. Oh boy.

"So do you, like, you know—go digging every—?"

"Weekend? Yes," she said.

"How did you know I wasnt going to say, like, every, well, day?"

She sat down right on the ground, or rather on the long grass on the ground. He sat down too, because if he was going to talk to her he didnt want to be standing up and talking down. A lot of women would not sit right on the ground. If there was a rock or a wooden box, maybe on them, but not kerplunk as they say on the ground, on the grass.

What was happening here was that Byron Huss was becoming attracted to this woman Shirley.

"I was wondering," he said. "I would have thought that I would never run into another digger, considering where I go. I mean the odds would seem to be against it."

"Why's that?"

"Well, because I dont have any system. Or maybe you could say I have a lack of system system."

She had taken off her glasses and was wiping them on the tail of her shirt. She had pulled her shirt out, and she had sucked in her breath to do it. Now she was looking up at him with blue eyes that were not exactly focused. That was another step in the—whatever this was.

"Keep talking, Byron," she said in a voice that was just what you would have wanted in such a situation.

"I mean," he said, "I know all about looking up under the ends of bridges, or where grass doesnt seem to want to grow right," he said. "All that stuff. I've read the magazines," he said.

"I think I know what you are going to say," she said.

And she put her glasses back on.

"But I decided, hey, there are millions of things just under the surface, that will never get found, whether you're scientific about it or not,"

"Right."

"So I just decided to go and dig. I could do this all my life and never hit anything. So what? There'll be people that come along after me. And stuff is getting lost and covered up all the time."

"Right."

"Does that make sense?" he asked.

"No it doesnt," she said. "But I understand exactly what you mean, because I feel the same way. I always thought there should be other people who felt that way, but I am sure glad that I know for sure now."

While saying this she reached over and touched the back of his hand for about four seconds.

He yanked a nice long green grass stalk out of its place and stuck it between his front teeth. So she could see that he was a normal person, a guy from the Valley.

"So, have you been out since this morning?" he asked.

He hoped that she would touch his hand again, or his arm. He wondered whether he could touch her shoulder.

"I got up around four-thirty and drove out," she said, twisting her face a little to look at him, who had the sun behind his head. "I've been working all day, didnt even stop for lunch, didnt bring any anyway."

"What a shame," he said. "You dig all day and dont find anything. You didnt, did you?"

"Well, part of the time I was digging for in rather than out."

He stared at her.

"In instead of out," she said.

"What does that mean?"

So she explained it to him. She liked to dig randomly for things, just as he did, she told him, because she thought about the world and its history just about the way he did. But for the same reason, she liked to dig holes and put things into them and cover them up. She liked to think about how many, maybe hundreds of years it would be before someone came along and found what she had put there.

She said she figured there was a kind of rule that evened things up in the universe. For instance when one person loses five pounds another person somewhere else puts on five pounds. Or five people put on a pound each.

"What do you bury?" he asked.

"Oh, all different things. I was engaged once, and I buried my engagement ring. This was six years ago. Seven. I buried the fresh water pearls I bought for my graduation. I buried the Seattle *Times* in an airtight tube. Money, sometimes. My baby's layette."

"Baby?"

"My baby died when she was four months old. What they call crib death."

She did not look away when she said this. She looked right at him with her face squinched up for the sun. The thought passed through his head that most normal people would have looked away when they were telling someone that sort of thing. The first time, anyway.

"What about when she died—?"

"I had her cremated."

She lived in the Uni district, in a house she had inherited from her grandmother. The mortgage was retired years and years ago, and she could manage the taxes easily. She worked at the University book store, not at a counter, in the office. She didnt live alone. She had a schoolteacher friend who paid rent on a room and her share of the kitchen.

She just kept telling him more and more. He walked around the house, looking at everything, not wanting to stand still anywhere. Outside the living room window was a dark verandah, and past the verandah was a big dark cypress, and past that was the freeway, and well past that was the glint of Puget Sound.

There were family pictures in frames on the walls, old folks in country clothes, big backyard lawn family gatherings, one kid's face a blur. There were no pictures of babies.

"Come on, I'll show you upstairs," she said, and took his hand for the first four steps. It was the old story, though he did not know it, the man following the woman upstairs. All the way up he had to be looking at her behind as she climbed. Oh, that.

His heart was pounding.

Byron was a shy man and Shirley was a shy woman. It took them weeks and weeks to do what a lot of people get done in a day or two. But eventually they did what they did. She had somehow had a child some time back but she was shy. But she lay in his bed, naked except for her laced-up boots and her socks. The covers were thrown on the floor, and he sniffed her body, he put his face all over her and sniffed. She smelled like earth.

He rented his condo to two guys who looked as if they might make holes in the walls, and moved in with her. During the week she went to work at the bookstore and he went to work at the planetarium. Before dinner, nice wide green leaves with Italian olive oil consumed on the verandah, she would take off everything except her boots and white socks. With her boots on she was five feet and a few inches tall if she stood up. He would take all his clothes off, and they would get over their shyness on the dining room table, or on the carpeted stairs.

That's none of our business, and quite all right. They were and are less than glamourous people, but people nonetheless.

On the weekends they put their shovels and other equipment in one of their vehicles and headed for the countryside. On Mercer Island they found a horseshoe, no telling how old. They put it on the lintel over the fireplace in the livingroom, heel upward.

One Saturday they were fooling around on the beach at low tide not far from Cape Mudge. She took his clothes off and he took most of her clothes off, and they made love on the smooth sand. There was no one else around as far as they could see, so they took a little stroll afterward, naked in the filtered sunlight. They got back to their clothes just in time because the water was returning shoreward. While he buttoned his shirt she rolled his belt and buried it a foot deep in the sand, digging the hole with her hands. He was caught up in the special feeling of the afternoon and decided not to dig it up.

Two weeks later she buried his knitted cap under the pine needles just west of Leavenworth, Washington.

Thank goodness it was still summer and thank goodness they got there in her four-by-four because next Sunday she buried his jeans near Union Gap. While they were there they bought some beautiful serrano peppers and that week they ate stew so hot they had to strip to their underwear at dinner.

He took to making outdoor love with his Paris boots on because he didnt want to lose them to the earth.

They would have made a nice picture, two short naked people with nothing on but boots and socks, strolling hand in hand in the forest. If there had been anyone in the forest to see them.

But they didnt spend all their weekend enjoying *al fresco* sex. He was still a digger, after all, and so was she, in her somewhat different way. He found an old wood stove oven door where there was no other trace of a farm house, and a few weeks later he got a 1948 Oregon licence plate, but nothing of value or beauty. She didnt dig up anything but stones and worms, but she was happy. He was pretty happy, and would have been very happy if he could make love to Shirley and find a nineteenth-century blue bottle, and get home without losing any of his clothes.

One Sunday in late August she buried everything but his boots and socks. On the way home that night the highway patrol pulled them over for speeding on the I-5, and when the policeman spied Byron sitting there in nothing but his boots and socks, he made a radio call, and the Mount Vernon police came and took Byron in. He spent the night with a blanket in the Mount Vernon cooler, and had to call in sick at the planetarium the next morning. Shirley was there with a bunch of his least favourite clothes in the morning to pick him up on his own recognizance, and when he went to court in the fall he got off with a fine. But something had happened to their relationship, at least from his side of it.

"I always think," he said one day after work, "about ancient temples and stuff."

"Dont I know it," she replied over her shoulder while she was stirring the stew.

"I keep thinking about how most of the buildings and cities that people built have completely disappeared from sight. They are either just some kind of dust, or they are bare designs buried in the dirt."

She stirred the stew.

"You want to set the table?" she enquired.

He started to set the table.

"Same thing with people, of course. Did you ever think about molecules of dead people?"

"Sure, all the time. I used to be obsessed for about a year in junior high about the molecules of dead people."

"I mean you might breathe a piece of dust that used to be a powerful land owner. You might eat an alfalfa sprout that grew over a lost grave."

She turned and smiled. He noticed that she had her weekend boots on.

"I think of the molecules of dead people a lot," she said. And she made an unreadable gesture with the wooden spoon. "I think of the *atoms* of dead people."

He sat up straight in his chair, and not just because one was supposed to do something between lines of dialogue. He was getting ready, though he might not have

240

known it for certainty, to make a quick move to the left or right. Forward and back were out of the question.

"Of course living people lose molecules, and atoms, all the time. When we comb our hair."

"Yep." Gesture.

"When we cut our fingernails."

"Yep." Stir.

"I lose quite a few of my molecules inside you from time to time."

He made an ingratiating smirk. She turned the heat down under the stew and washed the wooden spoon under the tap.

"Are you interested in losing a few right now?" she asked.

Lucky, lucky, lucky Byron, he thought as he followed her boots up the stairs.

The weekends got cooler and wetter, and outdoor poontang became problematical. They made romantic and inventive love in the four-by-four, of course. They sometimes remembered to bring their two sleeping bags and zipped them together. Boots inside a sleeping bag made for funny feelings, like memories of childhood, and like memories of childhood proscriptions.

huh?

Like certain young women at strip poker games, he would go on these excursions with some extra clothing on. But after a while she must lose interest in burying his clothes. Once he had to take his boots off to get his tight jeans on, and she managed to get her hands on one of them, but he smiled and took it back. They were made by Paris and he had paid a hundred and seventy dollars for them, his only extravagance.

She buried his cartridge fountain pen. She buried his cheap plastic digital alarm wristwatch. When she buried his prescription sunglasses he made a scene. She would not tell him where they had gone. He threatened to stay out digging through the night and all day Monday and so on if

241

she didnt tell him where they were. She asked him in various ways to indulge her. She showed him something she could do and that he had never even read about. Lucky, lucky, he heard someone saying in his head.

This had happened in the Okonogon Valley. When they got home she comforted him with apples.

He was just making that wonderful first cut with his fork at the point of his second wedge of pie, when she brought up the dead.

"Remember when you were talking about the molecules?"

"Glmfghh," he said, nodding his head to make sure she knew that he was saying yes or sure.

She picked at the crumbs on her plate for something to do during the dialogue.

"I always have this double feeling about digging up stuff."

He nodded, and looked at her over his plain glasses.

"Like, when you dig away all the sand, and there it is, the ancient temple at Licksore."

"Luxor. Temple at Luxor."

"Yes. That temple. I mean, when you put your shovel down and look at the sunshine shining on those paintings on those pillars for the first time in five thousand years—"

"Five thousand?"

"What does it matter? Thousands of years. Can I have that last bite?"

He stuck it into his mouth fast.

"Well," she said. "I always wonder. Are we looking at something really really old, or are we looking at something brand-new? Because a few days ago there was nothing here but desert."

"I think the temple is next to the water," he said.

"But you know what I mean, dont you?"

"Yes. In fact now I am going to wonder the same thing every time I dig something up."

"When was the last time you dug something up?" she said.

It was true, he hadnt found anything for months. He had lost quite a few parts of his attire, and some of his minor equipment. His Swiss army knife had gone a week ago. If things went on this way for very long he would be looking at a negative total on his lifetime's register.

He decided to say something to her about it for the first time. In the beginning her burying of his clothes had been kind of clever, or cute, kind of a nice love affair's early familiarizing jape. But the bloom was off the whatever. He loved her, as they say, but he didnt want to lose anything more like pocket compasses, eyeglasses and Swiss army knives.

"Honey, I wish you wouldnt bury any more of my stuff," he said, trying to put a loving look on his face. The eyes, of course, had to do it.

"Okay," she replied, chipper, brown-haired.

Now what, he thought. He got up and carried his plate to the dishwasher. Now what. He thought for a moment of picking her up and putting her on his knee, but then he hadnt read the *Post-Intelligencer* yet.

She saw this passing through his mind. She was wearing her boots and socks, and a short-skirted dress. That was all. What a waste, she thought.

"I have a hunch you'll be lucky this Sunday," she called to him.

He was sitting in the chair by the fireplace, reading the paper. He never bothered to start a fire in the fireplace, but he liked to sit beside it. If they had a big jowly dog it would be lying near his feet.

When he got out of bed early Saturday morning he found that he had wakened to a house and a day of solitude. She had left a note. It said that she had taken the four-by-four on a run to Portland. She'd be back after dark, so he should go to the Pike Street Market and get the fruit and other munchies for tomorrow's dig.

When she did get in, really late, he pretended to be asleep. She got her small body into the waterbed without causing strong waves. She smelled like blackberries and salal.

Sometimes Byron decided where they would go to dig, and sometimes Shirley decided. This time she gave no indication that he was going to have any input into the decision. She grabbed the keys and jumped into the driver's seat of the four-by-four. The vehicle was already moving when he scrambled into his seat.

There had been a day-long drizzle every day of the week, but this morning there was sun on the wet foliage, and after they had turned east into the Skagit Valley there was a frost on the shaded part of the grass by the river, rime on the narrow limbs of the willow trees there.

Byron noticed that Shirley looked intense while she drove, a little ecstatic, if you could say that. But she was quiet. Once he said that it was the first frost they had seen this year and she agreed. She said "Oh!" when a cat scampered off the road just in time. That was it for talking. This was not all that unusual. They were not chatterboxes on these drives as a rule. They were usually anticipating a dig, and more than that, anticipating the fresh air and the exercise of their back and arm muscles. But they usually said the inconsequential things that young domesticated couples say when out for a Sunday drive.

She drove past Sedro Woolley, past Lyman and Hamilton and Concrete. The landscape changed into countryside and then into forest. When they spied the glinting end of Shannon Lake, she turned left off the highway and started finding forestry roads. There weren't any logging roads left, and there weren't many forestry roads. Sometimes the road just fell away into a linear clearing among the trees, filled in with willows and bushes. But here they could see the tracks of off-road vehicles. Americans possess their entire country. Now they were in parts Byron had never seen before. They were climbing steadily, and he joined her in enjoying the bite of the four-wheel machine. They got to five thousand feet, according to the altimeter on the dash.

They were, he saw on his AAA roadmap, in the Noisy-Diobsud Wilderness. He didnt know what the name meant. When she nubbed the four-by-four against a gnarled pine and turned off the engine it was quiet. They were surrounded by lodgepole pines in clumps, rock out-croppings and sloping meadows. The sun was out bright now and all the frost had turned to wetness. Below he could see the Upper Baker Dam between Baker Lake and Shannon Lake. Above he could see the snowy volcano called Mount Baker. He turned and looked back toward their trail, and saw the other snowy volcano called Mount Rainier.

With volcanoes you dont have to dig. They bring the contents of deep earth to the surface for everyone to see. But now Rainier was quiet, and Baker was not noisy, though from time to time people claimed to see a puff of white steam above its mouth. A little farther south Mount St. Helens had turned inside out for a while a few years ago. It was interesting to dig around the mountain, looking for people's things that had been engulfed, as they say.

"Here we go."

"What?" He had been somewhere else. Digging had been the furthest thing from his mind.

"Get your stuff out," she said.

They hiked for a little while, their shovels over their shoulders, the pickaxe suspended from his hand like an assault rifle. She did not seem to be leading the way, but he seemed to be following her.

"Does this look okay?" she asked.

"What?" He had been thinking about the record low tide in the Sound.

"A likely spot?"

"Sure," he said.

Sometimes on these occasions she would go over a hillock out of sight and do her digging or burying there. Today it looked as if she was going to stay with him. That had embarrassed him the first few times, but now he liked it.

He found himself digging in a small bank of exposed tan-coloured earth. He stood on lichen-sheeted rocks and pushed forward with his long-handled shovel. The earth spilled easily out of the hole he was making. It was a random spot, of course. It always was, but was it really? That is, when it came to sinking the shovel's edge into the earth within a given area, didnt the digger choose this spot over the alternative one ten feet away? And now, didnt she sort of lead us to this area?

Nevertheless he was the digger, he was the autonomous archaeologist of the mountaintop. Almost mountaintop. Of course even the rookie digger knows that human beings have always congregated around water, in valleys or on coastlines. A digger who wants to raise the odds of finding something will stay away from mountaintops. Unless he's looking for Noah's Ark. Heinrich Schliemann exposed Agamemnon's golden face at the foot of a hill.

Schliemann found Troy after reading the extant poetry very carefully.

But these diggers in the Noisy-Diobsud Wilderness were not researchers, and they were not delving for glory. They loved the random and their reward was the hole itself.

Shirley was digging between two small rock outcroppings close by. He felt as if they were a family, frontier agriculturists in the wrong place but happily together. He stepped on his shovel's shoulder and turned over the light soil. He reached higher and scooped it away from the cutbank.

And he heard a thud.

Steel on wood.

He did not shout. No eureka. No holy shit. He stopped for a moment, as if debating the notion of continuing to dig. He looked over at Shirley, who was bent over lifting a stone out of her excavation. He watched as she carried the stone in both hands ten feet away, swung her arms and sent the stone on its little flight, removed one of her gloves in order to wipe her forehead with the back of her wrist, watched her turn to him and break into a sunshine smile. He returned to his cutbank.

The loose earth came away easily, but it also filled his hole over and over. Now the low winter sun was mountaintop warm and his shirt was wet on his back. He who had always done his digging slowly to promote contemplation was working fast. He saw a box half-covered with dirt. He dug. He put down his shovel and grabbed the wood where he could. He finally called for help.

She joined him silently. No holy moses. No jesus jupiter. They worked without words together and pulled the long box out of the loose earth, and it dropped out of their hands onto the hard ground.

He looked at her across the box. It was made of oiled boards of the kind used in the late nineteenth century in the west. Using the blade of his shovel and a big rock as a fulcrum, he prised open a board. He could see dark and cloth inside. He got all the boards off the top of the box.

He gazed on Agamemnon's face.

He saw his own face, rather, reflected along with sunglare in the dark glass of a pair of spectacles.

This was a coffin indeed, with a body in it. Most of the face was visible. The face was made of bone and some old yellow-brown leathery skin. The teeth were grinning but they were not all there. The feet were also visible, bone and leather and a long yellow-brown horn of toenail.

The rest of the fellow was covered with clothes and accompanied by artifacts. Byron Huss knew them all. The phenomenon was wearing Byron's dark glasses, his knitted cap, his jeans and belt, his plaid shirt, his work gloves, his cheap alarm watch and his elkhide vest. In the box with him were Byron's Swiss Army knife, his compass, his map case and his rattlesnake kit.

"Holy shit," he whispered.

He did not aim at taking any of his stuff back. He

didnt even want to touch anything, not even the cap. He had dropped his shovel and now he didnt have anything to lean on.

"Do you want to put the lid back on?" she asked.

So they put the old boards back on, using rocks to knock in the nails. Then he took her shovel and dug the hole deeper and wider in the cutbank, and using all their strength, they inserted the box. It was easy to collapse loose tan soil around it.

"Where is your shovel?" she asked.

"I put it in the box," he said.

He thought about using an old cowboy and Indian movie trick, use pine boughs to wipe out their footprints. But then he thought of two things—the weather would soon erase the signs of their visit, and whatever was being hidden, there was nothing wrong with what they had done. At least he tried to think these things. Thinking was not easy.

He was loaded with desire. It was more specific than that. He wanted her like crazy. He had wanted her very often in the past six months, and he had joyfully accepted the gift of her own desire many times in many places. But as he drove the four-by-four along Highway 20 he felt a desire that jangled his entire body. His foot on the gas pedal was shaking. She put her hand gently on him here and there as he drove. He turned on the radio and found Public Broadcasting, a male discussion of the national debt. He wanted to remove all the clothes from her small muscular body, including her boots and socks. He wanted her but he wanted her in their waterbed, with large fluffy pillows and the pulled-back eiderdown. He wanted roses in the room and Satie on the CD player. He wanted to get there fresh from the shower. He wanted to begin by lifting her abundant brown hair and kissing her high on the back of her neck.

LITTLE ME

June 17, 1988: *see "Staircase Descended"*

Three times a week I have my early afternoon meal at Daphne's Lunch, an ordinary place frequented by the less affluent workers of the neighbourhood and by the widows who live in the highrise apartments nearby. They know me there, and call me by my first name. In return I generally have the daily special. Today it was chicken soup and a patty melt. At Daphne's Lunch they make good soup and pretty bad patty melts.

I always take something with me to read, sometimes a magazine like *Saturday Night*, but usually a book. They know me as the guy who is always reading, I suppose, and not the garbagy drugstore paperbacks some of the shop girls open in front of their salads. Today I was about halfway through *Running in the Family* by Michael Ondaatje.

Always reading. Nevertheless I notice the fellow diners around me. It is a place for regulars. There is the fat old lady with the enormous bun of hair atop her head, and the cigarette holder clenched between her teeth. She looks like Roosevelt when she lifts her chin. There is the couple that always sits in the dead centre booth. I have never heard him utter a sound and I have never seen him meet any-one's eyes. He just sits there and eats his plain burger and drinks two cups of tea. His wife, or such I presume her to be, never stops talking. Not talking, exactly; rather she issues a constant stream of whispered curses between her nearly-meeting teeth. She has yellowish-white hair which she never washes but just pins back in sticky rectangles.

There are lots and lots of regulars. I never say hello to any of them. I am the sort of person who has to be intro-duced, and who soon forgets names if he is introduced. I do talk with the waitresses, and even get to know some of their names. If I get to know a name, I use it in a little bit of friendly fooling before I order the special. Once I ordered a toasted chicken salad sandwich instead of the daily special, and Delores had a hard time believing me.

Today I saw some people I had never seen before. Two of them I dont remember well at all. They were two young women enjoying Daphne's famous old-fashioned milkshakes in the can. The third person was an infant, I suppose you would call him, in a stroller. They had him parked at the open end of their booth, which was right across from mine.

I always look at children. If they are young enough I start an interchange with them. I offer winks and smiles and stuck-out tongues, and receive in return grins and stares, and once in a while a comic grimace.

So I looked at this child.

He was staring at me. Completely still, hardly blinking, with large serious eyes quietly open, he stared at me. And I was staring, I am sure, at him. Anyone watching us would think we were having a staring contest, a little child and a fifty-year-old man.

I usually dont stare. Over all the years I have managed to develop a technique of seeing enough without staring.

But on this occasion I was probably staring. I was certainly not doing the usual thing—looking away and then after a while back, and then away again. I was looking at this preternaturally quiet kid.

Or maybe I wasnt. Maybe I was looking at something more familiar. I say this seemingly pointless thing for this reason: the kid had my face.

I am not saying that an eighteen-month-old child had a wrinkled old guy's face. But he did not have an eighteen-month-old's face either. He had the large head and open face of a boy about six years old. He had the face I wore when I was six years old. I have seen that face hundreds of times in photographs, and since this afternoon I think I can remember seeing it in my grandmother's living room mirror.

I had a high forehead, large brown eyes, straight brown hair that lay diagonally across my brow, large front teeth with a gap between the two top ones in front. A large face with solemn innocence in it. I was looking at it for the first time in four and a half decades.

I left half of my patty melt and went home, forgetting to go to the supermarket. That is all right, though. It is far past dinner time, and everyone around here seems to have fended for themselves. I seem to have forgotten to eat altogether.

Sounds like Bowering is overacknowledging the idea that the author always writes about her/his own experiences

June 18, 1988:

I dont generally go to Daphne's Lunch two days in a row, but I was there today. Despite my resolve I had a cheeseburger and fries, with HP Sauce on the fries. I picked up that trick years ago, hoping the HP Sauce would keep my friend Artie away from my fries. It didnt work, and I found out that I liked it anyway.

But what am I doing, going on about HP Sauce? I rather suspect that I went to Daphne's Lunch to see whether that child with my face might show up again. I thought that I might have a look from another angle, with different weather and sky outside, in the middle of another kind of mood. I was thinking that I might fail to see the resemblance today.

I was rather hoping that, you might imagine. But I was also curious to have another look at my young face. If he still did look exactly like me at six or seven, I wanted to see more. I dont know what I was planning to do about it. It would not do to approach the child's mother and ask her where she got him.

But one feels that one might do something. I felt peculiar every time I remembered that face last night. I felt, I think, a little afraid. Nervous, at least. I do not often consult books about my feelings. I refuse to consider anything to do with astrology, C.G. Jung or blood sugar. But I thought I would see what I could find about one's double—as long as I did not have to go outside of the house to find such references. As long as it was literary references I was looking at.

Well, I found out we have a library full of double stories. They all wrote them, not just Joseph Conrad and Dostoyevsky and Robert Louis Stevenson. They all did. Literature seems, once you start looking, to be filled more than anything else with twins, shadows, mirrors, schizophrenia, robots, puppets, voodoo dolls, and so on and on.

Every society has double stories, and every age group has them. They mean a lot of different things, depending on whether the stories are about sex or religion or madness.

How lucky I am! I can have an unsettling experience in a greasy spoon, and simply look into my book room at home to reassure myself about it. One writer tells us this: that the double is not only strange, but also very familiar, because he was once within us. Another warns that we mess around with doubles at our peril because of the risk of being dominated by them. Still another cautions about a crisis of identity.

I learned after about fifteen minutes to skip through most of the stuff I was encountering. I kept seeing, as if they were staring up through the pages, the wide calm eyes of that infant with the child's face so familiar to my parents.

Oh, it was just one of those things, a fluke of lighting. Taking advantage of my distraction or tiredness. I have been having a hard time getting used to my new glasses. I wouldnt mind seeing the kid again, but it was just a lot of kaka.

Still, I wish that the usual idea about the appearance of the
Doppelgänger was something different. If you see it you are supposed to get ready to die.

But really, a *Doppelgänger* is a twin, a creature or apparition the same size and age as oneself. There arent any little kid *Doppelgängers* for grown-ups.

June 20, 1988:

They were there again today, the kid and his mother. She had the same friend with her as before. They were both wearing plastic jackets. Hers was shiny purple. Her companion's jacket was shiny pink. Her son, well I had to presume, presume? Presume he was. He was wearing little child clothes of some sort. You didnt really look at his clothes. His head is so big you dont remember what he was wearing.

When I was in grade three I was in a hospital room in Lawrence, with a boy younger than me. But the boy had a head that was half the size of the rest of him. He had to lay it on a pillow. That did not seem like a nice place to leave me. But I thought it was interesting anyway.

But this kid didnt have a head that big. It was just like a ten-year-old's head on a baby's body, let's say. Maybe not even that bad.

I didnt know whether I would ever see him again. Them again. I got as brave as I could and spoke to his mother when her friend went to the ladies' room. This is what we said, more or less.

"I hope you dont think I'm some sort of weirdo, staring at your kid."

"I didnt notice you were."

"It's just that he looks exactly like me."

"Oh, really?"

"I mean exactly like I looked, what I looked like when I was his age, or I mean when he was ten or eight. When I was."

"He's a year-and-a-half."

"Sure."

"Thursday."

"Anyway, he is a spitting image of me when I was eight in West Summerland."

"I dont see the resemblance at all."

"I wish I had a picture to show you."

Her friend was back from the ladies' room.

"Do you think Mikey looks like this guy?"

Her friend just giggled. She was a giggler, you could tell.

"I wish I had a picture to show you."

"Well, I never saw you a year and a half ago, so I dont think he looks that much like you. You're the second person this week to say my kid looks like them. Is this a new line for picking up young mothers?"

"Someone else? Did he look like me?"

"Not a bit. He had a long thin face, kind of pointed at both ends."

Her friend giggled.

The kid was staring at me with big calm eyes.

"How come he looks like that when he is only a year-and-half old?"

"Like what?"

I looked at her to see whether she was fooling me.

"He looks so old and wise. He looks like eight years old. He looks like an eight-year-old serious thinker boy."

"I sort of see what you mean."

Her son stared and stared at me. He could have been fifteen.

June 22, 1988:

No little me kid in Daphne's today. Just this talk that made me tired. Talk with the guy who walks in exaggerating how bad his back is aching. He sits down on the red banquette right next to me. I mean he has his little table and I have my little table, but we are sitting side by side on the long banquette. It is a banquette. That is what they call it. People fall off banquettes and later require steel pins in their ankles. I have heard that.

No little kids at all. But this geezer asks me whether I can see him.

"Nothing wrong with the light in here," I said.

"My wife cant see me," he said.

"I never get involved in other people's marital problems," I said.

"Not it," he said.

"I got my own problems," I said.

People talked this way to each other in Daphne's Lunch more than you might think.

"Oh sure, thanks," he said. "For nothing."

He always was a grousy old guy.

"I got this problem with a kid that's more than he ought to be," I volunteered.

Volunteered. How did I think of that word? I might as well admit that I have been having trouble thinking of words lately. Just now I remembered a word I wanted to use a while ago.

"Well, we all got our problems," the geezer said.

I just had to forget he was sitting beside me, and go ahead and eat my grilled cheese sandwich when it came.

June 23, 1988:

The little me was there today.

We sat there looking at each other for a long time. A long time. I dont know, maybe an hour. Maybe less than that.

He wasnt wearing glasses but other than that we sure looked a lot alike. Like twins maybe.

I dont know what he was staring at me for. Maybe he stares at everybody. Maybe he was seeing what he will look like in fifty years. Or thirty years or whatever it is.

He looks to be about twenty years old I would say. Smart-looking kid. Gets smarter-looking all the time. Time.

In my dream last night a smart young Jewish professor says "I do not use time to keep back space." I looked at his dark eye and tried to look like I knew what he was saying.

I dont even know what I was just writing. I do remember an amazing number of words, though, everything considered.

I figure I am still smarter than most people in Daphne's Lunch. Includes that little me fellow.

You want a battle of wits, kid?

Still, he's a nice-looking boy. I do have to say that, dont I? Given that I'm talking about myself.

No, I'm not. This is a person in a greasy spoon. Somebody's kid. Some kid. I cant remember what I had to eat at Daphne's today. The usual, I would say. Daphne is never there any more.

I am. Both of me.

June 24, 1988:

cereal
hamburger meat
toilet paper
2% milk
vegs—brocc. or cauli.
60 w. light bulb
tea bags
toilet paper

June 25, 1988:

Twenty-fifth. Holiday of some sort, but not June.

Light was coming through the window like Mom used to be. Very bright light. Coming in like an angel.

Like a god. Coins spilling off him. Skirt made of golden daggers.

In the lunch place. I saw a kid in a stroller or sitting at a table, same thing. I mean you get something. Good to eat.

They were angry at me. Someone.

Wanted me out of there.

Later I noticed a dog staring at me. This was just around the corner. He wasnt trying to scare me. Just looking at me. I thought okay.

I didnt think okay. It was just okay.

Dog didnt look like anyone.

I never had that kind. Havent got any dog now.

June 27, 1988:

dapne

he   xtwo

eyen   like

mi yen

.   hee

. i i

gett msf   2 get

THE DESCRIBED

She had always been the kind of girl who slouched, who sprawled in a chair, often with a knee hooked over the chair's arm, who walked with parts of her body moving back and forth in non-functional agitation. Now she was definitely not a girl, no longer a girl, and her back was very straight on the chair, and none of it touched the chair.

He wondered whether he would be able to speak, but of course he did.

"Well, now I have seen him," he said.

She sat straight in the chair, her long neck held perfectly vertical. She did not turn to him when she replied, but spoke as it were directly at the grey-painted wall. Her voice was not that of an intimate friend.

"You spoke with him?"

"Yes.

"Did you put a particular question to him?"

He wanted to sit down. He wanted to be asked to sit down. All he could do was pace a few steps. He had the sense to pace away from the direction of her gaze, not to impose himself on her ordeal.

Now what would he say to her? When they had first met, so unexpectedly, nearly violently, that hot day in the grove, he had been unable to speak, or at least unable to speak sensibly. As now he held his hat in both hands and unconsciously knocked its brim against his knees.

"I did," he said.

At last she turned her head silently and smoothly, the way a hawk turns to keep every prey's possible pathway in sight, and let her large brown eyes meet his. They were made only the more vulnerable by the fact that her hair was perfectly in place, pulled back from her forehead. She blinked three times quickly, then opened her large lips again.

"What did he—?"

Her voice failed, and she turned her face away from him and bent her long neck so that he saw her in all her vulnerability. A draught of cool air seemed to pass through the room, as if a door to a cellar had opened momentarily nearby. He wanted to take a step toward her. He wanted to lift his hand to her small shoulder.

He cleared his throat lightly.

"I think we can still find a way," he said.

She spoke into her hand, her face still turned from him.

"No. We should have known that it was hopeless," she said.

The two gold fish in the round bowl lay perfectly still in the water. There was not a sound, save a distant automobile engine gearing up and fading away.

"It is hopeless only if you—if we give up hope," he pleaded.

She still kept her face from him. He saw one of her hands lying like a dead thing in the lap of her brocaded dress. The other was out of sight, covering her soft mouth. Her ankles were crossed and seemed to be without life. He wanted to shake her and then apologize and kiss her.

At last she turned to face him. Wetness ringed her eyes.

"Surely you do not remember what the old woman said about hope?" she asked, her small chin trembling.

He would never know how to describe the effect on him of her trembling chin. He was a big man, but he had never thought of himself as particularly strong. Nor had he considered himself overly sensitive. The suffering of children, though, and now this trembling chin, dismissed his power of self-containment, and brought sour pain into his body, into the part of his body that did its thinking. He was not sure that he could himself speak without quavering.

"The old lady is not here. We are."

This dialogue would be so much—not easier but somehow a little easier to see one's difficult way through— if she would just rise to her feet, perhaps take a few steps, toward the window, if not toward him. Sitting there in her chair, as if afraid to put a wrinkle in her long maroon brocade, she effectively arrested his movement as well. It was as if they were frozen there for a painter's sitting or a tableau, and their very stillness promoted a greater pain in their sensibilities. If only he could break this spell—but he felt that any movement would break her, would push her off the smallest ledge of composure she had attained.

"Are we really?" she asked.

Her voice was edged with an unconvincing hardness that could not protect her tender heart from scrutiny. He was reminded of the frailty in her words when she first told him that she loved him. He had put the curved palm of his right hand on the back of her round head and gently brought her face to his breast. He wanted to hold her now, wanted her to rise from her chair and step one pace toward him. The summer's afternoon light bounced this way and that off the bevelled surfaces of the windows, and there would be somewhere in the room, he knew, a rainbow, or several of them.

Her question, he knew, was not philosophical. She was simply allowing her despair to show and hoping against hope for some reassurance from him. His own heart wanted to leap to her, brush that question aside, and promise a lifetime of protection.

"We cannot allow them to—"

But it seemed that she could not hear. Her eyes were open wide, and no longer bathed in tears. The light mascara she used was a trifle blotched, doubling the beauty of her vulnerability. He remembered all of a sudden a day at the lake cottage, the expression in the old man's face when he saw the two of them in the hammock. That was only a year ago. It seemed now as if it had happened to other people in another era, as if it had not happened at all, as if he had conjured it all out of hope or perhaps regret.

Night time at the cottage. They would never had stayed there overnight had it not been for the fire at the other end of the valley. He remembered wondering at the time whether the fire were a sign from the gods. But he quickly put that aside. They could never accept a boon that entailed also someone else's loss.

Now he was confronted by her loss. If she would only speak. If he could then find the words to drive the fear from her bosom. Her bosom—it was rising now as she took a fast deep breath. She was after all going to try to speak.

"It is not they who—"

But she could not complete her sentence, and after this, hardly more than a short phrase, she collapsed into her chair, no longer stiff of spine, her face in her hands, and her brocade-covered shoulders rising and falling with her gasping breath.

The sunshine through the bevelled windows sent discrete bars of light here and there through the room. One was now stretched and bent across her figure, as if nature itself desired to accentuate her unhappiness and its association with her extravagant beauty. In the slanted sunlight the faint hairs on her forearm turned to gold, and the gently tanned skin took on a darker cast.

He would have been hard-pressed to provide a description of his feelings at this moment. He was as always filled with desire for her, a kind of sweet hurtfulness that flashed through his body when she would take a step forward, her high hip pushing at the fabric in her dress. He was suffused with compassion for her tenderness and pain. And he was angry—he wanted to destroy anything, any person or force that brought her unhappiness.

"But we, you and I...."

Even as he tried to speak he remembered the first time he had seen her. She had been wearing a blue suit, jacket and skirt, and looked as if she had been born into a family in which women wore such things. The white collar that shone against the tan of her neck was only lightly laced, only a little wimpled. Her shoes were dark blue, pumps of rich leather encasing long narrow feet that he would later imagine touching his frame. Her hair was cut short in the back and spilled over her forehead. It was dark russet, perhaps what people meant by the word roan. Her eyes, when they met his, were absolutely calm. They were still and quiet but they could not be called expressionless. They were exceedingly deep, and he felt unbalanced for a moment, afraid that he was going to fall into them.

She noticed that too, and laughed lightly, a shiny star-movement in her eyes for a moment. He felt the heat of his blushing cheeks. Then someone was introducing them. There was a strange interplanetary voice behind him somewhere, as he looked dazedly into her eyes.

Three hours later he told her for the first time that he loved her.

And he loved her now, perhaps more than he did then, perhaps almost as much. But this was a different kind of love. Now he knew the history of her family, and the suffering she had endured every year of her life because of that history. Now he knew the responsibility of love, and more than that the responsibility of a human being who knows that he has the life of another in his hand, and does not know for a certainty how to protect it.

Now he must have been staring at the floor behind

those images of their first meeting, because he was aware of the rustling of her dress before he knew that she was standing. He looked up just as she spoke, with a voice deeper than he had ever heard from a young woman.

"You and I," she said.

Light was now pouring into the room, between the slats of the low jalousies and through the bevelled glass above them. There were rainbows everywhere. Petals had fallen from last evening's roses slightly drooping in their vase, pink petals on a white tablecloth. If one were to look with any kind of curiosity one would see small wine stains in the cloth, and if one were to look very closely indeed one might find the traces of some tears shed twelve hours ago.

He wondered what her three short words were intended to do, that echo, that painful phrase. Was she preparing to speak now, and if not, why had she risen to her feet?

The walls of the room bore the *gelb* seen everywhere in Austria. It was a rich colour in a room where the sunlight has been harnassed and domesticated and bounced from surface to surface. Ranged along each wall were the massively-framed chiaroscuro portraits of the bulbous men in her family, in its heavy history. There were a few women, but only a few. They were always in brocaded dresses of their periods, of a painted hue either somewhere between red and blue or between green and blue.

"I—"

The colours of those dresses were repeated in the oriental carpet that had seemingly been woven to order. Between the edge of the carpet and the wall the parquet floor shone brightly, as if someone had been waxing and polishing it within the past hour. Across from the paintings the windows made another row, and if one looked over the tops of the jalousies one could see that her family had been able to decorate the outside as well as the inside, to express their dynastic will with the very building materials of life. Outside those windows one saw nature to advantage dressed, and knew whose advantage was being considered here.

She had walked over to one of the windows rather than to him, and was looking over a jalousie, out at the long rolling lawn or rather sward, all the way to the pond with the overturned red rowboat on its edge, the rowboat that protruded from the shade of the oak trees, into the bright late-morning sun. There were lily leaves on the surface of the pond, and in the dappled light one could see white butterflies flitting as their momentary will took them over the surface of the water. There were dragonflies, too, that were visible from this distance only because the sun ran crookedly off their blueblack thoraxes, and because one, or rather two, had sat beside that pond often and had the time to notice all the varieties of insect life in the area, such as that bumble bee, heavy and furry black, now bumping its head against a wavering windflower just outside the window.

"I think—"

The oak trees rose high and nearly black against the pale blue sky. If there were any clouds they were in the half of the sky they could not see from these windows. It was, simply speaking, the late morning of a wonderful July day, the sort of day that lovers take as their due, that the afflicted of heart yearn for in drear January, that old women on porches meet with large straw bonnets and organdy shawls.

Now she spoke, though she was gazing upon the arboreal scene rather than looking at him. Her dull, low voice sunk through his body and weighed upon his spirit. Rather, she tried to speak, to begin to speak.

"Dont . . . do not . . . you . . . ."

How would he or anyone describe the communication of pain that belied the hesitancy of their voices? How describe the wound he now felt and knew would be with him forever, like the piece of shrapnel in the lung of the soldier who fought for only one day just a few steps up from the beach in Italy forty years ago and more?

It had been a grey and cold day despite the time of the year. The long clouds hung their dark bellies all along the coastline, and the soldiers knew hardly anything but water. Their feet had been wet since getting out of the boat, and the whole countryside looked as if it had been only for a recent while rescued from the Mediterranean. He knew that discomfort was a condition of victory, and they had been assured of victory since the troopship sailed from that other moist harbour on that other continent. But sudden metallic death was far worse than discomfort, so the wet sandy ground his body lay stretched upon—

What adjective could hope to capture that face he could see now only in profile, a light like that which bemused Vermeer caressing its smooth and gentle contours?

"I need—"

What figure of speech could tangle among the words an emotion that wound its way among the organs inside his body? We are told that language gives us mastery, that the alphabet can be combined in whatever way we require to make us masters of our experience. Yet he knew that he would never be able to capture the pain and pity and loss of this moment, of this morning. He didnt know when it happened, but she was turned to look at him now. Her deep, deep eyes threatened his disappearance. Her full lips were slightly opened, the top one having been dragged up the front teeth, which were glistening now in the light of the window.

His knees nearly fell out from under him, and he knew that he would not be able to try the steps he desired. He almost pitched forward onto his face when an object banged against a window from outside. A ruffled bird with a broken neck fell out of sight below the jalousie.

"I will die if . . . ."

She was looking at him now as if this were his last chance at something. Her eyes were large and round, and deeper than they had ever been. They were the colour of the reflected oak trees. He remembered the second time he had ever seen them, in the cafeteria of the Civic Art Gallery in the provincial capital. In her left hand she had been holding high the blue satin skirt of a dress she never should have been wearing in such a place, and in her right she had been holding a small paper plate with a lemon pastry and a small fork. Both hands were in the light that spilled down from the leaf-strewn skylight, but her face was in the shadow of a gigantic fern that seemed to explode from a Chinese urn. The scent of French cigarettes mixed with the odor of old plaster that always remained in the middle-range of one's attention in art museum cafeterias. She remained in her pose for only a moment before bending her long neck and descending into a seat at a table next to the green-tinted window. Her hair was pulled up tight, so that he could see how closely her small ears pressed themselves to her head, and how white was her long neck, the long neck that these painted relatives had tried to achieve. Now she was sitting before a pastry that might not receive her attention, and now she is at this moment disappearing out the door, and then she is at last using her fork to make the smallest wound in the lemon pastry and now her dark red hair is seen going past the windows, one after another. He wondered how she was able to sustain life with such a modest attitude toward food. Absurdly, he stared at the lemon pastry and silently begged the gods to urge her appetite. She touched her fork to the pastry from time to time, but never to her lips. She did not speak, but she was listening, and then it was that he noticed the old woman across the table from her. The old woman was talking, talking, all the while manoeuvring foodstuffs with complete candour, sticking strawberry short-cake into her speaking mouth now, and then licking the back of the fork. She listened to the old lady until they had decided that they had had enough rest now to take their bodies back to the rooms full of pictures, or to leave it at that and go to another part of the city to give clothing retailers their regard. He would follow, but he could not, and then he saw her go by the window, perhaps never to see her again, and as he watched her disappear past the corner of the building he knew that he would never be able to find the words that could describe his sense of loss, even of bereavement.